LA MARINA
BY JOHN RIGBY

Published in 2009 by YouWriteOn.com

Copyright © John Rigby

First Edition

British Library C.I.P.

A CIP catalogue record for this title is available from the
British Library.

1. RUTH

Ruth stood at the mirror putting on her earrings, the rubies Dad had got in Burma in the war, the ones he'd given Mum, but she'd said they didn't suit her. The scene outside was faintly irritating, the ranks of little houses, as uniform as a regiment, and their own house at the corner, a bit bigger but just as regimental, a Sergeant-Major's house. Ruth thought, why couldn't they have given these houses a bit of individuality like the officers' houses on the other side of Camp, but she knew the answer: originality was for officers, conformity for the Ranks and know your place.

She went downstairs, and Dad was still in his uniform – Regimental Quartermaster - Sergeant Evans: known as 'Q'. His uniform blouse was unbuttoned, and he was sitting there in his socks drinking tea out of a mug: Mum had tried to get him to use a cup and saucer, but he wouldn't give up his cookhouse mug.

He said, "Garrison Dance is it? - I'm proud of you, girl."

So he should be, she thought; I'm a credit to him.

"Colonel asked after you," said the 'Q' - "There'll be a few young officers at the dance."

"Condescending as usual, I suppose," said Ruth. 'Don't talk to me about officers."

Over at the NAAFI building, the music stopped, and Ruth had a chance to join her girlfriends, and to sip an orange squash. It was all excitement and so much to say: "Oh, I do like your dress Ruth," but she hadn't a chance to reply before the music started again and you could hardly hear above the din. It wasn't so much the drums as the blare of the saxophones - they always got a good band for the big NAAFI dances, a famous band: Harry Gold and his Pieces of Eight, one of those. It was a big camp, of course, and all the girls for miles around came to the dances, all the nurses from the hospital up Gobowen way, and the girls from Oswestry town, and all the WAACS and the other girls who worked at the Camp.

He was making for her, the chap in the blue blazer with the brass buttons, and he might have been an officer, she couldn't be sure: hardly anyone wore uniform off-duty in peacetime. She saw him from right across the room: he wasn't tall but he was solid, with a square jaw; and the packed Hall seemed to part for him.

"May I have this dance, please?"

Ruth smiled and swayed into his arms. It was a quickstep, 12th Street Rag, a good tune for dancing.

She said, and she had to shout into his ear "I haven't seen you here before."

He said, "I've just been posted. I'm Stan, by the way, Stan Phillips, Sergeant in Vimy Battery."

"I'm Ruth Evans. My Dad's the R.Q.M.S."

"Q" Evans? Well! I'll have to watch my Ps and Qs, then!"

"Oh, witty!"

He went into some intricate steps and Ruth was nearly caught off balance. He was trying her, showing off: he was a good dancer, a clever dancer, and he was trying to assert himself. He puzzled Ruth a bit; he was well-spoken, full of himself, without the awkwardness of a ranker, no wonder she'd thought he might be an officer. He could easily have been an officer, a National Service officer anyway, a temporary gentleman as the saying went; it was an old joke.

They came to the trumpet part of the Rag, and the trumpeter was making the most of it. Stan did a chassis, and he was easy to follow, he led well with a firm pressure on her back. Ruth loved dancing when she had a good partner.

The blare abated, and you could make yourself heard again and Ruth asked "Been in the army long?"

"Since I left Grammar School" he answered "I wanted to try for Sandhurst, for a Regular Commission, but it didn't work out. So I tried the "Back Door", joined in the Ranks and tried WOSB."

"What happened?"

"Failed." - he couldn't conceal the bitterness in his voice.

The music stopped "Can I get you a drink?"

There was a crowd, all jostling for drinks at the bar, but he was soon back with a beer, and a gin-and-orange for her. He didn't shove or anything, he just got served. He was authoritative, and Ruth liked that; she wondered how he'd come to fail WOSB.

Stan said "It's lively here. Do they often hold these dances?"

"Most Saturdays. I come with my girlfriends. We were all at the Grammar School in the town."

He said "Your Dad's had a long posting. All this time at the same place."

She laughed "Ten years. We're on the establishment like the furniture. The C.O. says he couldn't do without Dad."

A good Regimental Quartermaster Sergeant was like gold, especially in an Artillery Regiment with all that equipment, the guns and all that.

Ruth said "These dances are the best - there's not much else here, you know, just the Garrison Cinema, the Globe, and the Cinema in Town, of course. But it's not much. The

NAAFI's the centre of the Universe."

Stan said "The Sergeants' mess has socials, surely."

Ruth said "And the officers' Mess. They have their Balls - but I've never been."

No sooner had she said that, but she regretted it. He tensed up.

"Bloody snobs!" He said "The odds are stacked if you haven't been to Public School."

Ruth knew he was right. There were a few National Service officers, and a few Regular Officers come to that, who had never seen the inside of a Public School; but, mostly, Officers were Public School and true to type. Ruth could see them from her desk in the Regimental Library - many of them used the library, and one or two of the subalterns had made a pass at her, but she was damned if she'd respond. They were so condescending.

She talked to Dad about it, and Dad said there was a social divide. Dad might have had a `Q' commission, but he was a rough diamond, Dad, and happy as he was; he'd be uncomfortable in an Officers' Mess. Besides, he'd got used to Oswestry, to the big Gunner Camp; it had become home to him. He'd have to move if he took a Commission, and lose all his local contacts; all his perks and "little fiddles."

The `Q' was proud of his position. He'd be nothing in an Officers' Mess, but in the Sergeants' Mess he was Top Dog.

It was the Last Waltz, and they dimmed the lights, with the floor so packed you could hardly move. It was warm, summer warm, and there was a smell of B.O. and cheap scent; and it was the usual last waltz tune, all sugary and insincere, and the couples devouring each other, locked tight and necking while the music moaned.

Then it was the big percussion and glaring lights and God Save the Queen - the new, young Queen - and people still singing God Save the King, they couldn't get used to it, and all around the question "Can I see you home?"

Ruth said "I must get my bag; and say Goodnight to the girls."

Stan waited at the door until Ruth came, and they went out into the night. It was so warm outside, even at midnight, and, all around on the grass were couples interlocked, dark shapes, not even bothered, most of them, to move into shadow or out of sight.

"Let's get away from here" said Stan. And she felt the tug of his hand.

"You're going the wrong way" said Ruth "If I stay out too late, Dad will turn out the guard."

Stan laughed, but she was only half joking. A hard man was Q Evans, not a man to cross.

"Fair enough" said Stan "How about the pictures next Wednesday?"

"The library closes early on Wednesdays" said Ruth "It's a date.'

They were alone now, away from all the rabble, their heels hitting the dark path together, in step as was only natural for a soldier and a soldier's daughter. There was a figure, slowly pacing, and it was the guard on midnight stag not long now and he'd be back in the guardroom for bacon and eggs.

They came to the gun-park, with the rows of 25-pounders snouts raised to the sky. Stan said "You wonder why I stay in the Army? There's the answer."

He drew her to him, not roughly, but firmly, and she started to make a token resistance; but the gesture seemed futile, and she kissed him with a will. He didn't take liberties,

6

he just kissed her long and hard on the mouth, and his manhood was strong against her where they pressed.

He called for her on Wednesday, on his motorbike. He'd not mentioned the bike, and the roar and racket outside the house was the first Ruth knew about it. She ran to the door, and there he was, astride the beast, and grinning as he revved and blipped; and all along the row of houses there were faces at the windows, and he knew it.

Stan cut the engine and the bike subsided with a gasp. "You're not afraid of big bikes are you?" he said.

"Come in" Ruth said "I'm not quite ready"

Stan said "It's not a day to waste in the cinema. How about a spin? into the Welsh hills?"

She'd hoped he'd suggest that, now she'd seen the bike; she supposed he'd been planning it all along.

So, she tied a scarf around her hair, and put on more lipstick: she always wore the deep red nowadays, it suited her.

Stan was ready to go. He said "The bike won't let us down. She's a thoroughbred" and he patted her flank as though she'd won the Oaks. "Climb up" he said "Hold tight."

He pulled down his goggles and the bike snorted to a crescendo and away.

Ruth pressed hard against Stan's back, her cheek against his blazer and her arms strong around him. There was a brutality about it, about the machine, about Stan, and Ruth sensed the brutal female in herself. They were out of Shropshire now, and climbing into Wales near Llangollen; the bike scornful of the gradient, and Stan proud of the way he handled her, not showy, but taking the bends tight, leaning her into the turns and bringing her head up as she came out. After Llangollen they kept climbing; Ruth glimpsed a sign "Betwys-y-Coed" and they were heading for the Swallow

Falls.

The pub was in the woods above the village, and it was empty but for the Welsh sheepdog. The landlady came and Stan ordered "A pint of beer and a gin-and-orange", and the landlady said "Yes Sir." - Stan liked the "Sir". The landlady brought the drinks across to the inglenook, to where the fire would have been in wintertime, then she went back into the house; and all they could hear was a stream running, and birdsong through the open door.

Stan said "I like to get away from Camp. Away from pubs full of soldiers."

Ruth said "You might get an Officer or two out here. She thought you were an Officer..,

Stan glanced down at his cavalry twill trousers and his suede chukka boots, that were like off-duty uniform for Officers.

He said "Well - I should be an Officer. I'm good enough."

"Did they explain" Ruth asked "Why you failed WOSB?"

"WOSB - the War Office Selection Board - Oh, they'll never tell you. But I know it's a social thing. If you haven't been to Public School, they close ranks."

Ruth said "Some of those young Officers, those National Servicemen. They look nothing compared with you."

Stan took a deep draught of beer, a manly draught. He sneered "The men just laugh at them!. Officers my arse! Just catch any recruits laughing at me. I'd have their guts for garters and they know it." He took another drink and said "Isn't it lovely here?" and he added "I'll get another shot at WOSB. "

They heard a car outside, and they could see it through

8

the open door, a two-seater open sports with three young fellows, crammed together and laughing, having fun.

They came tumbling in, and one of them said

"I say, isn't it Sgt. Phillips? Good evening sergeant."

"Good evening, Sir?"

"What a lovely lady! You must introduce us, Sergeant."

"This is Ruth Evans, Sir. Daughter of the Regimental Quartermaster Sergeant."

"Of course. Forgive me, I should have known. The Regimental Library. Of course."

Ruth said "I'm flattered you noticed me." He said "A lot of people notice you, Ruth. By the way, I'm Jack, Call me Jack." He turned to Stan and said "Can I get you another drink, Sergeant? And one for Ruth?"

"Not just now Sir. I'm on the motor-bike you see. I must be careful."

Jack joined the other officers at the bar. Ruth looked at them, and she looked at Stan, and there was a difference; she didn't notice it immediately, but it went into her subconscious. Of course, Stan was on the defensive in a way, and the others were, well, sure of themselves; but there was something just that bit different about their cavalry twills, the way they moulded to the leg; and their chukka boots looked scuffed, not kept for best.

Stan said "Let's go and look at the Falls. They'll be pretty dry this weather, I'm afraid,"

They went outside, and the big bike was beside the little car, the aggressive bike and the sporty car, 'See what I mean" said Stan "Snotty-nosed bastards. He asked you to call him Jack - he knows I can't do that."

Ruth said "Oh Stan. I'm sure he didn't mean...."

"No, he didn't mean ... but, if I wasn't with you you could be one of them. It's different for girls."

She said "Oh, Stan. I do hope you pass WOSB. Next time,"

They rode slowly to the top of the Falls, and parked the bike, and walked together down the path. Stan reached out his hand to help her down, and he kept hold of her hand, and she felt the pressure of the ring on her finger, the emerald her mother had given her, the one she'd got in Singapore when Dad had been stationed there before the war.

Stan said "I love the feel of your hands, Ruth. They're soft. You can tell a girl by her hands."

Ruth said "It's important, - Grooming I mean. For a girl."

It was true; all the working girls, all the WRACs, the girls in the factories, in the kitchens, they made-up their faces like film-stars, but their hands betrayed them.

She said "Your hands are nice Stan. Strong. But not rough."

"It's important" said Stan "For a gentleman."

The summer evening was still bright, but the sunlight never reached the pathway beside the Falls; there was just a glint here and there on the water, but the banks were overshadowed. There was nobody about, and they came to where the water tumbled over the rocks, and Stan guided Ruth away from the path to a hollow beside a pool. It was humid and there were midges, and he said "Let's go into the sunlight." They climbed up on some rocks away from the trees; there were hills against the sky behind them, and, below, the forest obscured the rushing stream. Stan took off his blazer and sat on the dry grass and pulled Ruth gently down.

"You look so healthy" he said "I like a healthy girl."

10

He held her to him, and she came willingly. He said "Ruth. I want to make love to you."

She said, uncertainly "I don't know, Stan", but she did know, really.

"You're a virgin?" He asked, and she nodded.

"Well" he said "I'm a gentleman, Ruth. You must decide."

He released her; he didn't try to persuade her, and she stretched out beside him, where he lay beside her, strong and silent; and honourable in his way. Ruth looked at him, steady, to where his manhood was tight against the tight fit of his twills, a hard hump at his crotch. She said nothing; she reached across, and put her hand over the hump, and the hump jerked up, harder still, and the shock of it jolted her like an impulse through her arm.

Stan's hand met hers, there, over the hump, and his fingers were opening the buttons. He pulled the shiny, hard thing through, and he guided Ruth's fingers onto it, and he said "Your hands excite me, Ruth." Ruth turned towards him; she raised herself a little, and looked down at her fingers and the manicured nails, and at what her fingers were holding, and she remembered how careful she'd been to get the red lacquer perfect, and it was exciting, her fingers on him; her fingers tightened on him and her body tightened in a spasm, a sudden, delicious spasm, and, ah! she relaxed.

Stan said "I know a lucky girl who's had an orgasm."

That remark brought a shadow over the sun for Ruth - was it really the remark of a gentleman?

Stan said "I'll have to use a Sheath. A Frenchie."

Ruth knew about Frenchies, of course, how could she not have known in an Army camp? Frenchies were all over an army camp: used ones scattered everywhere, the morning after a dance. And Dad used to issue them by the gross to the guardroom, free issue to the men - voluntary of course in the U.K. but compulsory abroad. But Ruth had never actually touched one; she'd never joined in the jokes either, that even the girls made about them.

Stan opened his wallet and took out the packet; he tore the packet and took out the little pink johnnie which was just a crinkled bit of rubber, and he put the rubber on the tip of the hard thing, what a pity to disguise it, and he rolled it down quickly, so that it was a sheath, tight, a scabbard.

Then he said "I'll help you take off your panties" and he rolled them slowly over her girdle and over the bare space where the suspenders were pulling her stockings, and down to her ankles. She slipped one foot through, and then the other, and Stan held out his hand for them. Then, he did a curious thing, to disturb Ruth a little, though it was nothing really; he put the lace panties to his face, to draw a deep breath and get the smell of them, and the smell seemed to excite him.

Ruth was lying back, there, on the dry grass, bare under her skirt, and he reached and folded the front of her skirt upwards so she was bare to his gaze, and his gaze was silent and intent. She had an instinct to cover herself, she felt shy; but he said "You're even lovelier than I thought", and he touched the soft skin of her, with a soft touch.

She started to undo her suspenders, but he restrained her, and said "Leave them - I like them. I'll not snag your stockings." He smiled and she felt less tense. His hand, gentle and firm, motioned her to part her legs, and she moved them just enough to let him caress her, until the moisture flowed from her and the tension went.

Stan said "You're open. You're quite ready...."

She sensed an implied question and she said, reproachfully "I suppose you don't believe me - believe I'm a virgin, I mean."

12

"I believe you" said Stan.

Her blouse was tight, and would have been awkward to take off, but Stan undid the buttons, and reached inside, behind, and unhooked the bra. It snapped, as the tension left the elastic, and he pulled it out of the way to show her breasts. He bent his head over her, as if in reverence - he was leaning on one elbow, and he took one breast into his free hand, and he bent slowly and took the other into his lips. His tongue flicked quickly over the nipple, and his hand gently squeezed the other breast, and, oh! there was nothing Ruth wanted in the world, then, nothing, only his hard thing, his hard, shiny thing inside her.

"Please, Stan. Please - I want you!"

But he kept her waiting, deliberately waiting; he took his hand from her breast, and he moved it to where her legs had spread, now, wide to welcome him, wide and urgent for him; and he found the hard button, there, and he pressed and touched the little button, until she tensed her buttocks, and arched up for him.

"Please, oh, please Stan. Now."

She was pleading, and he liked that. Stan said "What do you want?"

"You know, Stan" she said "You know. I want you."

"And, what if I won't?" He was teasing. And she was pleading; he liked that. "Oh, Stan. I'd die."

Stan said "You silly girl. Perhaps I'm not in the mood...." Now, he thought, was the time, the make or break time, the time to break her in; like a filly. The time to show who was in charge, who was officer material, officer class.

Ruth started to agitate, to snatch at Stan "Oh Stan. Don't be cruel. Please. Please."

He was satisfied.

"Well then" he said "Just ask me. Ask me nicely."

"Yes, Stan. Yes."

Just say "Stan. Please. Please fuck me."

"Stan! that's not nice!"

But, when she saw him frown she said it fast, "Oh yes", she said "Stan. Stan. Fuck me, Stan. Oh, please, Stan. Fuck me."

Stan smiled, a smile of triumph. He pulled his trousers down to his knees, and he moved into the space between her legs. He took his weight on one arm, and deliberately, with the other hand, he guided himself into her; and, before he thrust, he made sure the frenchie, was down, safe and tight. He thrust home and held hard while she squirmed on it, squirmed with the ecstacy of it, and then he started to use it like a piston, every thrust deliberate, the power mounting and inexorable, until there was a gasp of triumph; and she, moving under the piston, wanted more, and more again; until his jerk, and quicker, quicker jerks, made her jerk too, and contract, tense, and contract, and relax; and melt away for ever.

Stan said "The sun's gone down. Better go."

Then it was downhill home, downhill all the way, and Stan went fast, dominating the bike, challenging her; and he thought he had dominated Ruth, but he was wrong.

The other families in Married Quarters used to curse Stan's bike. He was always at the Evan's gate, revving the bike and shattering the silence. It was a summer for biking, and good to get into the hills, and there was nothing on the road to touch the big Norton.

Stan didn't like town pubs, nor did Ruth. He liked a quiet pub in the country, a pub with atmosphere; or if it was a County town, one of the old Shropshire towns, they would go to the best hotel, the Feathers at Ludlow, one of those, and go into the lounge bar or the cocktail bar, whatever they called the best bar. There would be the horsey set in the bar, the women all braying and looking forward to the hunting season and sipping sherry; and the men drinking pink gin, though some of the women drank pink gin too.

Sometimes a few officers from the regiment would be in the bar, and they would give a nod of recognition, but Ruth never saw any other rankers besides Stan.

Often, they would walk; leave the bike and walk, somewhere far from anybody, away from people; and, it was such a summer, they never had to bother about the cold or anything, the weather was so good. Stan always made love; Ruth would have been disappointed if he hadn't. Stan was proud - he was a proud man, Stan -; he was proud of his power, and he liked to tantalise her; he knew what she wanted, and he liked to tease. What he'd really have liked was for Ruth to beg, beg for it like the first time, but, after that time, she'd never beg, not like that.

He taught her to put the frenchie on for him, while he lay back, with his cock up and hard; Ruth used to slip the frenchie over the tip and roll it down with little flicks of her fingers the way she rolled her stockings up her leg. It was always a private, sensual thing for Ruth, when she put on her stockings, a little squeak of private pleasure with her fingers, and the red nails on the nylon.

After she'd pulled the stockings tight so they were shiny - taut on her legs, and after she'd clipped the suspenders to keep the tension - she was usually sitting on her bed - after she'd done all that, she'd lie back across the bed, with her legs wide, and before she put on her panties, she'd caress herself, and she liked the look of her finger there. She always thought of that when she put on the johnnie for Stan, and she did it slowly to enjoy it.

Once - it was in the hills near Weston-Rhyn - while he

was lying there with his cock up, before she put the rubber on, she bent and took the cock in her mouth and rubbed a red ring of lipstick "There" she said "He's got his makeup on." She didn't care if it seemed shameless; she was a passionate girl, and that was it.

Stan said "You know. You are a natural lover." Ruth realised she, too, could play the game of tease and tantalise; so, she bent forward again, and this time she just nipped, not hard enough to hurt, but he felt it "You bitch!" He said. And, after that, he was so wild, driving it into her as if to get his own back; but what he gave her was a wilder deeper thrill; and she knew that, now, she was his equal.

No summer lasts.

The CO. asked to see Stan, and Stan went to the CO's office, and stamped and saluted; and Colonel Rudd told him the orders had come through for his WOSB and Good Luck!

He went to the other office and Captain Haggard gave him his orders and his Rail Warrant. The Captain said "You had a shot at WOSB once before, Sergeant?"

"Yes, Sir!'

"What was the problem?"

"Don't know. Sir. Thought I'd done well Sir."

"Perhaps you try too hard. Relax. Look as though you're giving the other chaps a chance."

Stan made no comment, but he thought "Smug Bugger! Give the others a chance? And what chance will I have then?"

Stan broke his usual rule, and went over to married quarters in uniform. He didn't stroll, he marched as he always did when he was in uniform, and he didn't march at Gunner pace either, he marched fast, more like Light Infantry, and no messing. He looked a Credit, he knew that: his boots were the shiniest, his uniform the best fitting - he'd not left it to the

16

regimental tailor, he'd had the alterations done in town, just like the officers; and he'd paid for them himself. His beret was just right, with the brass cap-badge glinting, with the gun and the motto "Quo Fas et Gloria ducunt" - where honour and glory lead.

When he passed any of the men, Gunners and Bombardiers, they jumped to it, whatever they were doing, and Stan liked that. He saw a Gunner, a sloppy individual, a National Serviceman, skiving behind a hedge, smoking, and Stan shouted "Bombardier! Take his name!" and the whole square jumped.

He marched past a gun-troop who were practising loading-drill at the edge of the square. The four 25-pounders were in line, with the gunners rigid and expectant, some kneeling, ready to ram, some standing, ready to load. The troop commander, a National Service subaltern gave the order, and all hell broke loose, but disciplined hell: crash the breech open; ram the shell and set the charge; close the breech; then, frozen expectancy again. Control.

"Number One Gun Ready!" yelled the gun-commander, a Sergeant, kneeling, arm in the air. "Fire! "

It was only dummies, of course, not even a blank, but Stan was proud of them; he'd trained that Troop.

Stan flung up his best bullshit salute as he passed the officer, who nodded, and called "Good morning, Sergeant" and touched his cap nonchalantly with his hand.

"Sloppy bastard" Muttered Stan to himself. He'd never put up such a sloppy salute when he was commissioned. Insulting!

Stan knocked at the door, and `Q' Evans answered; he had his boots off, and his tie, and he was munching a "wad" that looked straight from the NAAFI.

Ruth was drinking tea in the kitchen, and Stan said

"I'm off to WOSB!" and `Q' said, in his wry way "An officer is it? - I'll have to practise my salutes!"

Stan always suspected that he had been given the wrong advice at school - what could you expect from a dump like that, anyway - half the teachers had been conchies during the war, or bloody Army cooks, or Bevin boys down the mines; not like the Public Schools, where all the masters had been majors or higher.

Then Stan discovered you could get a Regular Commission through the "back door", by joining-up in the Ranks. The snag was, if you failed WOSB, you were stuck in the Ranks, a "gentleman ranker", a "poor little lamb who's lost his way", like Kipling wrote.

It went wrong for Stan, first time at WOSB - "not sufficiently mature! " they said. "My arse!" thought Stan.

But, they couldn't call him immature now, not any more. Stan had matured all right; he'd matured by four years' slog in the Ranks, and working himself up from Gunner to Bombardier to Sergeant, a spell in Germany and another in the Canal Zone. "Get some service in sonny" was Stan's motto; and Stan was admired as the man who could turn out the smartest gun crew in the regiment. And he'd learnt, he'd made sure of that: he'd learnt by watching, and he'd bought himself cavalry-twill trousers and chukka boots from Moss Bros; and he'd had his uniform tailored just so.

WOSB lasted two days and this time, second time around, it was familiar to Stan. He went by train and truck to Barton Stacey in the Hampshire forest. "Make yourselves at home, lads. Treat it as an adventure," they said. And, an adventure it was; the assault course, up the ladders, up the trees, swing on the rope, jump the ditch - Stan left them all for dead, all but a few, the ones as fit as himself. Then, there were the meals, an officer at every table - Stan was on his guard here - watch your manners, don't talk too loud, don't boast. A few drinks at the bar - sip slowly, nothing rash, informal, but on your guard; you never knew who was watching. Then, the tactical exercises; organise the group, show a bit of leadership. Stan formed them up, and called the Orders - not like a Sergeant, oh no, Stan was too canny for that; more like an officer, polite but firm. Then the interviews "Your motives for a Commission, Sergeant?" - "Serve my country Sir; self-fulfilment", all the usual blah. Then the written tests, not so easy those, a few puzzles, rather tricky; but he thought he'd done all right.

And then the result - Fail!

"Ruth. The bastards failed me!"

March around Camp, head high, feeling like Hell, the hurt of it; but keep smiling, don't give the bastards the satisfaction...keep smiling.

First the CO. "Bad luck, Sergeant" then the Adjutant "Bad luck!"

"Thank you, Sir."

And then, the next bombshell; couldn't they give him a bit of peace?

"Sergeant. Your posting's through. Korea!"

"Ruth. I'm posted to Korea - embarkation leave, and then Korea."

"Oh Stan!" she said "Oh Stan."

"Come away with me" he said "Let's spend my leave together. You can take some time off from the library."

Ruth said "Don't be silly. Could you see Dad allowing it?"

"Let's get engaged" said Stan, and thought a bit "Better still. Let's get married."

Ruth laughed "You always were impulsive, Stan - but I'm not getting married in a hurry. I need to think."

"If we were engaged. What would your Dad say then? To our spending my leave together?"

The 'Q' was surprisingly co-operative.

"You may be two years in Korea, Stan; a year at least" - perhaps he remembered his own loneliness during the war.

So, that was how they became engaged, and how they had a sort of honeymoon; and how the doubts that had been subconscious surfaced in Ruth's mind.

They went on the bike of course, with luggage in the panniers. Because they were going further, Ruth bought goggles and wrapped up against the wind, and heigh-ho for Torquay and the South-West. Stan bought her an engagement ring, quite a respectable diamond - Stan never seemed short of money, what with his Sergeant's pay; and his parents were comfortable and indulgent. Stan was never mean, you could say that for him.

They bought a cheap wedding ring to look respectable, and they signed the register as Mr. and Mrs. Phillips. It was late summer, and the hotel wasn't full; but the air was mild, and the days were filled with speed, over the moors, Dartmoor, and around the coast, Salcombe and everywhere.

There was another couple at the hotel, and, when the husband saw Stan's gunners' tie, he said he was in the infantry: he thought Stan was another officer, and Stan didn't disillusion him - Ruth was glad of that, and a bit ashamed of herself that she was glad. The girl was very lah-de-dah; she had bobbed hair and she sat on a cocktail-stool in a stylish way. She was called Annabel, Annabel Bilton and she sat on the stool - it was a chrome stool with a swivel top - as though she was posing on a pedestal, her ankles crossed under the stool to best advantage, and her skirt tight to show off her legs.

Annabel always drank Pimm's through a straw, and had a seductive way of sucking the straw that gave men ideas; and she was pert and bubbly as the Pimrns.

Annabel had a schoolfriend who hunted in Shropshire, Claire Fox-Denny. Did Ruth hunt? - "Oh Claire is so good with horses. I must give you her address." Puck Bilton had a super car, a Fraser Nash, and when he saw the Norton he said "Oh, super!" - they both said "Oh, super! " quite a lot. He was taken by the power of the bike. Annabel said "Oh Ruth, how do you manage on that thing? Your clothes, and everything. You always look so super. You're a miracle."

And Puck said "My Platoon Sergeant has a bike like that. A marvellous machine. He's famous for it." Then he stopped short, wondering if he'd dropped a clanger; and Ruth pretended not to notice. But she did notice, a sort of doubt behind the enthusiasm, as though a motorbike was, well, not quite the thing, you know.

Once, Ruth came into the bar, and she overheard Puck say "She's a fine girl; and well-bred. But him. I can't make him out. Seems a bit of a cad, if you ask me."

The nights were wild. The last morning, Ruth got out of bed, and stood, naked at the window, looking out to sea. She heard Stan in the bed behind her and he was punching the pillow in frustration "Oh, hell" he said "Fucking, shitting, hell! "

"What's up?"

'What's up? I don't want to go to fucking Korea. That's what."

"Can't you leave the Army, Stan? Buy yourself out?"

"And look as yellow as the North Korean Gooks? - Not Stan Phillips."

"What then, Stan?"

"I'll do my stint" He waited, and said, quietly "Ruth - please marry me now. It would make it easier in Korea."

She said "Stan. Stan. I must have time, I've got your engagement ring, and I must have time."

She looked out to sea again, and she looked at the mirror on the wall beside her; and she looked, quite dispassionately, at the reflection of a "Damned fine girl", quite tall, with the long legs and broad shoulders, very square; and the face with the generous mouth, and the short, black hair. And, she had to stop herself thinking "I can do better than this; better than wife of a sergeant, and follow the drum." She knew then that she'd never marry Stan, that she was officer material, even if he wasn't. She knew, then, as she faced the pitiless sea, that things had changed for ever between herself and Stan, that now it was she who was the stronger.

She crossed her hands over her breasts, and turned away from the sea, to face the mirror; to admire the sheen of black in her hair, and the way her breasts stood proud. She squeezed her nipples, hard, between her fingers, and she reached for her lipstick to tint each nipple to match her lips. And, where the lipstick rubbed each tip it tingled tight.

Stan was quiet and still - he was watching her from the bed, now, the last morning, the last time; and Ruth was greater than Stan, and she knew she would never marry him. But, Ruth was grateful to Stan, for opening the door on her soul; and he still excited her.

She went to the washbag and took out a frenchie and said "These rubber people are making a fortune out of us."

She pulled aside the sheet, and he was rampant - he was always like that when she came to him. He just lay there, and his cock was high and fit to burst. She put the frenchie over the cock, careful, and she pulled it down, the way she pulled up her stockings: not to snag; she always thought of that.

22

Stan must have been thinking the same, for he said "Put on your stockings, Ruth. Please."

Ruth smiled, and put on her girdle, and sat on the edge of the bed. She took a stocking, and pulled it slowly over her foot and rolled it upwards and pulled it taut; and then the other. She clipped the suspenders and each suspender was stretched over the skin between the girdle and the top of the stockings, where the tuft of hair was jet-black and springy, and already damp with desire. She stood tall by the bed, then she knelt on the bed, and, with a quick movement she swung one leg across him, to straddle him.

She said. "Just lie back, Stan."

He nodded, because of the ecstacy of it, but it was an uncertain nod because his initiative was slipping away.

Ruth raised up, on her knees and reached behind her and held the cock up hard; and then she slithered down on it, until it was home. She sat up straight, and as she felt the hardness, all manner of ideas went through her mind.

She remembered Annabel and what she'd said about Claire Fox-Denny who had such a lovely seat on a horse, and Ruth thought "I bet her seat isn't as good as this one", and Ruth said to herself "Why shouldn't I ride to hounds just the same as she, and go to Balls, and play the Lady?" and there, squatting there, one side of her in ecstacy but the other side dispassionate, she decided, yes, that's what she'd do.

"Stan" she said "Stroke my nipples". She didn't say Please, it was more like a command, and he did as he was told. She sat upright, like a good rider, and he reached his hands to her breasts and touched them until they thrust forward and the veins were blue around the nipples.

Ruth reached down, and touched Stan's nipples with her nails, and when she touched, the cock twitched inside her. Whenever she wanted him to twitch, and she wanted it again, yes, again, she touched him, and he was twitching so fast it made him pant. Then she remembered the first time, when he'd tantalised her, above the Falls at Betwys-y-Coed, when he'd loved to tantalise her, to work her up to it until she begged him, until he made her say "Fuck me. Oh please Stan. Fuck me" and he'd held back until she'd said it. But now, it was Stan, and he was saying "I can't bear it. Ruth. You've got to move. Now. Oh, Ruth" and she said "Wait Stan. Wait. I like it."

And he said "Oh, Ruth, you'll kill me. Finish it now."

And she laughed "Oh Stan. Remember the first time? It was me that begged. Remember?" and she said 'Do you want it, Stan?" she said "Do you want it?"

"Oh yes, oh yes." He said.

"Say Please."

Their eyes met, and he knew. And his eyes dropped, and he said, quietly, he said "Please."

But Ruth sat, steady, a good seat, steady, and ready for the fence.

She touched him again, and again, faster, and the cock was hot and twitching. "Oh please," he said "Please."

"Please what? Stan?"

"Oh fuck me, Ruth. Please. Ruth. Please fuck me."

She began to move, hard down in the saddle and knees very high, short stirrup. Grip with the knees - she'd heard the old horse-Gunners say it. Up down, up down in the trot, in time with the horse, up down, up down, and...down hard, down as the cock gushed, and all the shuddering, wonderful rush of it seemed to fill her, despite the rubber.

"Oh, Ruth" Stan said "Oh, Ruth. Why won't you marry me now?"

When she didn't answer, he said "Fuck bloody Korea!"

Ruth reached down, and held the rubber in place, and raised herself off him. She said "Only a year or so, Stan. It won't be long." But, as she said it, she knew it would be too long for her.

He took her back to camp, and the dreary year without Stan stretched ahead of Ruth. She started going out with the girls again, and it was girls' talk that irritated Ruth "Oh, what a lovely engagement ring!" and "Have you heard from Stan, lately?" Or, it was all about their own boyfriends, Bombardier this, who had a car, and Sergeant that, who had tattoos all over, what a giggle!, - all over his arms and chest at any rate "I don't know about the rest," - and they all giggled again. They went to the garrison dance, in the same little group, sort of mutual defence, until the last waltz of course when they'd let someone "see them home;" and Ruth knew they'd be off behind a wall, or anywhere - how far will she let him go this time? - and all prim and prissy again next week.

But Ruth could hardly bear to let them touch her - those rough hands, those sweaty hands - she could hardly even bear to dance with them any more, she had to force herself, or she'd have gone mad with loneliness. At least the engagement ring was some protection, so when it was "Can I see you home?" Ruth could say "Oh thank you, no - my fiancé's in Korea."

Once, some of the young officers came into the dance; they came in late, as they sometimes did after a good night at the Mess, and they were the same officers that had been in the pub near Betwys-y-Coed that time she'd been with Stan; when she'd wished that Stan was one of them and he'd said that she could be one of them if she wanted to, but, he couldn't not until he'd passed WOSB. But Stan hadn't passed WOSB, he'd gone to Korea, and now, she could be one of them, or loyal to Stan; she had a choice.

The officers recognised her and one said "Where's the handsome soldier then? Where's Sgt. Phillips'?"

"Korea," she said "I thought you must have known,"

He asked her to dance, and he said "You're not like the other girls here," and, later, he said "Can I see you again?"

She put him off, but, afterwards, she wondered what she'd have done if she'd found him attractive, and she smiled to herself. She knew damn well what she'd have done, and the engagement ring would have been off her finger, and into her purse.

2. GUY

Guy did his National Service straight after school; between leaving school and going up to Oxford. Some chaps did it the other way around, but it was better to be older at University; besides, he'd always been one for getting the worst things over and out of the way and saving the best bite for the last. Some of the Beaks at school had tried to change his mind, said he'd get out of the habit of academic work, and they were probably right; but Guy wouldn't budge.

So, Guy kissed Mary goodbye at Paddington, quite a respectable kiss, not like the night before when he'd kissed her in the car, and she'd let him go quite far, really; he'd unhooked her 'bra and she didn't stop him. She was a super girl, Mary, and he'd been taking her out for a year, off and on, during the school hols..

Guy chose the Gunners, though some of the other fellows at Radford rather poo-poohed that. They were going into the Cavalry or into the Guards, and, well, the Gunners might be O.K. for some people; but for an old Radfordian? Really? Weren't there a few chaps in the Artillery who were, well, not quite pukka, if you know what I mean?

But the Guns appealed to Guy, and, the train took him to Oswestry in Shropshire, no-man's-land. They sorted out a potential officers' Troop, but, to Guy's surprise, some of the men in the other Troops, working-class lads, were good company. There was the chap from Manchester, a real Lancashire lad, Gunner Davenport, Mick Davenport, who could have dropped Guy into deep shit if he'd wanted to. They had been on Guard together, Mick and Guy, and Guy had fallen asleep at his Post, a Court-Martial offence which might have cost Guy his hope of a commission. Mick noticed Guy sleeping, and he noticed the duty officer coming on his Rounds; he could have left Guy sleeping, but he didn't. He moved quick and quiet, the way they do in Manchester if the coppers are about; and he put a hand on Guy's shoulder to wake him and a warning finger on Guy's lips; and he saved Guy.

My God; it could have been CO's Orders, and a Reprimand, and, maybe, stopped from taking WOSB - my God, the disgrace of it. Every old Radfordian got a Commission, well, everyone except the real duffers whom Guy had never noticed at school.

Mick Davenport was cunning, and tough, and he'd come through a few fights in Manchester. He was as quick-witted as any potential officer, but they could never have commissioned him. He was broad Lancashire, not that that, in itself, would have barred him from an Officers' Mess, a Gunner Mess at any rate; but he was crude and loud, and he didn't give a bugger for anyone.

The NCO's chased everyone around from arsehole to breakfast time, as the saying went, but it was all bullshit really, and no worse than the Corps had been at school. Even square-bashing was fun but Guy had to admit he was looking forward to the day he got a batman; it was such a bore, bulling-up his boots and brasses. Of course he would pass WOSB, he never doubted that for a second - you got that self-confidence from being at a school like Radford. The best part of all was the gunnery, and Guy was glad he'd chosen the Gunners: the gun-drill on 25-pounders, the crash of the breech, and load, and ram; the frenzy of getting into action "Halt! Action Rear!"; the swing of the gun and the limber; loaded and ready to fire. It was fun!

Then Guy got his orders for WOSB; a detachment of them went down to WOSB together: train to Andover and truck to Barton Stacey, and the Major there sorting them into squads. Guy's squad was a mixture, mostly young National Servicemen like himself: some other Gunners, a couple from the Guards, and a Cavalryman; a Dragoon. And there was one oddball, a Gunner Sergeant from Oswestry, Sergeant Phillips, a real Regimental type, full of bull and full of himself.

At NAAFI-break, after the assault course, Guy queued for his coffee and his bun, and sat down in his denims, dripping wet below the knee. He said, half-mocking himself "It was a swamp under that rope-swing. I should have kept my knees up".

One fellow said "Don't worry. I don't suppose Tarzan passed WOSB," But Sergeant Phillips - he was still "Sergeant" though everyone else was on Christian-names - Sergeant Phillips barked out "How long are you going to stay muddy like that? Call yourself Officer material?"

Guy just looked at the others - it was no good trying to explain - some chaps had no sense of humour. Phillips was like that the whole time, sort of edgy, and the harder they tried to fit him in, the edgier he became.

The Major handed out the paper slips at the end, and most of them had passed. "Christ!" barked Phillips, as he read his. "Failed!"

For Guy, Mons Officer Cadet School was even better than Oswestry - there was still plenty of bulling-up and still no batman, but it was all go, and he felt so bloody fit. The rugger season was starting, and the rugger was super, like at Radford only better. The gun-drill and the square-bashing were something to take a pride in, and, even though they bawled at you till Kingdom-Come, the Sgt.-Majors were not bad fellows at all. They even called you "Sir" in recognition of your future status, though, admittedly, you called them "Sir" as well; and, as that old warrior, most outsize of Sgt.-Majors "Tiffy" Brittain told you "You are the only Bloody one that means it!"

They had a couple of free weekends, and Guy was able to get up to London and take Mary out to Quags - Quaglino's was Mary's favourite night-spot. It was dreamy dancing with

Mary, and she let Guy kiss her afterwards, and go further than she'd ever let him go.

Then - he could hardly believe it: the time had passed like an express-train - it was the end of the Course and Guy's Commissioning Parade: past the saluting base with the band thumping and blaring, and "Eyes Right!" to the Field Marshal on the Saluting Platform, and up to Woolwich to the Gunners' Headquarters, the "Shop," to be dined-in to the Royal Regiment of Artillery.

Outside, on the floodlit gravel stood the row of brass cannon, and, here, inside, sat Guy and the other new officers in that great Mess, full of Generals and Brigadiers and Colonels, with the military band playing, and "Pass the Port," and the Loyal Toast proposed by the Mess President, a General.

"Mr. Vice - the Queen!" and "Mr. Vice", the senior subaltern, proposed the Toast: "The Queen! "

All stood up - all in Blue Uniform: No.1 Mess Dress, or some in Blue Patrols, cut tight for horseback in the old tradition. Raise the glass - Emotion and Tradition.

"The Queen - our Captain-General!" - for, so she was, the new young Queen; not yet crowned yet Captain-General of the Guns.

Guy drank too much, of course; they all did, - and he slept the deep sleep. And, in the morning he said goodbye to all the others, who were off to Gunner regiments around the world, to Hong-Kong or the little Hell in Korea; or to Malaya which was worse in a way, with Hell always around the corner; to the Canal Zone, that strip of fly-blown sand; to Malta; to Germany; and to all the Gunner regiments in theU.K.: Ack-Ack, Field Guns, Light and Heavy, and Coast Guns, the Big Guns at the Forts.

But Guy was posted back to Oswestry, to train recruits.

What an anticlimax: all that opportunity to see the world and they had to give him this! Eighteen months more in the Army, a year-and a half of his life.

Guy went back to Oswestry in his car, to the Officers' Mess that had been so familiar from the outside when he'd been a recruit. Now he got his own room with a coke stove, and they gave him a batman, a skiving rogue called Gunner Porter. And, at Oswestry, Guy was dined-in again as always happened in the Gunners - there was the Mess at the "Shop" at Woolwich, and your own Regimental Mess, and you were a member of both.

A few people remembered Guy from when he had been a recruit, but not many - so many recruits passed through, they were just an Army Number on the Roll, and away. But Guy did get Sgt. Jackson as his Troop Sgt.; Sgt. Jackson had taught Guy his gun-drill, and Guy knew he could trust him. He saluted Guy, and they shook hands, and Guy asked about who else was still around that he knew, and he asked after Davenport, the Manchester lad.

Jackson laughed "He's a handful that one! He's done a spell in the glasshouse. But I hear he's got a stripe now: he's in Germany."

"And wasn't there a Sgt. Phillips? He tried WOSB."

"The man with the motor-bike? He was posted to Korea."

Guy said "Korea! Good God!"

Jackson said "He got off with the Qs daughter: got engaged to her." He paused, and added "Phillips didn't fit into the Sergeants' Mess. He thought he should have a Commission."

Guy said "It must have been tough for him. To want it so much; and to see chaps like myself get it."

"I'll tell you what, Sir" said Jackson "If Stan had been an officer, I would have hated to serve under him - you can't become a Gentleman by numbers."

"I know" said Guy "It's a bit unfair."

It was Christmas time and the last big Mess Night before most of the Regiment went on Christmas leave; Guy was the only newly-joined officer and they were dining him in.

Guy put on his Blues, his new No.1 Dress, and stood in front of the mirror. He thought he looked fine, though he wished he'd known about Blue Patrols before he'd bought the No.1 Dress. Patrols were supposed to be obsolete, but he'd fancy himself in Patrols; the bootees and the ceremonial silver spurs.

The evening followed like a religious ritual, conforming to the Dining-in at Woolwich in the way that a chapel service conforms to a service in a great Cathedral.

Guy introduced himself to the Colonel, the Mess President, Colonel Rufus Rudd. He clicked his heels, and bowed, and the Colonel offered him a drink. The Mess waiter, Gunner Flanagan, brought the sherry on a silver tray, and the Colonel signed the chit. He said "I hope you're happy here Guy. By the way, we don't use Ranks in the Mess. In the Mess, you call me Rufus."

"Yes, Sir... Yes... Rufus."

Rufus said "You know the adjutant? Capt. Haggard? Percy Haggard?"

Percy said "We've a tradition in this Mess, Guy. Newly joined officers do a little turn after dinner. Are you game?"

"A turn?" said Guy "What sort of turn?"

"Oh, anything - a song; a few jokes. Just a minute or two."

Guy said "I Pagliacci" - it was the first thing that came into his head, and Percy said "What the devil's that?"

Rufus overheard, and said, with a smile "They were operatic clowns, Percy. Poor sad clowns. Reluctant clowns. - All above your head, Percy."

Flanagan brought more drinks, and Rufus signed the chit; he said "It doesn't do to be too clever in the Army, Guy, or too arty. Just friendly advice. You're off to Oxford aren't you? After all this?"

- He's no fool, Rufus, thought Guy; no fool at all. He sipped his sherry and said "Cheers, Rufus! Thanks for the warning. But not all you Regular Soldiers are uncultured - only when it suits you."

Percy chipped in "Guy - be careful. Rufus is the CO.!"

Rufus said "Percy has old fashioned ideas about officers and Gentlemen."

The Duty Sergeant came in, all splendid with his red sash; he stamped to attention and announced

"Gentlemen. Dinner is served!"

Again it was like a Chapel service compared with the Cathedral of the Mess at the "Shop": just the one long table with the silver, and a small band, four-piece, playing airs; but, in a way, the microcosm made it more intense, more spiritual.

At the end, when the musicians had left, and only the initiated stayed in the holy-of-holies, then, after the loyal toast "the Queen - our Captain General"; then, it was Guy's "Turn". He emptied his glass, and refilled it, and emptied it again, and, thus fortified by Port, he gave them what they expected, the silly song, the dance, the prance, the prancing dance; and they all clapped and cheered and debouched from the Dining-room into the Ante-room; and, somehow, for no reason, Guy didn't follow, he just sat and he was alone: alone and unsober with the glasses, the plates, the crumpled napkins, the half-empty decanters, the guttering candles and his confused thoughts.

He could hear them all, happy as schoolboys; the noises of billiards balls whizzing and bouncing off the table, and upturned furniture, and the cheer when somebody won the obstacle race, under the carpet, and over the settee.

Percy came in, looking for him "Oh, there you are, Guy. Why aren't you in the Ante-room, with everybody?"

Guy said "Is there a law against privacy? That's not in Queen's Regulations." As he said it, he was ashamed of his brusqueness: Percy was too simple to understand. Besides, he didn't really understand himself, why he felt melancholy.

Percy said "Spoilsport! Look - you can't leave before the CO leaves. Why not join in the fun?"

"Fun you call it! It's all so bloody childish!"

Percy said "Many of these chaps were together in the war. At Alamein. Somehow, this horseplay is all part of that."

"Alamein? You'll be talking about Waterloo next."

Percy sat down, on the chair next to Guy. He said "Have it your own way, Guy. Waterloo, and Sebastopol and Ypres."

Guy said "Oh, cut it out, Percy. I know my Regimental History."

Percy said "We all know there's a childish side to it - when we're sober." and Guy said "Well, I'm not sober, far from it. Who could be sober after all I've drunk?"

Percy said "Oh, that! You did very well, Guy. We were proud of you!"

"Proud?" said Guy "I was ashamed. So, I've won my spurs have I? I've drunk a pint of Port out of a silver tankard, standing on the Mess table. And I sang a silly chorus. I'm so bloody ashamed!"

Percy said "Does Tradition mean nothing to you? Look, the other National Service officers are joining in...."

Guy said "Two years' National Service. The way to demoralise a nation."

Percy rose to that, he was getting angry. "Damn you" he said "The Army's saving the nation from itself; from the layabouts. We straighten them out."

Guy said "The Army will make a man of you," and he added "I'm bored; just bored. I'm less bored in here by myself than with the grown-up children next door."

Percy said "Oh Guy. Drink makes most men happy. Not you. Where's your sense of humour?"

Something got into Guy at that. He stood up, and took the nearest thing, a silver bowl, and plonked it on his head. Percy snatched it away, shouting "Stop it, damn you! That silver's sacred."

Guy said "That's my sense of humour! - Let's have a drink" and he shouted "Flanagan!"

- Flanagan came in "Yes. Sir?"

"Two brandies. Doubles."

Then Rufus came into the room, and Guy said "Oh Flanagan. Another double; for the C.O. ", Rufus said "I'm just leaving" and Guy said "You'll have the brandy before you go?" Rufus pulled up a chair and said "Guy I was impressed by your little turn on the table," and Guy said 'Do you admire a dancing bear?"

Rufus said "A dancing bear? You're drunk, Guy"

And Guy said "Drunk; oh yes, a little. Enough to recognise myself. I was the dancing bear."

Percy interrupted "I'm damned if I know what you're talking about."

And Rufus said "I think I understand."

Guy said "I danced on the table because I was expected to, not because I wanted to. Just like the poor bear."

Flanagan came in with the brandies, and Guy signed the chit. Rufus said "Thanks Guy. I hope you can afford this."

Percy said "Are we all bears, then, because we played the fool tonight?" and Guy said "Oh no. Only those of us who go against our true natures."

Percy said "It's all beyond me" and Guy said "Perhaps you're lucky not to be a bear. Just a natural, regimental officer."

Rufus had gone quiet. He was holding his hand over his glass, and he looked moody.

Suddenly he shouted "Damn you, Guy! Damn you!" and he seemed almost to be crying. Guy said "I'm sorry – Colonel; Sir; Rufus I mean. I didn't realise you hated it, just as much as I."

Rufus said "You won't be excused from dinner nights; remember that."

Percy suddenly jumped to his feet, holding up his glass and saying "I have a toast! The Regiment! Right of the Line!"

There was no point in ignoring it; Rufus stood and joined in, and so did Guy. Then Guy said "I have another toast! Rudyard Kipling!"

"Why Kipling?"

"Because he wrote the Regimental Anthem - Screw Guns!"

Rufus said, to humour him "All right. Kipling!" and the

three of them drank.

Then Guy said "Ubique!" and drank again, and Percy said "Ah. Some Latin we all know. The Gunners' motto. Everywhere."

"Everywhere" Guy said "Everywhere - to blow a hole in a man, and to splatter his guts on a wall."

Rufus finished his brandy and said "I must be going. By the way, Guy - excuse my talking shop in the Mess. You do know you'll have to stay in Camp over Christmas? The junior Subaltern is Orderly Officer over Christmas. It's a tradition."

Guy said "Tradition. That makes it right then. Tradition" and Percy said "You're learning, Guy."

Rufus said "Oh, Percy. Can't you hear the mockery?" and he shouted "Flanagan! My hat and stick, and my belt!"

Rufus left, and Percy said "Cheer up. It's not so bad really. Actually, I always volunteer to stay here myself at Christmas. It's like an extra leave allowance; although you don't go away."

"How do you mean?"

"Well; all duties cease between Christmas and New Year. So, you just hang around and enjoy yourself. It's one big party, really; and it doesn't count against Leave entitlement."

"Sounds promising."

"There's only one snag. The chaps who stay in camp do Orderly Officer. Turn and turn about. I do my share."

Guy said "All these parties. Who comes to them?"

"Well, there are all the local girls - farmers' daughters. And all the families back for Christmas. Rufus' daughter for instance - Prunella - she'll be back from Oxford."

Guy noticed with surprise that Percy looked shy, as though embarrassed to mention the girl. Percy added, quickly, to cover his confusion. "And, after New Year, when everybody's back in Mess - there's the Mess Ball. Now, that's something! "

Guy brightened up "There's a girl I'd like to ask to that. Her name's Mary - she's a super girl. I'll ask her up from London."

Percy said "You'll like Prunella. And you'll like it here at Christmas. The Mess rules are relaxed - lady friends allowed in the Mess, and all that."

There was a loud bang outside, and then another, and Percy said "Thunderflashes! Good Lord, they are priming the old brass cannon."

And Guy said "Idiots! Children; dangerous children. Perhaps you have to be a child to lead an Army."

And Percy said "You talk in riddles. Look. I'll have to go and sort them out. Stop them blowing us all up."

He went out, and Guy heard a few curt words, and some laughter; the noise subsided, and there were shouts of "Goodnight! " and Guy felt a grudging admiration for Percy the Adjutant.

Guy picked up a silver cup, from the table, looked at it in the mock-serious way of someone who has drunk too much, stared hard at the Inscription and read aloud "The Pride Cup for Gunnery" then, he reached for the decanter, and half-filled the cup with Port. He stood up, swaying a little and he spoke out, holding up the cup like a libation. He said "Now Gentlemen, we come to the highlight of the evening: Mr. Baker, our newly joined subaltern - Mr. Baker will sing and dance - dance and sing..." at that, Guy slumped muttering to himself "No better than a dancing bear. A bloody bear,"

Flanagan came in quietly and said "Are you all right,

Sir?"

"I'm all right Flanagan. It's late" and Flanagan said "Don't you worry, Sir. Gentlemen are often like this on Mess Nights. We expect it, Sir. Nobody minds."

Guy said "I'm not really drunk, Flanagan."

"Of course not, Sir. Lord - the sights I've seen. But, Gentlemen are always bright and shining next morning on parade. I admire that, Sir. Officers never let you down."

Guy said "You admire officers?"

"Oh, yes, Sir. I was saved by an Officer at Alamein."

Guy said "Tell me, Flanagan. Do you mind cleaning-up? All this mess?" "Lord, no, Sir. The officers depend on me."

Guy said "When you see an officer behaving worse than a child, throwing billiards balls around in here - do you still respect him?"

"Of course, Sir. It's tradition, isn't it, Sir?"

Guy said "Tradition! - Yes. Do the others - all the Other-Ranks in Camp - do they know what goes on here?"

"Of course, Sir. They expect it. They know the Officers won't let them down when it counts."

Guy said "Even temporary Officers like myself? - I wish I had your faith, Flanagan." "Tradition, Sir. Tradition will pull you through."

"Thank you Flanagan" said Guy "Goodnight" and, to himself, he whispered "I'll not dance to their tune. I'll be no bear."

*****

39

It was Christmas Eve, and Guy the Orderly Officer came into the Mess, after his Rounds. Guy had to admit it, there was something in what Percy had said: there was a warmness, and a comradeship in Camp, and not only amongst the officers - amongst the men too, the ones who'd stayed, who'd volunteered to stay; veterans mostly who must have felt something they could never have expressed, about staying. There was strong drink in plenty, but no drunkenness; more like a drowsiness, an alcoholic hibernation. Even the Guard were happy - they grumbled of course, grumbling was a Tradition - but, really, they were happy; and Sgt. Jackson, who was guard Commander this Christmas Eve was the right man for it.

Guy came into the Mess, took off his hat and Sam-Browne Belt, and loosened the collar of his No.1 dress.

There was a noise in the darkened anteroom, and it was Percy and a girl. There was a settee with its back to the door, and they'd been on the settee; and, when their heads appeared above the settee back, they were all rumpled. They saw Guy and were glad to see him.

Percy said "How's the Orderly Dog? _ I don't think you know the CO's daughter? - Prunella, - let me introduce Guy Baker."

Prunella smiled - she was a warm girl with an open smile. She said "Hello Guy - oh, you must be cold. Do get him a drink, Percy."

Guy said "Excuse my glad rags, Prunella. I'm duty officer. The only one in uniform at Christmas."

Prunella said "I've always liked uniform." Percy shouted "Flanagan! Is there any Christmas bubbly, Flanagan?"

Flanagan said "I put some in the fridge, Sir. Just in

case."

Flanagan brought the Champagne, and glasses, and the chit for Percy to sign. Guy said "You were right, Percy. Christmas in Mess is not at all bad."

Prunella said "An Army Christmas is wonderful. Especially abroad. Even Plum Pudding in hot weather tastes good at Christmas-time. All the parties; all the children's parties. Perhaps it's just nostalgia for my childhood"

Percy said "When will you turn out the Guard, Guy?"

"I was going to wait until midnight - Symbolic!"

Prunella said "Guy. What are you going to do. After National Service?"

"I follow you to Oxford - in the Army's good time.'

Prunella said "Thank heaven for National Service. It makes the men at Oxford so much more mature. A godsend to women."

Guy said, sarcastically "That's all right for you, Auntie!"

Prunella said "For you, too, if you only think about it. You will be more mature when you get to Oxford. Girls always look up to older men."

Guy said "This is lovely bubbly. I'm feeling the effect already."

Percy said "That's what Christmas is all about. Surely."

And Guy said "Oh, really? How about the little matter of the Babe in the Manger?" Percy said "You mean Jingle Bells and all that kind of thing?" He went over to the corner, to the wireless set, switched it on, and, when it warmed up it was playing "Jingle Bells."

Guy said "That's uncanny. Jingle Bells. Did you say

41

"Open Sesame" for that coincidence?"

Percy said "Why Open Sesame?" and Prunella interrupted, "Oh, Percy, you are silly! - Yes - Open Sesame. - Christmas is a bit like the Arabian Nights - all those Christmases abroad. When I was young."

Guy said "There were no sleighbells, no jingle bells in Palestine; for the Messiah, that first Christmas. Just dust, and the sharp desert night. In a way it was the Arabian Nights; but, before Islam, and Mahomet."

Percy angrily switched off the wireless "What the Hell are you two talking about?" Guy said, rather smugly "We're conducting a dialectic - about imposing a European Culture on a Semitic Tradition."

And Prunella said "Or vice-versa. One good myth begets another."

Guy called out "Flanagan! The other bottle, please, Flanagan."

Percy said "Let's play Gunnery" and Guy said "How do you mean? A busman's holiday?"

Prunella said "Oh, we play Gunnery at home sometimes. We all know the orders. Daddy taught us."

Percy took the Dinner Gong from its place in the corner, the brass Gong with the elephants. He said "You be Observation Officer, Guy. Imagine you've spotted the enemy. Prunella - you be Troop Commander; and I'll be Sergeant in Command of a Gun."

Guy started to give the Orders, the Orders he had heard so often, but Prunella interrupted "Oh, Guy. Not like that. It's got to be real - like Daddy does it. Like this" and she lay down on the floor behind a chair. So Guy lay down, feeling rather foolish, playing along; after all, it was Christmas and the time for games. He shouted out, rather lamely.

"Troop Target!" and gave an imaginary map reference, any old number that came into his head. Then all was pandemonium.

Prunella called "Halt! Action Front!" and Percy grabbed the settee and swung it violently around.

Prunella said "Load!" and Percy, was miming at loading and ramming, then kneeling with his arm raised "Number One Gun - Ready" he shouted.

Then Prunella, laughing with excitement, shouted, "Come on, Guy. Order Gunfire", so Guy shouted "Stonk! Stonk! Stonk! - which meant they could have the whole bloody Regiment firing at once, so Percy yelled "Fire!" and thumped the Gong so hard it sounded like Airburst.

They all flopped back on the chairs and settee, and drank more champagne. Prunella was as bubbly as the liquid, and Guy could see why Percy was so gone on her; she wasn't a beauty, but she was fun, and he could forgive her remarks about older men, she was quite right really. Guy said; he blurted it out and he was quite surprised at himself "You know, Pru, chaps like me - we've never known girls as friends; as ordinary friends."

And Prunella said "You mean - you want me to look after you at Oxford?"

Guy laughed "Something like that - oh, I've got a girlfriend - Mary's coming to the Mess Ball. But a chap needs a friend. A sort of favourite Auntie."

Prunella wondered about Guy, and thought he wasn't as ingenuous as he seemed, and said "I don't know if I like the "Auntie" bit.

Percy said "This is real fun. It's why I stay in Camp at Christmas" and Guy said - it must have been the champagne again - "You mean - it's Prunella keeps you here at Christmas!"

Then Percy said - and Guy wondered if it was a gesture of independence from. Prunella "I'm off for a stroll around the lines. Anybody coming?"

Guy said "Once is enough, for me. The Orderly Officer's done his rounds" and Prunella said "He wants to go alone. He wants to visit his beloved Guns on Christmas Eve."

When Percy had gone, Guy said "Christmas in the Army! This is fun. But, what about the chaps in Korea? Iced up in a dugout? They have to set fire to oil-drums to get any warmth. And the drums often explode: not so as you would notice, with all the high explosive going off. All tensed up, waiting for the Gooks, or waiting for a barrage as a Christmas present."

Prunella said "That's the Army. Here - or There. Heaven, or Hell."

Guy said "Take Percy. I admire him, in a way; but he's a Military fanatic."

Prunella said "It's the comradeship. They'll go miles to attend re-unions. The Desert Rats and so on. Sand in your Christmas pud is a shared experience. Like the blazing oil-drums in Korea."

Guy said "I don't think your father is a Military fanatic."

There was a sound at the door, and it was Rufus.

Guy said "This is really Christmas magic!"

Prunella said "Yes - Magic! We were talking about you Dad. And, before, we were talking about "Jingle Bells", and it came on the wireless."

Rufus was in his favourite old clothes, his old Duffle coat. He said "Hello Prune. I thought you were with Percy. I won't stay!"

Prunella said "Don't be silly, Daddy. Christmas Eve in the Mess, without the Traditional visit from the Colonel?"

Guy said "There's plenty of Champagne. I'll ask Flanagan to bring another glass."

Prunella said "Percy's gone to visit the guns. I expect he'll call in at the Sergeants' Mess and the Guardroom. But, mostly, it's the guns."

Guy poured, and Rufus sipped the Champagne. He said "I can understand Percy. Why he wants to visit the guns on Christmas Eve. The line of guns against the night sky."

Guy said "It's pagan. Worshipping a bloody lump of metal. A belching, fiery lump of steel - Moloch."

Prunella said "The guns are our friends. Dependable" and Rufus said "When a line of Guns is all that stands between yourself and Rommel's tanks, they are friends indeed."

Flanagan came in, and he looked nervous, alarmed. He spoke to Rufus. "Phone-call, Sir. The Guardroom. Urgent."

Guy jumped up "I'm Orderly Officer. I'll take it."

When Percy left the Mess he'd been in two minds whether to turn back; he knew he was being childish. That remark of Guy's, it had needled him a bit, made him look like Prunella's pet puppy. Those two with their smart remarks, Pru and that too-smart Guy.

So, he kept going, towards the Square and the Gun Park. There they were, his friends, snouts raised and ready. He glanced around: there was nobody, not even the Guard; nobody but himself and the Guns. He went over to the nearest gun, and stood close to the barrel and put his arm on the barrel as you would on the shoulder of an old friend. He stood there for a minute, then he stuck his hands into the pockets of his trench coat and walked slowly towards the Guard Room. The

45

guard recognised him - the soldier had his rifle at the slope and he gave the salute, slap-the-butt. Percy raised his hat; he was wearing the old tweed hat, and he called through the door of the Guardroom "Don't turn-out the Guard, Sergeant. Just a friendly call,"

It was Sgt. Jackson "Merry Christmas, - Sir."

Then there was a shout and the sound of running heels, and a soldier stumbling over the words "Sergeant. Sergeant. A truck. A truck's stuck on the level crossing."

Percy said "Follow me, Sergeant. And bring some men" and he started to run, down the hill towards the railway. There was the truck, across the line, and jammed against the mechanism of the gate. And from not so far away, came the chuntering rumble of the steam engine. Somehow, the truck had jammed everything and rumbling destruction was on its way.

It was a high truck, a 3-Tonner. Percy reached for the door and swung himself up, and the driver was Christmas-drunk and heavy over the wheel.

"Get this man out Sergeant" shouted Percy, and together they dragged him down to the ground, and the Sergeant pulled him clear. The truck wouldn't start, she was dead, and Percy shouted "Manhandle her! Push like hell." But, she was jammed, and the rumble of the train was rising to thunder. "Jump clear, Sir!" The Sergeant screamed. But, when Guy and Rufus ran up, the train was hissing to a halt, and the truck was bent and buckled, and Percy dead.

After the night - the night of no rest, and no peace; the night that should have been the most peaceful night of all nights. After the night of dragging clear the wreckage, and telephones, telephones ringing all night long, and trying to deal with the engine-driver and the Railway people. After that night, as the Christmas dawn crept into the Guardroom, and the electric light became somehow even harsher. After that

46

night, and in that dawn, Rufus sat on one of the Guardroom bunks; the stretcher was on the floor, with the body covered by a blanket.

Guy said "Nothing left to do Sergeant, but wait."

Sgt. Jackson said "Nothing else to do Sir" and Guy said "I still can't believe it. A couple of hours ago he was still alive, and celebrating Christmas."

The Sergeant said "It was like that in the war, Sir. You would be chatting with your mates - maybe having a drink. An hour later, they would be gone - bought it!"

Guy said "It should have been me, by rights. I'm Orderly Officer."

Rufus said "Sit down, Guy. You're shocked" and Guy said "It's a shocking thing." Rufus said "Perhaps its a glorious thing." He turned to Sergeant Jackson and said "I'm still confused Sergeant. How did it happen?"

The Sergeant said "The Sentry reported the vehicle on the level-crossing." "Didn't he try to get if off?" asked Rufus.

Sergeant Jackson said "He can't drive, Sir. And the driver was slumped over the wheel."

"Drunk'?"

"You saw him Sir. Drunk. He's in the cells."

Rufus said "What happened when you arrived at the crossing?

"We could hear the train, Sir. The Captain shouted out. He said..."

"Yes. Sergeant?"

"He said..." It sounds like the barrage at Alamein. The Stonk!" - We could see the engine, too, Sir. Its lights, and the furnace, and the smoke; even in the dark."

Guy interrupted "Did the Captain look scared?"

"Scared Sir? Oh, no, Sir; not the Captain. Just the opposite really. He looked happy."

"Happy?'

"Yes, Sir. Determined. Determined and happy. We pulled the driver out, and the Captain jumped in."

Rufus said "The driver will be Court-Martialled, of course."

Guy said "The driver's still alive. There's no justice."

And Rufus said, rather abruptly,

"Do you think Percy was thinking about justice?"

Guy said "It's amazing how soon we're back to normal! The road's clear; the line's clear. And Percy's - dead."

Rufus said "He'll get a proper funeral, a soldier's funeral. I'll see to that. And a medal - posthumous."

Prunella had been standing in the corner saying nothing, afraid of her feelings which were no feelings at all and only told her what she'd really known, that she hadn't loved Percy. She said "We played Gunnery, Daddy. In the Mess tonight. Percy acted out the Stonk at Alamein."

"I'm glad."

Prunella said "Percy will get his Medal, and there will be a gun-carriage, and a volley over the grave, and a Bugler for the Last Post."

Guy said, bitterly. "A medal! A decoration! A Christmas decoration for Percy!"

They buried Percy after New Year, when most of the Regiment had returned from leave, and winter had come down hard.   It hadn't snowed, but snow was threatening above, and the ground was hard below.

There was the flag, and under it the coffin on the carriage; the Regiment grim and proud; the slow march; the volley and the bugle. A few tears, not many; a relative? an aunt? Then action! Steel stud striking the hard, cold ground; and away! Quick march and away!

Afterwards, at the Mess, Rufus was Host, offering a word here, a drink there to friends, civilian and military "Thanks for coming;" and Prunella too, the Colonel's daughter, doing her stuff. Then, they all went, quite early, nothing left to stay for, and Guy said to Prunella "It's such a let-down. Afterwards."

Prunella said "Oh Guy. I'm sad. I'm sad that I don't feel as upset as I should. I ought to miss him more."

Guy said "Poor Percy."

"My God" said Prunella "I love the Mess - this warmth. I love the rich soil of England and the rooks in the sky; the trees waiting for Spring; waiting for life."

"It's a reaction, that feeling. After the funeral. Life and Death."

"The funeral? Hardly an hour ago. The flag and the coffin. Poor Percy, cold inside. Cold, and smashed."

Guy said "The slow march; that was well done. And the arms drill. Percy would have been proud of that. The Present Arms. The smack of the hand on the rifle-butt. The crack of the heel on the ground. Lucky the ground was hard."

Prunella said "Frozen hard - or baked hard by the sun - that's important. Oh, Guy. The Last Post on the bugle - it could tear your heart."

Guy said "The Last Post. Even cynics are moved by that. And the volley - then, it's all over. Everyone's in such a hurry to get away. Quick March and away."

Prunella said "And Percy. Left behind, Oh Guy! Why don't I care enough?" Guy said "Do you think they'll cancel the Mess Ball?"

Prunella said "They wouldn't do that. It's a tradition." She paused a second, then she said "Good Lord. The Mess Ball - I was forgetting. I was going with Percy. My God. "

And Guy said "Percy wouldn't expect you to act the widow. There'll be all the other fellows - and you promised to look after Mary for me - remember."

It was getting dark, and Flanagan came into the Anteroom to turn on the lights. Everyone else had gone: there was work to do, and some sort of return to routine, after Christmas, and after the funeral. Prunella went to the window, and, she's quite pretty really, thought Guy, with a soft prettiness rather like Mary - both of them nice girls, dependable.

Prunella said in a low voice, almost talking to herself. "I remember another military funeral, somewhere abroad - somewhere hot. The widow was distracted - demented; out of her mind with grief."

Guy said "I don't think you should dwell too long on it, Prunella."

But she took no notice "I remember the shallow grave in the hard earth. The gun carriage. The volley. Just like today - but hot; not cold like today." She was talking nervously, and Guy said "Relax Prunella. It's all over" but she said, impatient with him "Oh, you don't understand.... How long do you think it took her? To get over it?"

He replied, humouring her. "Oh, I don't know. A year? Two years perhaps?"

Prunella exclaimed, and her voice was loud where it had been a whisper. "A day! One day - that's all. Next day I was walking past her bungalow in the married quarters. She was with another man. I expect they went to bed."

Guy said "Prunella - you weren't married to Percy. Nobody expects you to observe mourning for Percy."

"No" said Prunella and she added "I'm looking forward to the Mess Ball. First the Ball, and then back to Oxford."

One thing Guy was determined to do during his National Service was plenty of reading: all the long books that he'd never got around to reading - War and Peace and Madame Bovary, and Les Miserables, and Vanity Fair, all those. The Regimental Library was in the middle of Camp. There was a big window, and a girl at a desk by the window; and, when Guy saw the girl, he felt an irrational shyness. He went over to the desk, and she looked up and "Oh!" was all she said.

Guy felt himself blushing, an awful, betraying blush, and he couldn't do a damn thing about it. He forced himself to speak, and it came out in a monotone "I'd like to borrow some books."

The girl smiled, and said "You've just joined the Regiment." She had an attractive voice with a Welsh lilt, the lilt of the border "I'm 'Q' Evans' daughter, by the way. My name's Ruth."

"I'm Lieutenant Baker - Guy Baker."

"I know" she said.

Ruth noticed the boy's confusion, and it was touching, exciting in a funny way, but she mustn't let him suspect. Her feelings were protective, almost maternal, which she found astonishing. He was a big boy - she couldn't think of him as a man - a big boy, and beautiful; healthy and strong and as dark as herself. Not that Ruth thought of getting to know him, beyond a few formal words - he was a baby, no more than nineteen; a National Service officer, who would be gone in a year. So, Ruth put the boy out of her mind.

Guy came out of the Reading Room, and he was

carrying some heavy books, Tolstoy and Dickens, she noticed the titles when she stamped them. She wanted to say something, but she couldn't think of anything; and Guy wanted to say something, but he didn't say anything either.

That night, after supper, and after she'd helped Mother clear up, Dad asked her "Heard from Stan lately?" and Ruth had hardly given Stan a thought. Dad put on the wireless, and there had been a big offensive in Korea, and she should have been nervous for Stan, but it was no good, you couldn't make yourself feel an emotion that wasn't there, you could only pretend.

That night, in bed, when she was starting to feel drowsy - drowsy and sexy at the same time, it wasn't Stan she thought about: she hardly ever thought of Stan, which made her feel guilty and she tried to make herself think about him; but it was no good. At first, after he went away, she did think about Stan but then, it was no longer Stan, it was some anonymous man she'd think about when she was drowsy and sexy, and she'd touch her nipples and, oh, she wanted the man of her dreams; and she was tempted to use something, a banana or something on herself. It had all started with Stan, and now, she'd grown beyond Stan, and there was no going back. Sometimes, she'd stand in front of the mirror, and watch her nipples tighten as she played with them; and her own sexuality, her own beauty, excited her. She could have had men, plenty of men like the other girls; men with rough hands and rough manners; but they revolted her.

Tonight, when she lay in bed, the face of her dreams was no longer anonymous - Guy was there and she couldn't have banished him if she'd tried. And her feelings were disturbing, too; not just lust, or physical attraction, but a strange yearning for him, wanting to protect him, almost maternal. It was Guy who filled Ruth's thoughts that night and every night, and Guy's manhood which filled her loins, and made her damp to think of his. And, when she glanced hopefully and often, out of the library window, it was Guy she wished for, the big boy, hoping that he'd be there, coming up the path, bouncing his stick.

Ruth had nothing like a plan. She didn't work out a plan or anything; she just found herself going out of her way, going the long way to the Library past the Officers' Mess. It worked; she'd meet him, and he'd give her the salute and he'd blush. It excited her to see him blush.

Then, there he was; a wish-fulfilment. There he was, coming up the path and bouncing his stick. There he was, coming to the Library to change his books.

Ruth knew, of course, why he was there; why he was renewing the books so soon. She knew she attracted him, and, she was attracted by him so strongly, despite all sense; and she knew that, if she left it all to him she'd have to wait forever, and so would he. So Ruth was decisive.

Guy couldn't understand himself; all this wanting to see the girl, and knowing he'd be shy and blush. He'd never been like that, not for years anyway, he'd never been shy with Mary, he'd always been the confident one. He'd got used to being the confident male, and here he was, back to blushing schoolboy again; it was not as if Ruth was his type of girl, and she must be older than him. He was used to girls like Mary, girls he'd kissed, peachy girls and dainty. But this was a big girl, a dark girl accented with red and black - red nails, red lipstick, black hair. And, on top of it all, she was a Sergeant-Major's daughter - what next? A Sergeant-Major's daughter, he told himself. But, what good was it? He couldn't get her out of his mind.

Most of the Camp was just wooden huts, but the Library was an old Manor House that had been requisitioned during the War. Ruth was at the desk, pretending she hadn't noticed Guy; then she looked up, and smiled when he blushed, and she said, "Oh back again. You must be a fast reader."

He said, "I must have chosen the wrong books" and she said "Are you bored by all the usual books? We've got some unusual books upstairs. Shall I show you?"

She led him up the grand staircase, which creaked. He had his cap in his hand and he climbed a little behind her even though the stairs were wide. They reached a landing and she unlocked a door, and when they were inside, it clunked shut behind them. "You see" she said, "Aladdin's cave".

It was a high room with high windows and bright with winter sun. It had been the main reception room of the house, a ballroom perhaps, and was still panelled between the bookshelves.

Ruth said, "These books are mostly donations - bequests and so on from old Officers of the regiment". Guy said, "How interesting", and Ruth said "Collections from all over the world. Some are valuable. Some against the British censorship laws. That's why we keep them locked up."

Guy imagined they must be something wicked and sensational, from the secret Presses of Paris or Stamboul.

Ruth laughed and said "I know what you're thinking. But there's nothing really naughty. Nothing more sensational than Lady Chatterley."

Guy said, "D. H. Lawrence's forbidden book! I'm told it's quite tame really. But I'd like a chance to read it."

Ruth pointed to the set of Library steps, "I'll need those" she said "to get it".

They were solid steps, carved and on casters; Guy wheeled them across, and set them steady with the chock. Ruth climbed to the top step - it was about eye-level - and Guy was holding the steps steady. Ruth swung one leg across and put her foot on a shelf to reach high, so she had one foot on the step and the other on the shelf, a wide stretch; and, as she stretched, her skirt rode up. "It's such a stretch" she said.

She reached higher still until her finger-tips found the book, and, as she stretched, her back arched, and her breasts thrust upwards in her sweater; and Guy saw her thighs and the strong muscles tensed. The skirt was stretched wide and so high that Guy's eyes were only inches from the skin where it showed above the stockings, where the suspenders pulled taut with the hint of springy fuzz, adorable fuzz that peeped from her panties.

It made Guy rampant as a stallion, but so uncertain that he hesitated.

"Catch?" Ruth said, as she dropped the book down to him, and "Butter fingers" when he missed, "Help me down" she said, so Guy held up his hand, and she gripped tight while her high heels clattered down the few steps to the floor. She kept her hand in his, then "Oh, you bvely boy" she said, and kissed him. It was just a kiss, no more; but the strength of her, and the life of her, was all in the kiss.

Guy had kissed quite a few girls: there was Mary, of course, and other girls, schoolgirls at parties; clumsy kisses. But Ruth had the power to kiss. Guy's physique was challenged by the kiss, it was almost a trial of strength, and Ruth was strong. But, even in the heat of it, he wondered about this girl he was kissing, a girl he hardly knew.

Ruth broke away and she said "I've been wanting you to kiss me", but Guy knew that really it was she, who had been the one to kiss him. He said "I was too shy" and Ruth said "That's what's so nice about you - so strong; and so shy".

"Can I take you out?" Guy said. He blurted it out, "To dinner or something?"

Ruth smiled, and said "It's not done: for an Officer to go out with an other - rank"

Guy said "But you're not" and Ruth said "Strictly speaking, I'm a civilian of course. But my Dad's a Sergeant-

Major".

Guy said "I'm only a National Service Officer. I can't see that it matters". Ruth said "We'd better go. Remember your book".

He picked it up from the floor and they went downstairs. "I'll have to register the book" she said "We don't stamp these special books. We just keep a record".

Guy said "Have you read it? Lady Chatterley I mean". Ruth smiled, "Oh yes. Everybody wants to read it because it's banned in England. It's not very shocking, really. It's rather sweet, in a way. "

Guy went out into the afternoon. He looked less shy already, Ruth thought; less of a boy. "Making a fool of yourself over a boy" she said to herself; "If you try to hold onto him, you'll ruin him" and she began to sort through the pile of books on the desk. Guy walked back to the Mess, and he felt like cheering and throwing his cap into the air, and all because he'd kissed Ruth, or she'd kissed him. But, he just walked into the Mess in his usual way, and there were some people having tea, some subalterns; and Prunella was there too. "Hi, Pru!" he said and she replied "Hi Guy - Why; it rhymes".

"What's that?" said Guy.

She said "Rhymes; Hi and Guy and why".

The Mess secretary's dog, a fat labrador was outside in front of the window, and he was across some bitch as usual and pumping away like fury. Guy said "The usual entertainment, I see". Prunella giggled, and someone muttered "Jolly bad form".

Guy took his tea and toast, and plonked them on the table next to Prunella. He said "I want to talk to you, Pru. I'm thinking of inviting someone to the Mess Ball". She said "I thought you'd already asked Mary". Guy felt uncomfortable at that, but he said "I've not actually sent Mary an invitation. I can put Mary off".

"Guy!" said Prunella; and Guy wondered if her tone of mock-shock was really all mock. "Guy, how could you? And who's the other girl?" She noticed the book. He'd just plonked it down and forgotten it. It was a curious volume, with old-fashioned binding, and the edges of the pages rough and hand-cut. Pru picked up the volume and read the title "Good Lord" she said "Lady Chatterley". She looked at Guy, as though he'd revealed something unexpected, and she said, half mocking again "Mysterious. First a mystery lady - and now a forbidden book. Where did you get it?"

Guy said "The Library. They've got a few surprises hidden away. Presented to the Regiment years ago". Prunella said "The book's still banned in England. It's ridiculous. I've been trying to get a copy for ages. I'm doing a special study of D. H. Lawrence at Oxford".

Guy said "I'll read it quickly; then you can read it. The book will be legalised sooner or later, and then nobody will bother about it".

Prunella said "You've only been here a few weeks, and the Library brings out its hidden treasures for you". Guy said "It was the girl at the Library" - Guy blushed as he said it; Good God, he thought he'd got over that.

Prunella said "Not the Sergeant-Major's daughter; the Qs' daughter?" and Guy said "Pru; she's the girl I want to ask to the Ball".

"Oh Guy, you couldn't! - And isn't she engaged to someone? A Sergeant or something?" Guy said "Even so, I'd like to ask her. And, Pru, I want you to find out what your father would think. Would Rufus welcome her?"

"Dad?" - Prunella paused to consider, "You know, I just don't know about Dad. You'd upset all the old Blimps".

"The Blimps I can manage. As long as Rufus welcomes her. If you welcome her, Pru". Pru said, "I still don't think she'd want to come. You can't imagine how hard it would be here for a girl like that, a girl of her background. But, if Dad says "Yes" - all right. I'll look after her".

"Thanks" said Guy, a simple word but he meant it. And Pru said "You were kind to me, Guy, about Percy. You didn't expect too much".

That night, Guy read the book; he sat up late and finished it. And next day he took it over to Rufus' house, for Prunella, it was an excuse to see her; "Finished it already?" she asked; but she was not surprised.

Guy said "There's nothing to fuss over. But it's worth reading. You know the plot, I expect?"

She said "Upper-class Beauty; attractive Working Man and all that?" Guy said "Well, it's more than that. It's a tragedy, in a way. Her husband has lost his sex, and she's frustrated".

Pru said "And now it's you who wants to bridge the social gap, Guy? I've asked Dad - that's what you've really come about, haven't you. He said it's up to you. He likes the girl." Guy said, "It's up to her, then".

The Mess Ball was the big event of the year. All the girls, all the farmers' daughters, and the girls from the Hunt expected an invitation, and each officer could invite a lady guest. The Ball wasn't absolutely exclusive - a few nurses from the hospital got invitations, and the same girls might be found dancing with the soldiers at the Garrison Hops. After all, there wasn't an unlimited supply of girls from the County Set; but still, the Ball was a Social Event with a capital "S", and exclusive enough.

Guy collected an invitation card from the Mess Secretary, and he carefully filled in the blank on the card:

Miss Ruth Evans. He put the card in the envelope, put on his belt and his hat; and his gloves, as it was frosty; and he walked over to the Library.

Ruth was sitting at her desk, and she noticed that Guy didn't blush, he just came up to the desk and said, "I haven't come about a book. I've brought this for you" and he handed her the envelope.

She said "Shall I open it now?" She slit the envelope, and Guy had that excited feeling about her, about her fingers on the envelope. She looked at the card, and "Oh" she said "I'm flattered".

Guy said, "Please come". Ruth forced herself to be casual, but the thoughts were racing through her mind; about what she might wear - supposing she looked tatty, or, worse, overdressed - and all those female vultures ready to peck at a girl from the part of Camp that was separated from the Officers' Mess by an invisible stream as final as the styx; ...... and Dinner ...... a Formal Dinner ...... supposing she did something shameful? Oh, not such a cliché as eating peas with her knife; something more arcane -she knew about never calling a napkin a serviette, but there must be a hundred other things like that, "Pass the Port the right way" and everything.

Ruth played for time. She said "Are you sure, Guy? Are you sure you're not asking me just out of kindness?"

Guy said "Ruth. I want you to come more than anything. The Colonel knows. He has approved".

She said "On one condition. Take me to the Garrison Hop on Saturday. Show that you can do for me what you're asking me to do for you". He said "There's the Rugger match. I might be late. Can I meet you there? Will that do?"

Saturday was one of those days that almost made Guy want to stay in the Army; from the moment Porter woke him at seven, and poked the stove, and topped it up with coke;

when he said "Good morning, Sir. Lovely day for the match Sir".

It was the day of the Big Match, the Fourth Round of the McIlwaine Cup, the Gunners' inter-unit Rugger Cup. Guy lay there, half dozing, and his first thoughts were of Ruth. A week ago, before he first admitted Ruth to himself, he'd try to think of something else, or of Mary; but now it was Ruth, all Ruth. He'd lie there, tense with desire for her, and with his manhood strong for her, just the thought of her; in the night, he'd half awake and Ruth would be almost real beside him.

And what of Ruth? True, she had kissed him, but what did that mean? He didn't know it, but it was the same for Ruth, and, in her mind, her lovely boy was beside her, and she was holding him,

Porter came back to Guy's room, "Not up yet Sir? Come on Sir, it's late". Guy washed, and shaved, and just had time for bacon and eggs in the Mess and an extra slice of toast for energy, and it was 8.30, time for Parade, and his troop all ready for inspection under Sgt Jackson.

The Sgt. put up a cracking salute "Good morning, Sir. Lovely day for the game, Sir". Guy put up his best salute - he hated the sloppy salutes some officers gave; they thought themselves superior, but it only made them look wet.

It was a good Troop, well trained. "You've done a good job, Sergeant. They could win the competition".

"Thank you Sir". The big salute, again, and the Sergeant raised his voice to the men "Now lads, Let's show our officer what we're made of", The orders came fast, and loud as gunfire: "Quick March! About Turn! Halt!" Never a waver, never a mistake.

Guy marched to the front of the Troop, snapped his stick under his armpit and said "Now, let's see your Gun-Drill".

Double-march, across to the 25-pounders. "Halt! Action Rear!" The frantic swing of the trailers; ready the limbers, and the guns; throw open the breach, and load, and ram.

"Number One Gun Ready..... Number Two..... Three..... Four." Dead stillness. Tense; the gun crews in position at the guns; standing; or sitting at the gunsight; or kneeling, arm in air - the signal "Ready". "Fire!"

Dummy shells, of course, but you didn't need much imagination to hear the crunch and to smell the cordite, and to see the smoke billow from the barrel.

"Well done! Well done, men", called Guy "Time for NAAFI Break".

At lunchtime in the Mess, all the talk was about the match. The opposition, a Heavy Ack Ack regiment had a couple of Star players, Rugby League professionals doing their National Service. One of them was a centre-threequarter, and it was Guy's job as wing- forward to stop him. Guy had been a good wing-forward at Radford, but he'd never had to stop a 14-stone black man who could run even-time.

Around the Rugger pitch, Guy was amazed at the turnout, the whole regiment seemed to be on the touchlines: the McIlwaine Cup was the big one.

There was Rufus, of course, and Prunella, and there was the RQMS, Ruth's Dad, on the bank, and Mrs. Evans, and, yes, Ruth was with them. As Guy ran onto the pitch, Ruth waved, and he had the mad idea that he was playing the match for her, like a knight in the lists.

The opposition were already on the pitch, and it was certainly Heavy Ack-Ack, very heavy. They booted the ball into the sky as though they were putting up a barrage, and, as it fell, the Black Bomber came behind it to crash over for a try; and to convert it himself. The Regiment was down 5-0 in

5 minutes!

It was all desperate defence, and by half-time Guy felt shell-shocked, he'd tackled so much; but they were still only 5-0 down. The heavy Ack-Ack began to tire, and the Regiment had a chance out of nothing: the Bomber dropped the ball from over-confidence, and the Bombardier on the Regiment's wing booted and chased to score in the corner. But the conversion failed and the Regiment was still behind, 3-5.

The winter light began to fade, and the spectators were shouting and willing the Regiment on. Even Rufus was shouting, and Prunella; and there was Ruth, on the bank shouting too. The ack-ack scrum-half held on too long, and Guy pounced and wrenched the ball away, and managed to hand it on to Gunner Dent who made off in a charge for the line. Guy hoped he wouldn't pass: Gunner Dent was no passer of the ball. "Go yourself!" shouted Guy "Run!", and the Ack-Ack team bounced off Dent as if he was armour-plated. But the Bomber got Dent, and he showed his class the way he did it, one of those Rugby League tackles like a Judo throw, that can stop man and ball for ever. Guy was close, and Dent had the sense to release the ball; and Guy had the presence of mind, dinned into him at school, to "play with the foot after a tackle". He tapped and picked-up, and held the ball, thank God it wasn't wet; he held it, and he dived for the line, with the whistle blowing for the try-, and they were all jumping for Joy on the touchline, and surging onto the field with the touch-judges trying to hold them back; and it didn't matter that the conversion was missed, it was 6-5 and victory. The teams had baths and tea; and everybody was polite to the opposition, until the Ack-Ack pulled away in their team coach, and then everybody had a celebration in the NAAFI. Rufus bought beers all round, and, after a bit, the officers left the NAAFI and went up to the officers' Mess. There were only four officers in the Regimental team, but all the officers in the Mess were celebrating and they all wanted to buy Guy a drink for the winning try; and he might have got completely drunk if he hadn't been meeting Ruth, so he just had a couple of beers, and spun them out.

About ten o'clock Guy said "Who's coming to the Regimental Hop?" A few of the chaps, the bachelors, said they'd come along; they were all in mufti, anyway, being the weekend: no officer went to the Hop in uniform to embarrass the men.

They had to push their way through a crush at the Dance Hall, and everybody wanted to congratulate Guy and to buy him a drink. Guy looked around for Ruth: the lights were low, and the music was mad, and the place so crowded. Ruth was being propelled around the floor by an off-duty Military Policeman, and then it was "Next Dance Please", and she rejoined the group of girls at the far end of the Hall. She hadn't seen Guy, who was pushing his way towards her excusing himself and bumping into people,

"Hello Ruth" he said, "Oh, the hero" she said gladly "Meet the girls"; and the girls said "We've heard all about the match. The way you scored the try".

Then, the music started again. You couldn't move fast in all that crush, and you couldn't communicate, with the blare of the music. So Guy and Ruth held together, and swayed together to the rhythm; tight together all the way down, with Guy's cock hard against Ruth, like a rhinoceros horn. Ruth rested her cheek on Guy's shoulder, and pressed her lips to his ear - and she said "Oh Guy", just that, in a way meant for him in all the noise.

They went over to the bar, and a girl asked Ruth "Have you heard from Stan?" - Guy pretended not to hear, but he felt jealousy like pain. Then, it was God Save the Queen, and the quaint formalities of pairing-off to go home; and, already, couples were clinched together in the darkness, seemingly oblivious to the cold.

Guy said "I'll go and get my car" but Ruth said "Don't be silly. It's not far, and I'd like to walk".

They walked hand in hand through the darkened lines, and, all the way, Guy was thinking, where could he take Ruth? to kiss her? - It was so damned cold.

They came to the front door, and Guy felt like laughing, it was so like his first date when he'd been a schoolboy and he'd asked "May I kiss you?"

But Ruth said "Won't you come in for a hot drink?"

Guy said "We'll wake your parents", and Ruth said "They are away for the weekend. They left straight after the match."

It was warm inside the house, with a fire still glowing. Ruth made some tea, and they sat, side by side, on the sofa. Ruth said "I expect you're tired after the match."

"Not really; though I feel a bit bruised and battered. That black chap felt like a rock dug out of a coalmine."

Ruth sipped her tea and said "The Mess Ball. You know, I feel nervous about it already. All those important people."

Guy said "You're a lady Ruth. It's natural to you. You don't have to worry."

Ruth said "You don't understand, Guy. That's your habitat - the Officers' Mess and the County Set. My evening frock, for instance. Most girls like me wouldn't even have one. How do I know if mine will pass muster?"

"I see what you mean" Guy said "I hadn't thought about it. You had better show me."

Ruth went upstairs, and came back with the frock. Guy said "I can't really pass an opinion unless you put it on." Ruth started to go back upstairs, but Guy said "Don't go back in the cold. Change in front of the fire. I'll turn my back."

So, Guy faced the wall, feeling rather ridiculous, then "Ready!" she said, and he turned. It wasn't an expensive frock, but Ruth made it look expensive the way it set off her shoulders. Even to look at her made him feel excited. "Turn around" he said. The back was cut low, and Ruth's bare back was strong and lovely. "Oh, Ruth. You're splendid" he said.

Ruth said "Tell me honestly about the dress. You'll do me no favour by flattery."

Guy said "The basic dress is very good. And you look marvellous. But - all that fussy stuff. You'd be better off without it."

Ruth said "It's cheap lace. I'll get Mum to take it off."

Guy said "You look good enough for Vogue; I promise."

Ruth smiled with pleasure, and held up her arms to him, and kissed him gently. She said, quite simply "I've fallen for you, Guy. You must know that."

Guy felt confused and mad for her, and almost stammering "Ruth. I can't stop thinking of you - If you only knew - But, what about the Sergeant? Your fiancé?."

Ruth said, quietly "Stan's a problem. My problem, Guy" and she added "I wanted to tell you - Stan and I made love, Guy. Does that shock you?"

Guy said "Is he the only one?" and Ruth said "The only one - up to now."

Guy said, and he had difficulty finding the words "I've no experience. Is that shameful in a man?"

"Oh Guy" she said "So touchy, and so serious! I'm going to be the luckiest girl in the world. Help me off with my frock."

The frock dropped to the floor, and Ruth stepped out of it. Guy had a primitive urge to grab hold of her but that would spoil it; he just lifted the frock from the floor, put it over an armchair, and looked at Ruth, enjoying the sight of her, feeling predatory and constrained at the same time. She stood there in her bra, and girdle, and the taut suspenders: and her nylon stockings, and the evening shoes that went with the frock.

All Guy wanted was to hold her, and he lurched for her clumsily; but she restrained him and said "I'll help you change."

Guy took off his jacket, and shirt, and sat on the sofa to untie his laces; and Ruth dropped on her knees in front of him and helped him to pull off his chukka-boots.

"Your socks, too" she said "You'd look silly just wearing socks."

He unbuttoned the cavalry twills and Ruth helped pull them off; inside the trouser band she saw the label "Huntsman's - Savile Row" - no wonder they were such obviously Officers' bags. There he was, sitting in front of her, still uncertain; sitting in his jockey-pants all bulging tight up at her, and a damp stain on them as round as a penny.

"Oh Guy" she said "Oh, Guy" and she wanted to grab hold of him to kiss him, to do anything, everything, just for him.

She took off her bra, and took his hands and placed them on her breasts, and he could feel the nipples swelling and standing under his touch.

She said "I want to touch you, Guy. I so want to."

So, gently; forcing herself to be slow - she wanted to hurry, but she made herself slow - gently, she pulled his jockey pants down, over the lump of him, and the hard force of him was there, proud and free in front of her; and she felt

66

she was kneeling before him like the handmaiden of some God. She bent forwards and he was looking down on the grace of her shoulders, and her black hair where it shone in the light; then he felt the lightest touch, a light touch as terrific as a turbine, and she had touched him, there, touched him there with her lips. She bent forward, and touched her lips to the swollen shine of him there, the shine swollen at the tip; she looked up, to see if it was what he wanted, and she held the root of him, and her fingers were tight to make him swell; and she moved her lips, and stroked him with her tongue, to make him rear up with the power that was throbbing through him.

And then, a thought occurred to her "Guy! Contraceptives? You won't have any, I expect?"

Guy said "I've never needed any - I thought that you - ?"

Ruth said, sharply, "A girl doesn't keep them. Not unless she's shameless." She thought a minute "I wonder if Dad? If Mum and Dad have any?"

She went to her room, and put on her dressing-gown against the cold; then she went into her parents' room, and rummaged in the cupboards; and then she came downstairs, laughing. "I found them in an old ammunition pouch. Enough rubbers for a regiment."" Guy said "The `Q' goes up in my estimation all the time."

They lay back again, together on the sofa; they were warm and drowsy in front of the fire, and it was a big sofa. Guy said "Ruth. I seem to have a sort of madness about you. I'm always hoping you'll be there, around the next corner."

Ruth said "It's like that for me, too. It's a wonderful thing to happen to a girl." Guy said "I didn't think you felt the same way."

Ruth said "A girl doesn't show it. She can't afford to

show it. But, whenever I saw you, I felt the excitement; I had to try to control it. Hoping you would notice me."

Guy said "It's mad. I can't go and fall in love. Not at my age."

Ruth said "We mustn't spoil it by promises; or responsibilities."

They held together for a time, saying nothing, just happy in front of the embers. Then, Guy turned to kiss Ruth on the lips, he held his lips to hers, and the kiss added yet more strength to his stirring, and she felt him, hard, against her.

She touched his cheek and said "It's going to be wonderful, Guy." She loosened the girdle of her dressing-gown and Guy was proud, not shy, with his manhood proud and high. Ruth said "Guy, I want you to see the secret part of me. Your part of me.

She raised herself above him, where his head rested on the sofa, so she was kneeling, one knee at each side; and she reached down to her vagina, and parted the lips for him. Guy said nothing, but his breath came fast. She said "You see the little button? The button's hard for you, Guy."

Then Ruth said "You should put on the rubber, now." She opened the packet, and put the rubber on him and guided his hands to pull it down. They changed places, so that Ruth lay beneath him, and he entered her while she smiled up at him, encouraging him.

She said "Lie still, inside me."

Guy lay still for a minute, then Ruth began to contract herself, in spasms until he felt a wildness that made him want to thrust, and he had to do it, to start to thrust; and when he came to the end of the thrust, he jerked again, harder, and Ruth said "Yes. Oh, yes, Guy, yes", and he thrust and faster thrust, until her eyes showed tears of happiness; then, slow at first, he felt the slow surge of the juice from the roots deep inside him, until, whoosh! up the channel, up the tingling tender channel of him; up; and he made his strongest thrust, hard, held hard; held hard there while he jerked, in a spasm that shot out of him, pumped out of him. And, the jerk of him inside her was something precious for her, precious between Guy and her; Guy and Ruth only; and her soul went with her body as she moved with his body; in a spasm that went on and on, beyond sensation into Paradise.

They stayed still, for a long stillness; then Ruth said "My darling. You'll have to come out - while the rubber's still tight." She guided his fingers into her, to hold it tight and she said "The loo's at the top of the stairs. To flush it down."

Afterwards, Guy said "I've grown up, Ruth. Grown up in a night" and Ruth said "I'm so happy it was me you grew up with."

Guy dressed, and they kissed goodnight, and he went out into the cold moonlight, past the brave silhouettes of the guns.

Then it was the Mess Ball. It was the evening of the Ball, and the 'Q' had his feet up in front of the fire; he was studying the racing page in the paper, and he had his tie off, and his blouse unbuttoned as usual. Good God, it was nearly seven o'clock: they'd been upstairs for hours, Ruth and her Mum, and, though he pretended not to understand, the 'Q' knew why they were taking so long. Ruth was getting ready for the biggest night of her life, and she was like a filly that had never been raced suddenly having to run in a Classic.

The 'Q' looked at his watch and called out "Know what time it is?" - the Lieutenant would be here any minute.

The 'Q' hadn't been quite as indifferent to it all as he pretended. He'd gone to see the C.O., quietly, no fuss, and he'd asked the C.O. about it. The Colonel didn't answer directly; he said "How does Ruth's mother feel about it, 'Q'?

How does Mrs. Evans feel?"

"I'm not sure, Sir. She's ambitious for Ruth, of course, Sir."

The Colonel said "I've know Ruth a long time. She's grown up in the Regiment, just like my own girl. Like Prunella. Ruth is a thoroughbred, `Q'. It's not fair to curb her."

Upstairs, Ruth was putting on the final touches. She felt excited; excited and nervous. She wished Mum would stop fussing, she said "You've done a marvellous job on the frock, Mum. Guy was right: that lace was awful."

Mrs. Evans went downstairs at last, and Ruth sat at her dressing-table studying her nails; the red lacquer was perfect. The eyeshadow, the eye liner, her hair; all were perfect. She heard the knock at the front door, and the sound of voices; then she took her lipstick and applied it, deep-red and deliberate: a sign of defiance, a sign of courage. She broke the seal on the bottle of perfume Guy had given her, the perfume he'd chosen, the right perfume; a small bottle but expensive. "Here" he had said "You'll need perfume for the Ball, Ruth. If there's one thing that a bitch will bitch about it's scent."

Ruth opened the bottle: "Balmain." She breathed it in, strong and heady as lust. She knew that she should only wear a touch, but it was more than a touch she put behind her ears, and at her breast, and on her wrists. She closed the stopper tight, and put the bottle in her new evening bag, the one Mum had gone all the way to Shrewsbury to buy; a pretty bag, sequinned, shimmering and expensive. She snapped the catch, snapped back her shoulders, and went downstairs, to make her first "entrance", her entrance into the little sitting room, the trial "entrance" for the big one, at the Mess.

Guy said "I'm proud to be with you, Ruth - you should be proud of her Mrs. Evans - and 'Q'."

The Q' almost got to his feet, and that was the best compliment. All he said was "That's my girl", but he was proud of her, all right.

They went into the cold, and squashed into the little sports car, the M.G., with Ruth hoping that her frock wouldn't be crushed. Outside the Mess, the duty Bombardier saluted, and opened the car door for her, and almost blurted something when he saw who it was.

Prunella was waiting as she'd promised, and she showed Ruth to the Ladies' Room, while Guy handed-in his belt and hat, and waited for Ruth and Prunella to emerge. Then Guy took Ruth on his arm to introduce her to the Mess President in the traditional way. Ruth knew Rufus already, of course, and Rufus said "Ruth - I'm delighted. I hope you'll honour me later on with a dance" - he was a man you could respect, Rufus, a gentleman.

The mess waiter, Flanagan, came with the sherries on the silver tray, and Guy looked around. Prunella was with her usual crowd, the hunting crowd, and more people kept coming into the Ante-room, it was getting packed. Then the Duty Sergeant opened the double-doors, and stamped to attention, and called "Ladies and Gentlemen. Dinner is Served."

Extra tables had been squeezed into the Dining Room, and all the Mess Silver was on display, with cut- glass at each place- setting; and crackers because it was a party.

Guy looked for their place-cards: Second Lieutenant Guy Baker, R. A., and Miss Ruth Evans, down there, at the end of the main table beside "Mr Vice". The silver and the crystal were sparkling, even in the low light, and a starched napkin stood like a cockade on each side-plate.

There was a call for silence, and the Padre said the Grace like rapid fire; then, all was hubbub and hilarity. The meal followed the formality of a Regimental Dining-In Night:

71

so familiar to the Officers, and vicariously familiar to so many of the ladies, who had followed the Flag; a formality that was strange to others, to the debs or would-be debs up from London; and strange, too, to Ruth, whose family had followed the same Flag, but as outsiders. Ruth didn't allow herself to relax: success was more important tonight than fun, though she hoped that fun and success would go together. So - no elbows on the table; but, when she looked around, there were one or two elbows on the table, self-confident elbows, which puzzled her a bit. There were glances; men appraising her, admiring the girl they had not really noticed at her library desk; and envying Guy; perhaps they were wondering why they had not tried their luck.

A waiter was at her shoulder with the tureen; the band struck up, and the wine- waiter offered white wine, Meursault. He poured, and Ruth sipped; and Guy thought how pretty Ruth's fingers looked round the stem of the wine glass. It reminded him of her fingers on his own stem; he felt a secret stab of sex, and the excitement that he always felt for her. She caught his smile, and guessed what he was thinking and she felt happy.

They brought the Roast, and the Red Wine, and it began to get very lively. A chap across the table, a full Lieutenant, a Regular, must have had too many sherries; he was throwing pellets of bread in the air, and catching them in his mouth like a seal. Prunella joined in, and snapped up one of his pellets before he caught it, and she got a cheer and a laugh. Ruth clapped, and thought - I wonder if I'll ever have the confidence to do that. She envied Pru who would never have to wonder: Pru with the clever brain and the kind eyes, who was such a good friend for Guy, and such a good friend, now, to Ruth, for Guy's sake.

The Roast was Venison, and there was Pheasant too, and the wine a big Burgundy, an honest Beaune. Ruth said "This wine is marvellous, Guy" and Guy said "You've got the right instincts."

Ruth was careful just to sip, it would be so easy to drink too much, and spoil everything. The band struck up the Regimental Anthem, "Screw Guns", and the Gunner Officers started singing the chorus, and some of the ladies too, those who knew the words - the tune was easy, the same as the Eton Boating Song. Prunella joined in, and waved to Ruth across the table, and Ruth sang the words she'd heard so often, in so many Artillery camps. She found she was enjoying herself.

It was still the Christmas-pudding season, so the lights were doused and the Chef- Sergeant brought in the Pudding all flickering with the blue flame of the Rum, and the trumpeter blew a blast to welcome the pudding. Then, there was Port in decanters, and Stilton cheeses, scooped and Ported, and then the Toasts "Mr Vice - The Queen."

Everybody rose, and lifted their glasses, and then, a very rare event in a Gunner mess, Rufus proposed a second Toast.

"Ladies and Gentlemen, to an absent friend. A very brave friend, Captain Percy Haggard."

Then, it was time for dancing, and Guy was thankful that there would not be the usual tedious, half-sozzled session over the Port.

It was later on, between dances, that one of the Regular Subalterns started to get stroppy. It was the same chap who'd thrown the bread pellets, which had been funny; but he'd only been half-drunk at Dinner, and now he was aggressive. His name was Baird, Lieutenant Roger Baird R. A. whose whole life was the Army; and he resented National Service officers with brains.

"I say, Ruth" Roger said, and there was an edge to his voice. "I say, Ruth. I thought you were engaged to my old Troop Sergeant, Sergeant Phillips." So, here we go, thought

Ruth, this evening is not going to be all Roses, after all.

"I still am.... in a way."

"Only in a way?" said Roger "Really? - engagement ring and all that?" - He looked pointedly at the ringless finger.

Guy said, quietly "Come on, Roger" but Roger wouldn't go quiet that easily, not for any National Serviceman. He said "I'm a Senior subaltern, remember that."

Ruth said, and her tone was bitter-sweet, "Oh, Guy. You'll have to get some service in - like Dad. My father's a Ranker, Mr Baird."

"As if I didn't know" sneered Roger, and Ruth said "My Dad admires officers; at least, he admires officers and gentlemen. Gentlemen never pull rank off-duty."

Roger said "When I think of that poor sod - I'm talking about Sergeant Phillips. He's out there in Hell; in Korea with the Gooks coming at him over the hill. He's dreaming of his girl back home - but his girl's out with one of the Toffs; out with a temporary gentleman."

Guy said "Careful, Roger. You've drunk too much." Roger squared up to Guy, elbowing him, and Guy thought oh God he's going to get violent. Ruth said "Wait a minute!" She opened her bag and took out a photograph, and held it under the light for Roger to see. It was a photograph of Stan, with a Eurasian girl on each arm, and the tarts were not wearing much more than their lipstick. And Stan, smug as a polecat, had his arms around the girls, each hand cupping a bare breast.

Roger said nothing; he just gave a vicious look and moved away. Guy said "Where on earth did you get that snapshot?" Ruth said "One of the girls has got a boyfriend in Korea. He sent her the photograph."

It got later, and the music got sleepier; and dancing was little more than just holding tight, and swaying in the dark.

The saxophone player was good enough for Quags; it made Guy want to take Ruth to Quags, and, oh, everywhere; she was such a splendid girl, a girl for a man to be proud of - at Quags, or at the Cafe de Paris, or anywhere. Holding her tight, tight to the music, his lips to her ear, he whispered.

"Oh, Ruth. I think I'm in love with you," and she whispered back "You silly boy, you mustn't! I won't let you."

"Why?"

"Because so many boys tie themselves down too early. I'm too old for you. Let's just be happy now. No strings."

That was how Guy's year of happiness began, and, in the manner of happy years, went away with the wind.

Guy was due some leave over Easter, and an old schoolfriend had offered him a flat. "Let's have a week in London" he said; and Ruth said "I thought your parents lived in London - I thought your home was London."

Guy said "Not really. Woking is not really London. This flat is in Central London. Well - almost."

"You just don't want your parents to meet me."

Guy paused; he'd tended to forget Ruth's sensitivity; the idea that he could be ashamed of her was so ridiculous. He said "Don't be an ass. You'd be bored silly, out at Woking. "

And so, it was Eastertide and the open road, the A5, Watling Street; the M.G. nicely- tuned and humming along; and London. They found the flat in no-man's-land near Euston Station - the friend who had lent Guy the flat hadn't pretended it was salubrious, but he'd left milk and bacon in the fridge, and a note "Have fun! "; so, they fried the bacon, and had fun in the bedroom, and Guy 'phoned up a few friends to fix up a party.

Next night, it was Easter Saturday, and everyone was meeting at the Scarsdale Arms. It was crowded, and Guy elbowed for drinks - there was a smart woman, middle aged, on a bar stool, with a well-mannered poodle under the stool; and she said to Ruth so that Guy could overhear "My Dear - what a lovely man you've got! And you look so chic yourself!"

All the fellows were at the Scarsdale with their girls, all dressed for evening, the men in dinner jackets, and the girls pretty and fresh-faced as though they had come from point-to-point. Some of the girls had been watching rugger if their boyfriend was playing: everybody had been at rugger on Easter Saturday; except Guy who'd been in bed with Ruth.

They were asking Guy what it was like in the Gunners - most of the chaps were National Service Officers on Easter leave. There was Chris, home from Berlin and the British Sector; and Desmond in the Guards at Caterham - Desmond could afford it - and Julian in the Cavalry at Bovington, testing tanks.

There was Jill who said her secretarial course was super; there were lots of super girls, and if he knew any boys in London, there were all those super girls looking for boyfriends - all the boys were out of Town, in the Army, and wasn't it a bore? Didn't Ruth think it was a bore?

Ruth laughed and said "It suits me. I'm with the Army myself, you see."

"What luck!"

Guy looked at the other girls, and he looked at Ruth, and he thought she was like a queen amongst handmaidens; they were all pretty, but Ruth was the queen. Her colouring was so intense, compared with theirs: the black hair and the creamy skin; the square shoulders, and the bare, beautiful back. The other chaps kept eying Ruth, and Guy felt a pride to be with her; and a lift in his loins when he looked at her.

They left the Scarsdale, and drove to the Cafe de Paris,

where it was the usual thing, not a proper Dinner really, just a supper: bacon and eggs with your champagne.

It had to be the Cafe de Paris because the Kitt girl was doing the Cabaret, and you had to see Eartha Kitt that season. They had a table on the balcony, the best place to see everything, and the best place to be seen. Half the officers in the Army seemed to be on leave in London, all crammed into the Cafe, the same chaps, many of them, who had been at this school, or that school, Marlboro or Radley - Guy knew them by sight from Rugger matches. So, he nodded to them as he danced with Ruth, or someone would pass a remark like "I see Radford lost to Cheltenham this year," and one chap said "Hello, Guy. I say, what a smashing girl!" and he overheard someone else saying "Do you see the girl with Guy Baker? - Wow!"

It was so exciting, such fun; and Ruth was happy dancing, leaning back on Guy's supporting hand. She said "Have you noticed, Guy; how all you Public School men seem to know each other? You're a world of your own."

It was Cabaret time, and time for another drink. The lights dimmed, and the drums rolled, and the black-velvet singer moved into the single, intense, pool of light. She shimmered in white satin and white fur against the bare, black, skin and she sang all her old songs; and she looked like a small feline predator, a black pantherette. She was an Old Fashioned Girl, and a girl who could have had all the young bucks in London if she'd wanted, and most of the old bucks too. She didn't seek applause, she just accepted it as a tribute; and Guy was struck by the similarity between Eartha and Ruth, the two proudest women in that Cafe, the Black Diamond and the White.

Ruth had never been to a London theatre, so, on Easter Monday they did a show. They could have done the obvious thing, and gone to one of the big musicals, but `Pygmalion' was on, and Guy was curious to see how Ruth would react to the Cockney flower-girl turned Duchess, and to the Professor who helped it happen. Afterwards, Ruth said "Guy. I sometimes feel a bit like Eliza Doolittle."

Guy said "Eliza had brains - and ambition. Bernard Shaw wanted to show what a girl could do, if she had brains, and ambition."

Ruth said "She was pretty. That helped,"

Guy said "Oh yes. That helped a lot."

Ruth thought a bit, and she said "Guy. Do you ever feel like Professor Higgins? Are you trying to make a Duchess out of me?"

Guy thought a bit; then he said "You remember, the Society Ball? The Ball was a Test for Eliza. You passed that Test at the Mess Ball, Ruth."

Ruth said "I knew I was on trial."

Guy said "The next Test - at the Cafe de Paris. All those society men worshipping you as if you were a Duchess - just like Eliza."

Ruth said "Could I pass as a Duchess?"

"Yes, Ruth. You can do anything now."

Ruth said, a little shyly "I'll always love you, Guy."

"Then why, why, won't you marry me?"

She said "I'd be a dead weight Guy. Through all your years at Oxford. For years afterwards."

Guy thought a bit, and he said quietly, "But Ruth. If you're honest. It's not just that, is it? You couldn't bear the years of scrimping."

Ruth started to deny it but the denial was still-born; and she acknowledged what had been in her subconscious. Would she ever again giggle with the girls at the Garrison Hop, and allow those sweaty hands on her back? She shuddered. And Stan? It came as a shock to think of Stan, the Gentleman Ranker; Stan, who'd bridged the gap. Stan was a bridge already washed away, and, for Ruth, there was no going back.

And what of Guy. Oh, she loved Guy with a love that made her ache. But Guy was such a baby.

Ruth said "Oh, Guy. Why couldn't you have been older? Just five years older?"

For Ruth, and for Guy, that night was the night they glimpsed the heaven that poets have described, but only a lucky few have experienced on this earth.

They kissed, and Ruth's love for Guy was the protective love of the she-wolf for her cub, a love that would protect him with her life. Her tenderness touched Guy, and he, too, was almost moved to tears of love for her.

As she kissed him, she put her hands to his face, and her touch jolted his desire, as it always did.

Then Ruth lay on the bed, with arms outstretched and with a smile of welcome.

Guy undressed, and stood at the end of the bed, just looking down at her, with his cock pointing like a weathercock to the wind. He opened the packet, and Ruth said "Let me do it." She knelt forward on the bed, and kissed his cock, and tickled it with her tongue. Then she held it hard, with her fingers around it, and, thrusting her breasts forward, she pressed it hard against her so that the dribble wet her nipples.

Guy said "My God, Ruth. You make me mad."

And Ruth said "You make me mad, Guy. Oh, God. I love you, Guy."

She took the rubber, and put it carefully over the tip; and Guy looked down at the long fingers, and the red nails where she flicked down the rubber, tight and taut.

Ruth said "Oh, Guy. I don't want to wait."

She lay back, and he came down on her, and she was wide, and he was straight. She said "Just stay there. I want you to stay there as long as you can."

If he moved too soon, it would be all over too soon, and he'd spoil it; so Guy stayed still, thrust-up and still; and Ruth said "I'm happy, Guy. So happy. Please make it last."

She raised her head to him, to where he was arched above her, and she kissed his nipples, and ticked each nipple so that his cock twitched and jerked inside her; and, with each jerk she gasped with pleasure. Then she lay back, supine, and reached behind him, and pressed her finger behind his cock, where it came from his body, at the root, and the pleasure of it was like an ecstacy for him, until he could hold himself no longer, and he said "Ruth, Ruth I've got to fuck you." And she said "Yes. Yes. Oh, Guy. Fuck me. Yes."

So, Guy moved, and thrust, wishing it could be forever, taking his weight on his arms, and looking down on her as he moved and thrust, hard and strong; strong and hard; straight; twisting sometimes; hard and twisting; and, she, twisting with him; her eyes glazed in ecstacy; and, he, hard, hard; hard and fast; a surge at the root to give him warning; and "Now!" he shouted "Now!" Still, the surge was held by the Dyke, the Dyke of his Will and by the deep breath he held for the Dyke; until the pressure, the weight of the surge was too great for Dyke, or for Will, or for Breath. And, Guy thrust forward in triumph, trumpeting like a Bull Elephant on Must. "Now!" he shouted "Now", as Ruth went into the long, long, spasm of that glimpse of Heaven she would never forget.

That summer. In England, the careless, carefree Summer; and, in Korea, another humid, insect-ridden season, full of boredom, and fear, and more boredom; and, for Sergeant Stan Phillips, bouts of sin in Seoul!

Ruth's world and Stan's world no longer impinged - not in any sort of communication, either postal or telepathic. Ruth hadn't heard from Stan for months; she'd had no news, and Ruth's own letters had petered out through lack of response. And now, Ruth scarcely thought of Stan.

Then, it was rumours of Armistice from far away across the world, and the bitter battles gave way to an embittered peace. Stan was posted Home.

Stan wanted his motor-bike and he wanted his girl, and both were in Park Hall Camp at Oswestry. Stan was posted to Woolwich, to Permanent Staff at Royal Artillery headquarters, "The Shop", and permanent staff at Woolwich was a cushy posting, with plenty of Married Quarters, comfortable quarters for a Sergeant.

Stan got a leave-pass, and he wangled a Rail Warrant, and, in the autumn, he knocked at the door. The 'Q' answered the door "Well - if it isn't Sergeant Phillips - Come in, Stan."

"Is Ruth in?"

"Well, no. Not expecting you is she? - Come in and have a drink."

The 'Q' brought out the bottled beer, took off the Crown corks and poured. The beer was a bit frothy, and, as he was waiting for it to settle, the 'Q' said "Korea must have been a shit-hole, from what I've heard."

"A shit-hole. Yes." Stan said "Sometimes it was frozen shit. And sometimes you couldn't see the shit for fucking mosquitoes."

The 'Q' said "In the war, in the Desert, it was flies. At Tobruk and that. The flies were worse than the fucking Jerries. You couldn't see the shit for fucking flies."

"There were flies in Korea, too," said Stan "And there were as many fucking Chinese as flies. I hate Chinese; and I hate flies."

The 'Q' said "Here's Ruth, now. I'll tell her you're here."

The 'Q' went outside. "It's Stan" he said "Careful, now."

For a second, Ruth wanted to run away, to hide. A year ago she might have done so; but now, she braced her shoulders and went inside. She stepped into the parlour and closed the door behind her. "Hello Stan."

He jumped up, and made a clumsy move to embrace her, but Ruth just offered her cheek to be kissed.

"Oh, aren't we high and mighty!" Stan sneered.

Ruth said "I see Dad's given you a beer. I'll get one for myself." She hardly ever drank beer, but this seemed like the right occasion. She went into the kitchen and said "Dad, you've left your beer in the parlour." She took a bottle, and a glass, and was half hoping that the 'Q' would follow her, but he didn't.

In the parlour, she opened the bottle carefully, so the beer didn't fizz, and she tilted the glass while she filled it, to minimise the head.

Stan said "I see you've learnt some clever tricks."

Ruth said "Stan. Was it awful in Korea?"

He said "Boring mostly. Boring and empty. With occasional periods of Hell."

Ruth said "I wrote to you at first" and Stan said "I'm sorry. There didn't seem to be much to write about" - He felt the void between them; they both felt it. He said "Look, I'll get the bike out. Let's go for a ride; like we used to do.'"

She was on the point of refusing, but, she thought, he had a right; she ought to go. At least one day; she could spare

82

him one day.

Stan went to the M.T. park, to the sheds where they'd stored the bike as a favour; where they'd drained the battery and everything. He'd let them know he was coming, and they had it all ready, acid and charge and ready to go. He'd warned them, but he hadn't warned Ruth - he wanted to surprise her. The M.T. Sergeant had seen the bike right, kept it safe in the corner of the big shed under a tarpaulin; in the corner by the gun-trailer.

"Back already, Stan?" said the M.T. Sergeant - "Got some service in!" - he was a bit oily, a bit scruffy, like all M.T. blokes, a veteran of the War; and all he lived for was engines - loved 'em. He tinkered about, inflated the tyres, checked the oil. "Give her a try" he said. She started third kick, and Stan was away.

Ruth had put on a coat, and slacks and gloves. She said "It's cold Stan. Better not to rev. her too hard. "

"Get on" said Stan. He had not cut the engine, but was on the saddle, blipping her, making her roar, to challenge the whole Camp.

"Right" said Ruth, and she straddled the pillion.

Stan didn't go far, just into Oswestry town, taking the bends beautifully as he always did, leaning the bike into the bends, and using the camber. It was Saturday and late lunch-time, a half-hour to closing-time and not many people about. They went into the Hotel, into the snug bar by the fire. Stan ordered a pint and a gin-and-orange, but Ruth interrupted "A dry sherry for me, Stan. A Fino."

"A Fino is it? You've been learning your way around."

"Yes, Stan. I've changed."

Stan said "You always had it in you - to be a lady, I

mean."

Ruth said "I don't know about being a lady, Stan. I just know what I want."

The bar extended between the main Lounge, and the Snug. The barman came through with the drinks, and Stan got up to collect them from the bar. He took a long drink and said "Beer like this; pubs like this - they make me feel secure. A million miles from Korea."

He sat, looking into the glass, as though he was looking for some meaning in the liquid, and he said "You say you know what you want, Ruth."

Ruth said "Perhaps I should have put it another way. I know what I don't want." Stan said "I notice you're not wearing my ring."

"No, Stan. But I've got the ring. I'd like you to have it back."

"So that's it!" - Stan's pride was hurt "You could have spared me all this. Let me know before."

Ruth said "I should have written. But you never replied to my letters. Besides - I knew you had to come to Oswestry; for the bike."

She opened her purse, and put the ring in his hand. He sat, looking at it, and Ruth said "No hard feelings. Please, Stan."

There was a sound of people coming into the hotel, and voices in the Lounge-Bar. Someone said "Just time for a pint before closing." Another voice replied "I'd rather be playing rugger. But a pint's better than nothing" - and it was Guy.

The voice said "Ladies' Night at the Mess tonight. Of course you'll be with Ruth; you lucky guy." - the same old pun, as familiar to Guy as an old friend.

"So that's it!" said Stan, and his voice was full of bitterness "Officers! - I'm not good enough. Officers!"

Ruth put her hand out, to try to calm him "Please, Stan."

"Don't say please to me! Bloody National Servicemen! Bloody subalterns!" Ruth said "It's not the boy's fault."

Stan was raising his voice "National Service subalterns - we had 'em in Korea. We had to wet-nurse them, I can tell you. Poncing about like God Almighty. But they shit themselves when the Chinks came at us. When the shit was flying."

He was shouting now. Guy poked his head around the door, saw Ruth, and Stan. He said "Oh! - Excuse me," and was moving away, when Ruth said, quickly. "Guy. Do you remember Sergeant Phillips?"

"Oh, yes" said Guy uncertainly, and Ruth said "He's just back from Korea." Stan said "I remember you, Sir. We met at WOSB,"

Guy managed to say "Of course; I remember, Sergeant. You went out to Korea."

Stan said "You must have had a cushy time, Sir. Here in England" - he didn't try to keep the sneer out of his voice.

Guy said "I'm no hero, Sergeant. Not like you."

Stan said "I was engaged to Ruth - but I expect you know that."

Guy nodded; and Stan went on "Was it, you know, Sir, conduct becoming to an Officer and a Gentleman? - while a Ranker was away on Active Service? For Queen and Country? To steal his girl?"

Guy took a deep breath and mumbled something incoherent, something about being sorry.

Ruth stood up quickly, full of anger. "Oh, so you're sorry, Guy. Sorry! That's a nice compliment!"

Guy said "Will you be coming tonight, Ruth? To the Mess, I mean" and Ruth said "If I'm still invited? - It's what's been arranged."

Star said "Oh, high and mighty! The Officers' Mess! What does your Dad think of that?" Then he turned to Guy, and said "I thought there was something about Honour, Sir. I suppose it didn't even worry you - that I was in Korea?"

Ruth said "Stan. If you want to blame someone, blame me."

Stan said, sneering to cover the hurt in his voice "Getting off with the Officers while the poor bloody Ranker does the fighting. In bed with an Officer while I'm fondly believing you're waiting for me!"

Ruth said "Hypocrite! I hoped we'd part as friends." - She opened her bag, and took out the photo, the one of Stan and the two tarts.

Stan stared at the photo "The bastard!" he said "The sneaky, rotten bastard!" He lifted his pint glass, and drained it. Then he turned to Guy, and said "She's a whore, Sir. You're welcome to her."

Guy lost his temper at that, and grabbed at Stan; but Ruth restrained him, and Stan said "Careful, Sir! Striking a subordinate! - That's a Court Martial offence."

Stan left, and they heard his bike like a final roll of drums.

That night at the Mess was a night of tension. Afterwards, when Guy tried to kiss Ruth, she held apart, and said "I've made it awkward for you, Guy." He tried to reassure her, but she said "Guy, remember what you said to Stan. You said you were sorry. Sorry about me."

Guy said "I just blurted it out. I had to say something. I didn't mean it."

"In a way, you did mean it, Guy."

"Rot!" said Guy - he was desperate to convince her.

She said "They are talking about us; down in the Sergeants' Mess. It's awkward for Dad."

"What are they saying?"

"That I'm high and mighty. Think myself too good for them. Too good for Mum and Dad."

Guy said "The Q and your mother - they don't believe that?"

Ruth paused "I don't know, Guy."

Guy said "I'll be demobbed soon. In the spring."

Ruth said "That's just it, Guy. What sort of a position will I have here, without you? No entree to the Officers' Mess; no welcome in the Sergeants' Mess."

Guy said "What, then?"

"I'm not sure. But, maybe, now's the time to make the break."

Her words cut deep. Guy tried to protest, but she kissed him quickly, and went into the house.

Guy didn't sleep much; he worried at the problem all night and all the next night; but the problem was still unsolved on Monday morning when Porter came in, and plonked down his boots and webbing, and said "Nice morning for the Passing-out Parade, Sir."

Then, all was bustle and bullshit, and Guy had no time to think as his Troop had won the Competition again thanks mostly to Sergeant Jackson. So, it was march past the saluting base, Guy at the front, Troop Commander of the winning troop, once more.

"Eyes Right!" he bellowed, like Stentor. - "Eyes Right!" - miss one pace, then snap the hand to the peak of the cap, the salute; looking Rufus straight in the eye on the rostrum; then "Eyes front!" like Stentor again-, miss one pace; and snap of the head to the front, and hand away from the cap, and into the swing of the March.

Then, all the Regiment in Line: "Present Arms!" - the crash of the hands on the sling and the slap of the palms on the butt; and - stillness!

Then "Commander of the Winning Troop! - Advance to collect the Cup!"

Guy alone. Stamp and March, and Salute again; alone; in front of a thousand eyes; and Rufus shaking his hand and saying "Well done, Guy!"

Then, March-off-Parade and "Fall Out!"; and hurry to the Mess, carrying the cup, hoping for a drink before lunch, he needed it; but here was the Q, coming up, and saluting and "Can I have a word, Sir? - Ruth's gone, Sir."

"Oh" - the flat "Oh", but the turmoil within.

The Q said "Please - let her go, Sir. Give her a chance."

Guy said "She doesn't want to see me?"

"She thinks it's better, Sir."

"I see" - Guy tried to keep the hurt out of his voice, the desolation. He said "It will be hard for me, Q."

"Yes, Sir."

"Tell me Q. Is it a secret; where she's gone?"

"Secret, Sir? Lord no, Sir. No harm in your knowing. Seeing as she trusts you, Sir. Trusts you not to chase after her."

Guy said "It will be hard Q. But I won't follow. Not if she doesn't want me." The Q said "I didn't say that, Sir. I didn't say she doesn't want you."

Guy said, and he almost smiled, in spite of everything "You do have a naive trust in gentlemen; officers and gentlemen."

The Q said "I trust you, Sir - My Missus has a sister, lives on Merseyside. Birkenhead. Not far from here, really. Ruth's always been her favourite."

"Good Lord, Q!" - Guy forced a laugh, a little, dry laugh "Merseyside! Good Lord. A funny place for Ruth to go!"

3. RUTH AGAIN

"Why don't you come to the Dance on Saturday?" One of the girls at the Library said - Ruth had got a job at the Library, in Birkenhead. "I don't know what's wrong with you" the girl said "A pretty girl like you. Don't you ever go out?"

Ruth smiled "Oh, yes. The pictures. Now and again." – Ruth's Auntie liked to go to the pictures.

Saturday came around, and Auntie said "Ruth. I'm worried about you. Why don't you go out? You don't seem to see any young people."

The phone went, and it was the girl from the library. She said "A crowd of us are off to the hop at the Rugger Club. Come on, Ruth."

Ruth hesitated, and the girl said "The Rugby Club - they have these dances - a band; plenty of men - all full of beer, of course; but fun."

"All right!" said Ruth.

There seemed to be a thousand people at the dance, all crowding at the Bar, to get a drink, and you could hardly hear the music for the row. The men all looked huge, and steaming after their shower; and beer in pint pots, and beer in gallon jugs was passing to and fro over everybody's head from the bar.

Someone anonymous held out a glass for Ruth, not a pint pot thank heaven, and filled it with beer and grinned at her. The girls from the library pushed their way into the other room where there was dancing, and they started dancing around, two girls together, waiting for a couple of men to break them up; that seemed to be the idea. It was like a livestock market, a display for the customers, and Ruth began to wish she had never come. Most of the girls were just wearing cheap skirts and tops, and Ruth felt overdressed; really, she'd expected something a bit more fashionable than this. She was wearing the black frock she'd bought in Harvey Nicholls that week in London with Guy - it seemed like another life, that week in Heaven. She felt the shadow of regret, as she'd felt it so often since she left him, and "This is a mistake" she thought: all those hunks of beefcake, sweating and ready with their sweaty paws; really, it was no better than the Garrison Hop.

She noticed one or two red faces approaching, and she knew she would be asked to dance, so she started to move away, back into the clubhouse. Escape - she'd call a taxi; never come back.

A tall figure was blocking her way. "Excuse me!" Ruth said.

"Certainly" - the voice was courteous "I say. You're not leaving, are you? - I want you to meet my friends." And, before she knew, Ruth was sitting on a chair with a drink, not a beer, but a dry Martini. "I could tell you were a dry Martini girl" said the big man - "I'm sorry, I didn't catch your name."

She told him, and he announced "Everybody - meet Ruth. By the way I'm Paul. But everybody calls me Buff. Short for Buffalo, you know."

"Hey, Buff" said Tony "How did you find her? I thought only Grimmies came here by themselves."

Buff said "She's certainly not a Grimmie, is she?" and he put a protective arm around her shoulder.

One of the girls, Tony's girl, was perched on a bar stool, and she said in a plummy voice "You men would all be after Grimmies, if we weren't here to keep an eye on you."

All the men laughed, but no one denied it. Then, Louise, the one with the plummy voice said:

"Come on, Buff. We've supported the Club. We've done our bit of slumming. Let's go to Tom's place."

Buff said "I say, Ruth. Do you want to come along?"

"Who's Tom?"

"Tom Vernon? Oh, he's a millionaire."

Ruth stood up, and Louise said "I say, what a super frock", and Ruth said "It's Harvey Nicholls" - she said it as though she went there every week. Louise wrinkled-up her nose and said "Everyone seems to go to Harrod's - makes me not want to set foot in the place."

Ruth shrugged her shoulders, and, when she noticed the effect that had on the men, she shrugged them again. They all piled out of the Clubhouse together, Buff and Tony and Louise and all the others; and there were already a dozen couples in the shadows, in the empty stands, snogging and the girls giggling. Ruth thought "I'll never do that, and be called a Grimmie; and be condescended to by girls with plummy voices."

The cars were outside and Louise was driving her Daddy's Bentley. She said "Hop in Ruth - and Buff"; and as soon as they were in the back seat together, Buff had his hand on her knee. Ruth didn't do anything about that, she just ignored it, and, eventually, he took it away.

Louise said "Tony and Buff and most of the others. They're not millionaires yet. So I provide the transport." She was handling the car well, a brute of a car, a brute with impeccable manners. Ruth thought, the car's a bit like these men; a bit like Buff.

She said "I had a boyfriend once who had a big motorbike, a Norton. You should try one of those, Buff."

They drove along a sea-front, with the sea a vague line far out, across the sand. They pulled into a driveway beside a big house, with great pools of light spilling out, and snatches of music. There were other cars in the drive, Jaguars, Mercedes; expensive cars.

"Hello; Hello, Buff" someone called "Hello Come in!"

Here was opulence. Ruth had seen it on the films, High Society, those films; the opulence of New Money. Ruth wasn't sure if it was vulgar, or if such ostentation had a style of its own: all marble statues, and hunks of silver and gilt; and velvet everywhere. Down the whole length of one room there was a Bar, all chrome and slabs of glass; a thousand bottles glinting on the shelves, and a thousand goblets waiting to be filled.

There was a gramophone in the corner, and someone had put on some music, not very loud, a Rumba or something, the Calypso Boys; Buff took Ruth in his arms and swayed around a bit, and while he swayed he exchanged remarks with the other couples who were dancing.

"Hello Buff. Heard from Bunty?"

Buff said, in mock surprise "Bunty? Who on earth do you mean?"

Ruth said "Is Bunty your girlfriend Buff?" and Buff said "I think she is - she's gone ski-ing."

"What about you?" said Ruth,

"Me?" said Buff "I can't afford it."

Ruth said "Really? I can hardly believe that."

And Buff said "True - most of us here aren't qualified yet: Lawyers, Accountants. We're not rich yet. Except Tom of course. Tom and a few others."

They went over, and sat at the Bar, on high stools. Louise was sitting on the next stool, popping stuffed olives into Tony's mouth, while he caught them like a trained seal;

93

Ruth found herself admiring Louise's style.

Louise said "See. Tony's a good boy. Getting his reward" and Tony said "I expect more of a reward than a stuffed olive."

Louise said "Well. You'll have to work for it, won't you?" - She was just a bit hard, Louise, a hard beauty. She said "Tony and I will get married, someday. He knows he's got to get rich to keep me."

Tony said "Daddy and his bloody Bentley. That's Louise's style, and I'm expected to keep her in it."

Ruth said "Do you see a lot of each other?"

Louise said "Not really. I'm a model. I work in London most of the time." "I'd like to try that" said Ruth.

Louise looked at her more closely "It's not all glamour" she said "Damned hard work really. But, yes. You could do it."

There was a chap standing by himself in the corner, surveying the scene. He seemed to be enjoying himself in a quiet way, as though he liked to be a spectator. He came across and said.

"Buff. Do you mind if I ask the lady to dance?" He bowed, with an old-fashioned bow, and clicked his heels German-fashion.

Ruth stood up, and she was nearly as tall, and she could sense that he was admiring her shoulders, which came just below his chin. He said "I'm glad that Buff brought someone new. We always seem such a clique. I'm Tom Vernon, by the way."

Ruth said "It's all new to me, and fun. Thank you for welcoming me."

He said "You would be a credit wherever you went."

Louise overheard, and she called out. "She'd like to be a model, Tom. Don't you think she'd make a splendid model?"

"I might be able to arrange that" said Tom, and he returned her to Buff, with another bow.

They brought in some food. "Just a few bits and pieces" said Tom. A butler and a maid went around with salvers of canapés that might have come from the Ritz; lobster and caviar. There was plenty to drink, as much as you liked, anything you wanted; but nobody was getting drunk, and that surprised Ruth. A few couples were drifting off, up to the bedrooms, but it wasn't blatant; not like the coupling on the grass outside the Garrison Hop at Oswestry.

"Let me show you around the house" said Buff. And Ruth thought "If he thinks I'm a pushover, he'll have to think again." She made a joke of it "Won't we find all the rooms occupied?"

"I'll just shout "It's only Buff'- they won't mind."

He led her into a darkened sitting-room and called out "Buff's here" and turned on the light. A couple blinked up at them from the sofa; the couple were still fairly respectable, after all it was a sitting-room not a bedroom: full of French Baroque, and chandeliers dripping with crystal, and a fortune in Aubusson on the floor. Buff waited a minute for Ruth to look, then he turned off the light with a cheery "Have fun!" and they went into the dining-room which was unoccupied except for a great gilt Eagle with wings outspread.

There were a few men in the billiards-room, playing snooker, or watching, and one said "Hello, Buff. Fancy a game?" In the swimming pool, people were swimming, and floating around, drinking and talking. The pool was down a few steps, and marbled like a Roman bath; with steam rising and lit by lamps fashioned like flambeaux, held aloft by link-boys of cast bronze.

Buff led the way upstairs, up the marble stairway with the marble busts on the balustrades, and, outside the master bedroom he shouted "It's Buff - may we come in?"

It was Tony's voice, mumbling something from inside, something about you awkward bloody Buffalo and always putting your bloody hooves in it. They went inside and Louise was sitting up in bed, holding the sheets as a gesture of modesty; she wasn't upset or anything, just exasperated.

Ruth felt embarrassed, but Buff insisted on showing her the bathroom with the golden cherubs - cherubs for taps, cherubs for Spouts, - after the manner of Manikin Pis in Brussels; and a bath as big as a lake, plenty of room for two. Louise said "We'll be having a bath together. - Care to join us?" And she was only half joking.

Buff said "The other bedrooms are rather the same as this one" and Ruth said "I'll take your word for it, Buff. You've embarrassed me enough."

He called out at the next bedroom, and there was no reply. It was empty, so he led her inside, and pulled her towards the bed.

He said "You've really got class. Do you know that?" - He'd sensed how to flatter her. She let him kiss her, and fondle her a bit, and it was quite nice - it was so long since she'd been kissed; but she said "Buff. I'm not going to let you do much more than this."

"You can't be serious!" - He just didn't believe her; so, when he did try it on, when he put his hand under her skirt, and she saw the obstinate look, the Buffalo look, she struggled free and said "I meant it, Buff!"

But Buff wasn't so easily tamed; he was a wild Buffalo after all. The door was closed, and, if she'd shouted who would have bothered? He held her in a grip and she said "You're not going to rape me? - A gentleman like you?"

He looked ashamed, and Ruth said "And what about the girl who's ski-ing?"

The remark hit harder than she'd expected; it was a bit below the belt. She said, and she knew it was cruel "I expect she's in bed with the ski instructor. They always are."

"You bitch!" he said, and Ruth was shocked, and rather frightened at his reaction. Buff was hurt, and he reacted by mauling her, pulling her to him, and she almost gave in; she thought, was it worth it - really, was it worth it, trying to fend him off; what was she trying to prove? But, she did know that she was proving: never, never against her will, never!

Buff was a wild buffalo now, obstinate and a bit drunk, so Ruth brought up her knee, to his groin, and the shock of it made him release her, for her to twist away.

Downstairs, Tom said "Where's Buff - you look as though you need a drink." Ruth said "I had to deal with Buff. He's drunk too much."

Tom said "Do you want to go home? I'll run you home in my car if you like."

Tom picked a Mercedes from a row of cars, and opened the door for Ruth. He drove slowly. He said "Don't worry about Buff. He won't be a wild buffalo for long. He'll be quite domesticated. You see, Bunty will be back. Back from ski-ing."

Ruth said "I made a joke, a silly joke really, about her getting off with the ski instructor. That's what turned him ugly."

They pulled up outside the little house, and Tom said "By the way, what's your 'phone number?"

"It's my Aunt's number" she said. "I'm staying with my Aunt, you see."

She gave him the number, and he wrote it in his diary

97

under the dashboard light. Then, he got out of the car, and went around to open the door for her.

Ruth became Tom Vernon's mistress.

Tom waited a few days, after he had brought Ruth home, then he sent the Rolls for her, and a chauffeur, with everybody in the street peeping from behind net curtains. They had dinner, just the two of them, at the Adelphi Hotel in Liverpool; in a discreet corner of the Restaurant, and not very busy, midweek: no need even to consult the wine-list, the waiter knew what Mr Vernon liked to drink, a Chablis followed by a Cotes de Nuit. Tom said "You must be bored - working at the Library. I've arranged a modelling course for you in Liverpool."

Ruth started to protest - he'd certainly moved fast. He said "It gives me pleasure- helping my friends."

So, Ruth left the Library, and went each day to Liverpool, to the modelling course; sometimes she crossed the Mersey by Underground train, Birkenhead to Liverpool, and sometimes, when she wasn't in a hurry and when the weather was fair, she took the Ferry boat to Liverpool Pier Head, and walked up the hill, past the Liver Birds, into the City.

They learnt deportment, and how to walk-on, and how to show the clothes; and it came easily to Ruth, as Louise said it would.

The usual crowd were always round at Tom's: Buff and Tony and Louise, and Buff's girl Bunty, who'd been in Switzerland; and, once, at one of Tom's parties when it had got wilder than usual - it was after Ruth had become, very definitely, Tom's girl, and could decide who was invited, and she had the run of the house - Ruth had the idea for a bit of mischief. Ruth went into one of the bedrooms - she pretended she thought it was empty, but she knew Buff was in there with Bunty, and Ruth had the mischief to catch them at it; she was getting like that, fond of mischief.

Ruth went into the room, and feigned surprise, and there they were: Buff forcing himself to grin and pretending it was all a jolly romp, and he was kneeling on the floor practically naked, and Bunty was astride him, riding him, and kicking with her heels. Buff looked so silly, but Bunty was unembarrassed, and said "Hello, Ruth. Come and join the fun. This old Buffalo is strong enough for two."

She gave Buff a slap, and he bellowed, and Ruth thought: well, we know who wears the jodhpurs there.

After a party, Ruth usually stayed the night at Tom's. She'd tell Auntie the party had gone on all night, which was a way of maintaining respectability.

That night, after the funny scene in the bedroom, Ruth went down to the pool- while his guests danced, and drank, and ate, Tom often spent his time swimming. She changed into the costume she always kept there, and, while they were splashing around, she told Tom about Buff and his Rider upstairs. "I'm not sure that I like that" he said.

The last car drove away, about three in the morning, and Ruth and Tom went upstairs, up the empty stairway, past the marble busts. They were relaxed after their swim, and the house was warm, it was always warm; so they lay down on Tom's bed, naked. Ruth lay back, head on pillow, legs spread wide for him. He was a good lover, a generous lover - he was a generous man, and it showed in his loving as it showed in everything else. He caressed her, and brought her close to her climax, and "Yes" she said "Yes, Tom, please." It was the truth, she did want him. He entered her, strong and gentle, and he fucked her to give her pleasure, and, because her pleasure was important to him, his pleasure was great as well.

Ruth wasn't completely happy - if only Tom had been Guy! Someone as ambitious as Ruth is never truly content; but, at least, she was living in her element. Luxury had become Ruth's element.

Wherever they went together, Ruth was admired - Ruth and Tom, they made a brave couple: when he took her to the Races, the National in the spring, and Ascot in the summer. He was a big racing man, Tom.

Wherever she did a modelling job, Ruth was admired as much as the clothes, and she couldn't help liking that. Many of the jobs were in London, and sometimes Louise would be modelling on the same show. Ruth used to take the train up to London or Tom would go with her, drive her in one of his cars, the Rolls or the Merc, whichever took his fancy. He came to a few dress shows, and sat amongst the Buyers, the Fashion people, and afterwards he would whisk her away for dinner at the Savoy or some restaurant, Genaro's in Soho, or the Boulestin. He suggested the Cafe de Paris, but Ruth put him off the idea - somehow, she didn't want to mix things up; she wanted to keep this life separate from her old life with Guy.

Once Tom chartered a 'plane, Starways out of Liverpool Airport, and he took everyone, all the gang over to Le Touquet and they spent most of the time at the Casino; and, when they weren't at the Casino they went down to the seashore and ate crepes suzettes which they bought at a stall. Tom gave Ruth a few gaming chips, and she tried Roulette which soon bored her, so she watched the Baccarat and the Chemin de Fer; and, after a bit, she sat down at a table herself, and had some luck. There were more English people than French at the Casino, and a few men tried to make a pass; but, when they found out she was Tom's girl, they backed off.

In the Casino, Ruth felt at home, just as she felt at home in Tom's place and the places he took her, the established places, the places of privilege. Tom liked the Casino - he seemed to be more lively in a Casino than anywhere, less detached; more involved, as if gambling gave him a kick like alcohol. That was why Ruth liked going Racing with Tom: all the gambling, and the people in the

County Stand; morning coat and topper, binoculars and Champagne; and all the ordinary people in the crowd looking up at them.

Tall girls were getting most of the modelling work, and Ruth's picture was always in Vogue, modelling for this or that Fashion house; and, once or twice, she was in Tatler, at the big social occasions with Tom. In Vogue, of course, she was anonymous, just a face and a figure, but, in Tatler it was "Mr Tom Vernon and Miss Ruth Evans, enjoying a glass of Champagne," at Royal Ascot, or Henley or at a Charity Ball.

The old crowd were still together, the old crowd and the hangers-on; they'd meet every Saturday at a pub, the Basnett Bar in Liverpool or the Ring 'o' Bells on the Wirral. Then they'd go to someone's house, usually Tom's, or they'd go to a Club, the Bowler Hat in Birkenhead or to the Aero Club. Or they'd go out to dinner to a Hotel, the Grosvenor in Chester, or to one of the Robley restaurants where they had dancing and a cabaret; and pink linen and obsequiousness. Wherever they went, it was always the best table for Mr Vernon, for Mr Vernon's party; and all the women, all the waitresses and all the others, would try to get noticed by Mr Vernon. But it was Ruth who was Queen, and Ruth blossomed on it.

Ruth despised these women, the way they threw themselves at Tom; she'd never have done that. It was just wealth they were drawn to, the glamour of wealth, for, in himself, Tom had little glamour, he was too self-contained.

Once, at a club, Ruth was dancing with Tony, and she thought Tom was with Louise, but he'd gone out and Louise said that the Manager's wife was showing Tom around the place. Ruth felt herself getting jealous, but she said to herself don't be a fool, you've no rights over Tom; it was hurt pride that made her angry. She pretended not to care, and had another dance. Then Tom came downstairs with the woman following, and her husband pretending not to notice. The

101

woman was attractive in a hard, blonded way, and full of satisfaction as she came downstairs.

Afterwards, in the car, Ruth said "Everyone saw you go upstairs with that woman."

She thought they might have a row, she wanted a row, but Tom just said quietly "Do you mind?"

Ruth said "I mind being made to look a fool."

"I'm sorry" said Tom, and Ruth found her anger giving way to amusement. She said "Was she fun?"

Tom said "Too wild for me. She had so many tricks - she must have worked in a brothel."

Ruth said "You better have a good bath before you come near me again."

Then, it was Autumn again, and another Rugger season - watching the games; and parties, always parties on Saturdays after the game.

Ruth went home for Christmas, the first time she'd been home, even though it wasn't far. Mum and the `Q' had made a few visits, of course, to see her, and to see Auntie: but this was the first time Ruth had been back to Oswestry.

Tom didn't like Ruth going. At Christmas? What a time to leave him. "I'll be back for New Year's Eve" she said "I promisee"

Back at Oswestry so much had changed; not the Camp, but the people. People always changed so fast in the Army. There were so many new officers. Guy had been demobbed months before - she knew that; otherwise she would not have come. He'll have done a term at Oxford already she thought. At Oswestry, Guy was forgotten: National Servicemen left no more impression than rain on the desert sand.

One night after Christmas - between Christmas and

New Year - there was a Party at the Officers' Mess, a Dance, and Ruth went past, to look, anonymous in the dark. There they were, all excited, some faces she recognised, all the cars driving up and the Bombardier saluting. And all the girls alighting, chattering, hugging their friends "Hello, hello!" so happy and excited. How sophisticated she had thought they were, Ruth remembered: all those farmers' daughters with ruddy cheek and country style.

And the dresses? Ruth wondered that she'd ever admired and envied their provincial idea of haute couture: not-quite-a-perfect-fit.

There was one face she did recognise, Prunella Rudd; and, a sudden panic – that wasn't Guy surely? But no, she needn't have worried, for, when the gentleman turned full-face, he was an older man than Guy.

As she watched, there in the dark, she felt unwanted, a Sergeant-Major's daughter: no place for her at an officers' party unless she was invited by some Prince Charming. But, in another sense, she had travelled way beyond the Officers' Mess; as far as Xanadu, and she could never return.

On the Sunday after Christmas Ruth went out alone, through the deserted lines into the sullen morning. There was a truck outside the guardroom; the Guard-Sergeant had come out for a breath of air, and was standing by the polished shell-case that served as a firebell. He recognised Ruth, and threw up a cracking salute - he'd no one else to salute - and she smiled, and waved. It was frosty, and Ruth was wearing her Red Fox coat, the one Tom had given her for Christmas. She passed the rows of guns, and went towards the Regimental Library. There was a scuffle in the undergrowth, then a dog emerged, followed by Prunella.

Pru said "Ruth! It's been ages!"

Ruth asked, trying to sound casual. "Have you seen anything of Guy?" and Pru said "Oh yes. At Oxford. He seems to be enjoying himself."

Ruth said "I'm glad he's happy, Pru" and Pru said "The next thing you know, he will be inviting you to Oxford - to a Commem. Ball, or something."

Ruth said "I wouldn't go, Pru."

"Spoilsport! - of course you would go!"

"No" said Ruth. "I couldn't go through all that again. I got too fond of him."

Pru had noticed the fur; she said "My God, Ruth. What a lovely fur coat. It must have cost a fortune."

"It was a present."

Pru said "Of course, I've seen your picture in Vogue - and in the Tatler."

Ruth had Sunday lunch with Mum and the `Q', then she 'phoned for a taxi. There was nothing to keep her in Camp, nothing at all.

New Year's Eve was Ruth's greatest triumph; it was like a Coronation, and she was Queen.

Ruth's frock was as black as her hair, tight and self-supporting; very reticent and very expensive: Tom had seen her modelling the frock, and had insisted on buying it for her. Ruth had a room of her own, now, at Tom's place - not Tom's room, but one of the other bedrooms that became, really her private dressing room where she could bathe and change, and keep all her expensive things - so she wouldn't have to keep them at Auntie's place. Of course, Auntie knew all about Tom, but it wasn't mentioned.

The New Year Party was in Liverpool, where the boys, the Rugger crowd, had taken over the Drill Hall, the big Territorial Army Drill Hall, which they'd hired for the night. Everybody joined in the preparations, it was part of the fun:

Ruth went over in the afternoon, to help with the streamers and blowing up balloons, and, oh, that was a wonderful time, like a kid's party.

It was a fancy dress party, and Ruth was going to the party in the latest model frock. To sacrifice the frock was unthinkable, so, with a Welsh Witch's hat, and a broomstick, Ruth became the sexiest, wickedest witch.

She stood in front of the mirror in her room at Tom's place, her hands crossed over her chest above the bodice, and her fingers splayed out and red-tipped like the rays of two suns; she felt a suggestion of sexuality at her own beauty, and a thought came to her, unbidden: "If only it wasn't old Tom again, tonight.,'

If Guy ever did invite her to one of those Balls at Oxford, like Pru said, would she really have the willpower to refuse?

Tom was turned out as a Regency Buck, from his high collar and stock down to his patent-leather pumps; but, above the collar, he was still the same Tom, and Ruth caught herself thinking, how dull. But, it was no time for introspection, as she was whisked away in the Rolls through the Mersey Tunnel; and into the crowd at the Drill Hall, that you would never have guessed was a Drill Hall; it was so disguised by lighting and bunting. And, there they all were, all the gang and everything pulsating around Ruth.

"Hello Tony; Hello Louise, Hello Everybody."

"Here comes Buff!" They shouted; and there he was, a whisk tied to his rear for a tail, and blinkers and a real bridle and reins. Bunty was togged-up like a jockey, what else, and she shouted "This buffalo has changed into a racehorse" - she was in white jodhpurs and silk Racing Colours, and looked disturbing and sexy.

Tom said "Bunty - do you know you're wearing the

105

Racing Colours of the Aga Khan?" Bunty replied "Oh, yes. He's a friend of mine" - and she might not have been joking.

Most of the men drank too much that night, and it was all such fun, it was delirium. The cymbals crashed at midnight, and everyone was kissing in the dark, and whoever it was who was kissing Ruth, it certainly wasn't Tom. The man said "My God, Ruth. You make me mad!" - It was Mike, one of the chaps from the Rugger Club, a big ladies' man; but with not much money; yet to make his way in the world like Buff and the others.

They had Auld Lang Syne, and crashing into each other as they held hands and sang it; then somebody cut the balloons down, and everybody was popping balloons and kissing everybody else, and shouting "Happy New Year."

Ruth had got separated from Tom, and she didn't care; and here was Mike with a glass of champagne for her; at least it fizzed like Champagne and Ruth was past caring how it tasted. There was a Club Lounge at the Drill Hall, and it had become the snogging room for the night, darkened, with couples stretched out on the sofas. Mike collapsed into an armchair, and pulled Ruth down; it was only festive fun - festive, sexy, fun.

Mike said "What will you do, when you split from Tom?"

Ruth said "Modelling I suppose. In a bigger way. London."

Mike said "You'll find another chap like Tom. Rich."

Ruth said "You think I'm just a gold-digger don't you?"

He said "Perhaps."

Ruth said "There was a boy once. But I wouldn't tie him to my apron strings."

They had another dance, then Mike found Tom, and handed Ruth back to him. Tom said "I've been wondering where you were." Which irritated Ruth: such a banal remark. She almost wished he had made a fuss.

On the way home, Tom said "Let's go ski-ing. In February. Let's ski."

A crowd of people from the Rugger club were going ski-ing; they went every February: the more established people; the people who could afford it.

Was it a year since Bunty had gone ski-ing, and left Buff behind? A year since Ruth met Tom? The richer ones went ski-ing, and the poor chaps, the articled clerks and so on, next year's lawyers and accountants, were left behind to keep the Club flag flying, and to play in the teams.

Nobody had got married yet, but that would be the next stage, and, already, Tony had forked out for an engagement ring for Louise. Ruth wondered if Bunty would wait for Buff - God help him, he'd be on a tight rein, and she would probably bitch him pretty soon.

Ruth thought: What if Tom proposed? - My God, she knew that he never would; but if he did, would she sell out for money and a life of luxury?

Ruth said "I've never tried ski-ing. I'd be a drag on you" - Tom had a reputation as a skier; he was a good sportsman, and he'd had a lot of practice.

"Don't worry" Tom said, "You'll join the ski-school. You'll soon learn."

The idea took Ruth's fancy. They were in the Mersey Tunnel when she said "I'll need ski clothes - anoraks, ski-pants, all those things." At least, she knew about ski fashion, the magazines were full of it; she'd even modelled ski clothes, and she'd felt a fraud.

Tom said "Go to Harrod's and get yourself kitted out. Charge it to my account."

In February, the Rolls took them to Manchester Airport, and, after the flight, the mountain railway pulled them up, into the heavens, out of Interlaken and up to Wengen, with the Jungfrau towering above them, and the valley in the mist below. It was a new excitement for Ruth to hear the tinkle of the sleigh-bells and the crunch of snow under skis, and to see dazzling whiteness under ice-blue sky.

They got off the train at Wengen, and their places were filled by a hundred skiers on their way further up the mountain, jostling and laughing in the hurly-burly of comradeship; all helping one another with their skis. The racks of skis rattled, and the little train went off, climbing on its cogs, and "Come on" said Tom "Just time for a run before dark."

The Regina Hotel was the top hotel, proud of its respectability, so, as a formality, Tom was sharing a room with Tony, and Ruth was sharing with Louise. It was just for convention's sake: most of the time they just swopped beds, and Ruth was with Tom. As usual, Buff hadn't been able to get away "Next year, perhaps," he'd said; and Bunty was in a room on her own. Last year, Bunty had gone away with other friends, but, now, she had attached herself to Tom's party.

Ruth went down, to the nursery slopes, to the beginner's class. All the others went off, up the mountain, while Ruth was left floundering with a few fat puddings of girls, nearly all English; and she made up her mind right away, that she wasn't going to stay.

A girl, she knew, must have accomplishments to hold her own in society, and one of those accomplishments had to be ski-ing. Louise and Bunty, especially Bunty had a long start on her, but Ruth had caught up in other ways; and now it was ski-ing.

This was the price of ambition, she thought, as she flopped down yet again in her impatience. She felt like giving up, out of frustration, but she forced herself to smile and she tried again.

She waited her turn in the little group on the slope, and watched the instructor as he demonstrated how to dig; dig, your edges into the snow until your ankles hurt. Then, as Ruth went down the slope, slowly and at last under control, she thought - how many things, little things, big things, you had to learn to hold your own in Society. It was two years since she'd started, two years since she'd met Stan. She'd come a long way, and she wouldn't stop now.

The class ended, and the others went away, talking eagerly of hot chocolate and kirsch cake: Ruth had caught the aroma from the cafe near the station. She waited until the Instructor was alone and she said "I want to learn quickly. Please teach me" and, when he hesitated, she said "I'll pay." She deliberately opened her eyes wide to make them melty, and she said "I want to be able to ski - by tonight."

He just laughed, he couldn't help himself.

He replied in English, Alpine-guttural "Tonight? - It's not possible. In one hour, two hours perhaps, the sun will go down, and the piste will freeze. It will be dangerous - ice." She said "Two hours tonight, then. And tomorrow."

He shrugged his shoulders. "Tomorrow should be my day off. Tomorrow - It is possible! To ski a little, is possible."

For two hours, until the sun dropped behind the mountain, Ruth worked and sweated so that she had to remove her anorak; until the instructor pitied her, and asked her why she drove herself. He said "Is this a holiday for you, or a penance?"

She just kept going; she could see all the other people having fun, and here she was, labouring like a coolie, having to trudge back, up every little descent she'd made. "Tomorrow morning" she said "I'm going up in the train."

Afterwards, Ruth met the others at the cafe in the village, all crowded together and steaming and drinking hot chocolate. "My God, it's hard work" she said, and they all laughed.

The moonlight was on the snow when they dined. The wide windows looked out, over the valley and the mountains; the orchestra played Viennese waltzes, and the Swiss waiters were the best-trained waiters in the world. Ruth sipped her Hock from her tall-stemmed glass, and she thought of the little house in the married quarters and her mother darning socks; and she now knew what life could offer, and she'd never let go.

In the morning, the others went off while Ruth pretended to re-join the beginner's class; but, really, Ruth met her instructor, her private ski instructor. Ruth had to smile at herself: all the jokes about ladies and private ski instructors, and this boy was quite pretty really; but, all she wanted of him was his power at ski-ing, she wanted that as avidly as another woman might desire his power of sex. Besides, he had rough hands, workman's hands, hands that reminded her of those rankers' hands with their clumsy pressure at the Garrison Hops. She was reminded, too, of the cruel remark she once made to Buff, about Bunty and a ski instructor, and she felt a pang of shame.

They took the train up the mountain: it wasn't very full: there were just a few laggards and their skis, and a few non-skiers going up for the views and for the sun. The instructor, Max - he told her his name was Max - put their skis on the rack, and they rattled up the mountain, up to Scheidegg where they got off. "It is too steep, higher up" Max said. Even this slope, which had looked gentle from below, now looked terrifying to Ruth, as she looked down.

Max said "Too many people break a leg. Go slow" - and he showed her how to traverse across the slope, using her edges; in control. He made her hold her skis in a wide V-shape, a wide stem as a brake, but, even then, Ruth couldn't control the turn; she built up momentum alarmingly and "Sit down!" shouted Max.

She went down that first, long slope, stopping in the deep snow at the edge of the piste, and turning there laboriously for the next traverse. At the bottom, there was a wide area, open and almost flat, a mountain meadow in the summer; and there Max showed her how to run parallel and to turn parallel "Drop and swing!"

Ruth fell the first time, but, then, it got easier, and she began to enjoy the sensation of ski-ing. They came to where the snow-track was narrow and steep between pine-trees, and Max made her remove her skis and walk, clump, clump, in her heavy boots. Then, the slope became gentle again, and he said "It is safe here," and they let the skis take them on the long run, down to the village.

"Again" said Ruth "Again. I must go up the mountain again." So, they went a second time, and a third, and it was getting easier all the time. There was a drag-lift. "I must learn to use that" said Ruth, and Max sighed, she wasn't ready for it; but, he showed her: "Keep your skis parallel. Don't let them cross; don't let them run away."

Ruth tried, and, the first time, she came off, it was inevitable; she almost let her temper get the better of her. She knew she should laugh it off, with all the good-humoured people who were passing by, expertly, on the drag-lift, while she struggled in the snow-drift alongside; and she did force a laugh, and force herself to try again.

At the tope of the drag-lift there was a restaurant full of people, all packed together and trying to make themselves heard over the hubbub; and kids jostling to buy cokes, rich kids, born on the right side of the piste. Outside, on the terrace, over the yawning valley, people were stretched out on loungers, faces up to the sun, expensive women all sun-tanned and sun-bleached, all in the most expensive ski-wear; and skis piled everywhere, and ski sticks.

A couple of skiers came out of the trees, experts wearing the official anoraks, and they were guiding a huge roller down the piste, rolling the piste for the afternoon skiers.

They went down the slope, swinging the great roller in wide arcs, like some elephantine waltz; and the two skiers themselves seemed to be in waltz-time.

Max came out, onto the terrace, with coffee and plates of food, pasta, and Ruth found herself devouring the food like a she-wolf. Oh! the air and the exercise and the big experience of it all! Down, down, deep away; sun and snow, and all the beautiful, lucky, people.

Ruth finished her coffee and said "Come on." Max frowned, and said "It's very steep," and Ruth said "Teach me a jump-turn!"

She managed to scramble down to a side-piste, away from the main ski-run, and, reluctantly, Max showed her how to keep her skis close, always parallel, and to flex her knees; and to lift her heels and twist into the turn.

"Edges" he shouted "Your edges must bite!" - and the strain on her ankles was like Chinese torture.

The first time, Ruth hardly managed to get round, and the gradient pulled her down like a runaway express. She fell close to rocks, and Max said angrily "No. No. You try too much."

Then, Max threatened to leave, to stop the lesson, to go home; but Ruth turned her big eyes to melt him. She did it deliberately; she knew she'd cornered him and it wasn't fair; but, she couldn't afford to be fair.

Ruth kept trying, and, quite suddenly she could do it; it was just a shimmy, really, like a dance-step; swing, dip, control; edges, edges, edges. She stopped and looked up- up, up, at the high slope and the faraway restaurant perched up on the mountain; and Max stopped beside her, making a sudden, triumphal stop from speed, throwing up snow like an explosion. Ruth pulled off her goggles and laughed; she laughed, up at the sun, a laugh of triumph.

"My God" said Max "Not even two days. Just part of two days, and you can ski! Impossible!"

They skied down together, down into the darkening valley. Max went a bit ahead to show the way: around this hummock, watch that rock, an easy bit here, now straight down and hold your sticks under the armpit; and, now, the last drop into the village: Hey - Hop - Hey - Hopla - Turn - and Stop! Bravo!

"Thank you so much, Max" Ruth said, and paid him, and added a generous extra. He said "I'll see you around? and she said "Of course." -It was a dismissal.

The others weren't at the cafe, so Ruth shouldered her skis, and walked to the Hotel. The porter took her skis, and helped her off with her ski boots, oh, the relief! Like being freed from shackles. Then she went slowly, all stiff and aching up the stairs for a bath. She hesitated - which bathroom should she use?

The door to Tom's room was locked - funny! "Hey, Tom!" she called "It's only me. Open up!"

Then there were noises, funny noises, whisperings; and it was Bunty's voice, nobody could mistake the plummy stridency, whispered or not.

Bunty! Bunty with Tom, and she's trying to get off with him! Ruth started on the angry words, but she found she didn't care. What the hell! Bunty and herself - birds of a

113

feather, surely? So, she called out, through the closed door "Oh Tom. Bunty's with you. Don't let me spoil the fun - I'll see you at Dinner."

Louise was in the other room, and, when Ruth told her about it Louise asked "Do you care?"

Ruth said "It's curious. What I care about is not caring. In a way, it's a relief."

Louise said "I'm only sorry for Buff. Poor Buff. One buffalo can't compete with a thousand horsepower Rolls. And Tom's going into the horse racing business, did you know? Bunty will like that."

Ruth said "If I say she's welcome to him, it will seem like sour grapes."

Louise said "Bunty will marry Tom. She'll marry him if you don't."

"I could never marry Tom" said Ruth; and she meant it.

"Poor Tom" said Louise "Poor Buff."

Ruth had a deep, deep, bath, and through the bathroom window she could see the moon rising over the Jungfrau just like in the song. After Dinner they all went along to watch the ski jumping by torchlight; not a high jump by competition standards, but spectacular in the dark, with the skiers shooting out of the dark trees into the arc-lights. At the last jump, the jumpers carried flaming brands like gods from a saga; and, all the while, incongruous music filled the forest from a Tannoy; cuckoo-clock music "Wengen du Silberhorn."

At first Tom was all formal and embarrassed, but Ruth felt super and free, really free for the first time in ages;so, she kissed his cheek and said "I don't mind about Bunty. Really." He chuckled and squeezed her hand.

Next morning at breakfast Ruth announced "I'm skiing with you all today." Bunty looked cross, and Tom said "Ruth,

114

it's too dangerous." Tony said "Honestly, Ruth. It's a hell of a piste up there.. Kleine Scheidegg. Narrow and craggy down to Scheidegg; a tough run for an expert." Bunty said "Louise and I always wait for the boys at Scheidegg. The top bit's too tough for us."

``I'm going up all the way' said Ruth.

Tom became angry, really angry; he was hardly ever angry, and it made Ruth, perversely, almost sorry that she was going to lose him; to see him like that, all animated, so unlike himself. He shouted "Ruth, you're bloody well not coming. Two days! That's all the skiing you've done, I'm not going to let you kill yourself."

Louise said "Let her come up to Scheidegg. It must be miserable by herself down here. She can always take the train down again."

Ruth said "I skied down from Scheidegg yesterday.

Tom said "That's impossible. Don't try to fool me" and Ruth said, "I'm coming all the way with you, Tom. You can't stop me."

The little train, all crowded and jolly, moved upwards, out of Wengen, and the only people who weren't jolly were the little group in the corner of the carriage who were tense and silent - except for Ruth, who was looking at the majesty of the mountains. Most people got off at Scheidegg - Bunty and Louise got off, and Louise tried once more to persuade Ruth "Please, Ruth, be sensible", and she even tried to pull her out. Then, it was steep, and straight-upwards on the cogs, clunk-clunking, up, up; and there was ice in the air. Stop! "You can go back, Ruth" said Tom, but he knew it was hopeless. The two men got out, and got their skis from the rack; but, they didn't get Ruth's skis, or help her or anything which must have made quite a conflict in such gentlemanly minds. It was an opportunity for irony not to be missed "Thank you so much, gentlemen" she said.

Tony said "We can't just leave her. She might get killed."

Tom said "Be damned to her! It's her own bloody fault." He skied off, and Tony followed him reluctantly.

It was the first time Ruth had seen the men skiing: Tony was good, poised and balanced; it came easy to him. And Tom, well, she had to admit it, Tom was bloody good - strong and direct.

The men had already dropped down the first slope, and, in a minute, they were just two small figures far below. Then they stopped, and Ruth knew they were waiting for her.

She felt no fear, just a great exhilaration. She looked down; Oh, how she wanted to go straight down, like the winner of the Downhill Race, but she wasn't fool enough to try that. More than anything, she had to prove that she wasn't being irresponsible. She forced herself to remember everything that Max had taught her: control; slow control; edges. So, she took the first 100 metres slow and steady, with tight, slow turns; no jump turns. She stopped beside a rock, and they were still there, the two men, far below; and the piste ahead was wider and less steep.

Not over-confident, no, that was the trap; but sure, and concentrating; all muscles braced at her Will; ankles braced against the strain, and never mind the ache; edges cutting into the slope, and, lift the heels and swing, parallel, parallel for God's sake, and don't cross the skis; dip the knees, and, again - the whoosh of snow, and, again; swing and turn; like dancing.

Ruth skied up, beside the men. They said nothing; then Tony said "I suppose it was your little joke - pretending you couldn't ski. Pretending this was the first time."

Tom said "You even put on an act when I took you to the nursery slopes; to the beginners class. Pretending to fall about.

Ruth said "I wasn't acting, Tom. I had private lessons from Max. All day. The last two days."

"Max can work miracles said Tony.

"Oh, I'm coming skiing every year" said Ruth "It's wonderful."

The next stretch was nasty, not wonderful at all, just a mountain path between pine-trees, with packed snow, and patches of ice; and rocks like sharks' teeth sticking up through the snow. When she looked at it, Ruth couldn't help feeling afraid. She said "My God. I haven't learnt how to cope with that. Here's a chance to show your chivalry."

Tom said "Do it in stages. Don't lose control: there's no room to turn"

He showed her, going ahead for her to copy, and, whenever he gathered too much speed, he put his skis across the slope, to check the momentum. It was difficult, and Ruth had one fall. Then, they were running on free snow again, and, when Bunty and Louise looked up, they saw Ruth and the men coming down into Scheidegg together.

After the holiday, after those marvellous days of exhilaration, and they were back home, everything was just the same again: so much the same, and so different. Everybody started announcing engagements, and arranging weddings. The first wedding, at Easter time, was Tony and Louise; a lovely spring day, and the church so pretty with the blossom, and Louise in white lace; and a marquee for the reception of course. Everybody had a marquee, and champers; and all the men were in morning coats with only different flowers in their buttonholes to distinguish them.

Then, Tom went away for ages, on business, he said, and Ruth didn't hear from him. She telephoned his office, and she even went round to his house to collect some of her things.

It wasn't just his being away, but he'd always told her about it, and this time Ruth knew in her heart, she already knew that this was the push-off. It was only Pride, really, that made her care, and the thought that people would be pitying her - my God, she wouldn't stand for that!

At least, she didn't have time to brood. It was the Spring Fashion Collections, and she was getting more and more modelling work; in London mostly. She seemed to spend half her time on the London train.

Then, one day, she was in Liverpool, and she happened to meet Louise in Bold St., Ruth hadn't seen her for ages, what with Louise just being married, and all the rushing to London. At first Louise seemed lost for words, and then she just blurted it out "Oh, Ruth. Have you been asked to the wedding?" - and then it all came out, about Tom and Bunty and how they were to be married.

Ruth said "I'm not upset about it - really. Now I've got over the surprise. Drop a hint for me - I'd like an invitation to the wedding."

But, she never got one; Bunty said no, which, of course, was final.

Ruth found herself worrying about Buff; funny, she had a soft spot for Buff, and she knew he'd be hurt, the big booby. She went along to the Rugger Club, and there weren't many people about, as it was out of season. But, the bar was open, so she bought herself a drink. A few people started to drift in; not Buff, but Mike came in, the chap who'd made a pass at her on New Year's-Eve; it seemed such ages ago.

He said "Let's go for a drive." He drove across the Wirral peninsula, and parked in a quiet spot, overlooking the Dee estuary. He kissed her, and it was nice; he tried to take it further and she said "No" and he said "Why? Don't you like me?"

Ruth said "Of course I like you, Mike. And you're attractive. But I won't have casual sex."

Mike said "After Tom - what's the point of bothering?", and Ruth couldn't make him understand. So he drove her home, and wished her luck.

It wasn't that Ruth was missing Tom, but she did miss everything that went with Tom. Nothing exciting seemed to be happening: there may have been parties, but, if there were, Ruth wasn't asked, and, perhaps there weren't any, and everybody was staying at home. Then, after Tom's wedding - after it all became public - even the Modelling jobs became harder to find. Ruth had always known it was a risk to stay freelance, and to stay in the North of England; but, when she'd been with Tom, she'd been able to pick and choose, she got so many offers, and she'd turn down as many as she accepted. She telephoned the Fashion Houses and the Model Agencies "Sorry, Dear, we're very quiet.

We'll let you know...."

Merseyside, which, only a few months before, had seemed full of Life and Excitement was just a bore. Ruth was going mad with boredom, and pretty soon, it would be worse than that: she'd be broke, and she'd not sponge on Auntie. At the last resort, Ruth thought, she could go back to Library work, but, really, there was no going back to that, just as there was no going back to Army life.

She went across to Liverpool, to the Kardomah Cafe, and down into the basement where the old gang used to meet for coffee - they'd all come out of the offices for coffee, and pick up the girls for parties. The gang would always take over the big table in the middle, and the whole life of the place used to revolve around that table. But now, the table was occupied by strangers.

Ruth paused at the bottom of the stairs, and she saw Buff sitting alone at a small table; stirring his coffee, and looking down at his cup as he stirred.

She said "Hello, Buff", and he was glad to see her. He welcomed her with something like his old grin, so she sat down and he ordered her a coffee.

Buff said "We're like two abandoned ships" and Ruth said "Were you asked to the wedding?"

Buff said "Not me. I heard it was splendid. - Well, you'll have seen it in the papers." Ruth said "I would have loved to go" Buff laughed "All that champers and caviar. They could have spared a bit for us."

Ruth said "You may not believe me, Buff, but I don't envy Bunty. It's hard for you though. I'm sorry, Buff."

Buff said "I keep telling myself I'm better off without her - of course I am. But I can't help it. I'm miserable."

Ruth said "She was two-timing you with Tom - even when we were away skiing." Buff said "The trouble is, she's so attractive. A splendid Consort for a Prince." Oh, yes" said Ruth "Until a King comes along!"

Buff said "How's life treating you, Ruth?"

"I'm bored, Buff. Bored, and broke."

Buff said "You need a change. We both need a change, come to that. But I can't get away. Look - I've got a friend. He's a manager with Butlin's. He could get you a job as a Redcoat."

"A Redcoat?" - the idea seemed so bizarre.

Buff said "Quite a few well-known people do a summer or two as a Redcoat - Athletes, Footballers; and Stage People."

"Well!" said Ruth "I'll have to think about it.

"Yes said Buff "Think about it." Ruth thought about it,

120

and was sent to Skegness, the oldest Butlin's Camp. It wasn't the place she'd have chosen, but it was already mid-season, and the only vacancy.

Forget the glamour: working as a Redcoat was bloody hard work. It was so like the Army, that Ruth felt at home from the start: from the first Reveille that came over the Tannoy "Good Morning Campers" to that sugary Dream-Tune "Goodnight Campers" at Midnight. The Red Coat of her Uniform reminded Ruth of the Red and Black jersey of the Army Physical Training Corps, and the Skegness Holiday Camp had been a Military Camp during the War. It was as though some dotty Commanding Officer had ordered an Army Camp to be decorated in pastel colours, and everybody's military duty was to enjoy themselves.

Redcoats lived in Chalets like Campers, and Ruth found herself sharing a Chalet with Beryl, who was peroxide blonded, and so indifferent to the attentions of all the men that she let them all screw her, she didn't care, while she carried on polishing her nails, or something - "What the hell", she said, she'd not had an orgasm for years, and why disappoint the boys when it was so little trouble to her? Beryl was always so glammed-up with skin-cream you couldn't tell what was underneath, what with peroxide and false eyelashes and lipstick: she liked to be admired. Whenever Ruth went back to the Chalet, she never knew who'd be on the lower bunk with Beryl: one of the Redcoat men, or one of the Entertainers, the theatrical crowd.

One night Ruth got back late, very late, after Lights Out, and the Camp guard had made his patrol with his Alsatian. After she'd had her shower, and they'd turned off the Chalet light, Beryl talked. She said "It was my uncle. He just raped me one day, when I was twelve. Since then, I've never thought it was worth fussing about"

"Because you lost your virginity?" said Ruth.

121

"Oh no. Not really. I mean Love. It's not worth fussing about Love. It's a sham." Ruth felt a deep pity for this girl. She said "I'm not a virgin, Beryl. But I can love,"

Beryl said "A lot of the Redcoat girls - the glamourous ones. They've been girl friends to Billy - Billy Butlin. Or of one of the other Directors."

"Yes" said Ruth" I can understand that. I'm not surprised, really."

Beryl said "Billy always treats his girls well. Some of them really fall for him, you know."

Ruth said "Money?"

"I don't know about Money. A car, maybe. But, always a job, if they want one. And, he goes out of his way to keep in touch. He'll be visiting the Camp this Summer. You'll see."

The popular idea of a Redcoat's life was Seaside and Sin, but, the reality needed energy and stamina thought Ruth, that's for sure. You weren't going to get away with any Sin, or any other mucking about during duty hours: you were paid to entertain, and that's what Billy Butlin expected you to do - dancing with the old chaps, and getting the Glamorous Grannies out onto the floor; and, if an attractive young man asked you to dance, it was one dance only. If it was a Camp employee that asked you, even if it was his time off duty, you had to put him off after one dance.

There were a couple of fellows from University, doing holiday jobs, just boys really - not Redcoats. They were clerks in the Camp office, cashing-up and counting the takings. They were called Jimmy and Peter: Jimmy was one of the boys in the queue around Beryl, and Peter was the self-contained one: when he was off-duty, he used to laze around one of the Camp pools, reading a book; he'd swim a bit.

One night, it was their late night - the clerks took it in turns to go around the bars at night, and collect the takings.

After they'd been to all the bars, the Pig and Whistle and all the others, all those bars, all packed out and noisy and awash with beer; and everybody singing, and the piano banging-out "Roll out the Barrel" and all the other songs; and, after Jimmy and Peter had had their free pint here and another one there - every barmaid wanting to pull them a free pint so as they wouldn't notice the pound notes tucked into the cleavage and never rung-up on the till; after all that, when Jimmy and Peter were singing too; then, Jimmy took Peter into the big dance hall where they were doing the Olde Tyme, the fifth time around of the Palais Glide, and Ruth said "Hello, Peter. Can you do the Palais? Come on!"

Then it was nearly midnight and time for Auld Lang Syne, and, at last, Ruth's time was her own for the first time since breakfast - after all the kids' games on the lawns, and the swimming sessions, and calling the numbers at "Housey-Housey"; and the Variety Show where the Redcoat girls made up the high-kicking chorus-line.

The last Campers were calling to Ruth "Goodnight, Dear - see you in the morning", and Peter said "Can I walk you back to your Chalet?"

It was a warm night, and, across the sand-dunes, the moonlight was on the sea. Peter said "Let's paddle"; Ruth took off her shoes and let the seawater ease the soreness from her feet - three hours of the Valeta and the Palais Glide were hard on the feet. They stood side by side in the shallows, and held hands, and Peter said "May I kiss you?" It was touching, and old-fashioned.

They walked back carrying their shoes, and stopped outside Ruth's Chalet door. Peter said "Good Night, Ruth", and they touched lips again, and he went. Inside, Beryl was on the lower bunk, alone thank God; she said "So, you've been baby-snatching" - it wasn't really a criticism, but, it was true, and Ruth thought, why did she have such a soft spot for innocence?

It was always a big occasion at the Camp when Top Management came from London. Often it was Billy Butlin himself: he liked to visit all his Camps. He would arrive like Royalty in his Rolls, and the Campers would make an occasion of it, lining the route; he'd present the prizes, or there might be some big event going on at the Camp, Bathing Beauties or Beauty Queens: regional finals. Billy would be a judge, and the lucky winner might get her big chance, especially if she was susceptible to Billy's charms. The Redcoat girls just loved it when Billy paid a visit, but, this year he sent Arthur Chandler instead, who everybody said was the financial brains behind the Butlin Empire.

Arthur came in a Rolls like Billy's but he wasn't a showman like Billy who had come over as a young man from Canada, and had worked on fairgrounds and coconut-shies. Arthur wasn't a showman, but he was nearly as rich as Billy. He didn't swank about it, and he didn't throw his money around, and give it to charity like Billy. True, Billy had a house like a Palace in Jersey - but Arthur had a house in London full of priceless paintings and furniture.

They held a Gala Lunch for Arthur, and, when Ruth was presented to him he said "You're new, aren't you? I like to meet the new girls."

That afternoon, it was a game of "Housey" and Ruth was calling the numbers, and Beryl came in with a message "His nibs has invited you for a drink. This evening."

Ruth said "I can't; I'm on duty at the Olde Tyme Ballroom."

"He's thought of that" said Beryl.

There was a cocktail lounge which the Camp Management used, but Arthur was there alone; there wasn't even a barman.

"Let me get you a drink" he said and Ruth said "Fino,

please."

"I see" he said "Dry Sherry before Dinner."

Ruth said "We don't have Dinner. Just High Tea - with the Campers."

"I know." he said "Would you care to Dine with me?"

Ruth smiled "If you'll give me time to change. I can hardly go out in a Red blazer."

Arthur poured two Finos. He's rather an old-fashioned gentleman, thought Ruth - as though Butlin had gone out of his way to find someone like that. He said "I know it's a stale gambit. But I've seen you somewhere. In Vogue. And in Tatler - with Tom Vernon, wasn't it?"

Ruth said "And now I'm a Butlin's Redcoat. And I'm enjoying it."

Arthur said "The jolly Camping life can become tedious. If it goes on too long." Ruth said "I'm no stranger to a simple life."

He said "But you've developed expensive tastes. Don't you miss the champagne and caviar?"

Yes, she did miss it all; not so much the luxury, but the glamour and excitement. But she wasn't going to admit that. Arthur's turnout, she'd noticed, was impeccable: lightweight suit, and muted tie; gold cuff-links; gold watch; hair line receding, and a Mediterranean suntan he'd not picked up at a Butlin's camp.

He said "I rarely stay on Camp these days. We can dine at my hotel."

Ruth went back to the Chalet and took her dress out of her suitcase - it was a bit crumpled, but it would do: Heavens, she'd worn nothing but uniform for a month. She took her time over her makeup and her hair - she would keep him waiting, not too long, but enough. Beryl came in and said "I see you're going Man-hunting" and Ruth said "Big-Game."

He was waiting in the Rolls, driving himself. It was getting dark, but there were still Campers about and some kids gathered around the Rolls. He didn't get out for Ruth, he just leant across and opened the door from the inside; and as they passed the Camp gate, the security guard saluted. How like a Guardroom, Ruth thought, almost expecting a "Present Arms!" They drove along the front at Skegness, to the Hotel, and they were shown to a table in the Dining Room.

Arthur ordered the meal without fuss, and a good wine to go with it, nothing flashy, not a champagne or anything.

Arthur said "Why did you come to Butlin's, Ruth?"

Ruth said "I'm a Model. Business was bad. A Redcoat's job is seasonal; You know that. I'll be free in the Autumn."

"What then?"

"Back to modelling, I hope."

Arthur said "We do keep a few Staff over the winter. At the Camps it's all seasonal - but we keep a few in London." He added "We're planning for the future: Abroad. - The Continent. The Caribbean, even."

Ruth said "You mean, like the Club Mediterranee? And isn't Pontin opening in Majorca?"

Arthur said "Butlin's has got to keep up: Holidays abroad for the masses."

The waiter brought the main course; Duck, nicely served, and not too greasy. After he'd gone, Arthur said.

"How about it, Ruth? How about the winter at our London office?"

Ruth paused to consider. They both knew it was a

126

proposition. She made up her mind, and smiled at him "It sounds exciting. But I've nowhere to stay in London."

It was Arthur's turn to consider. The next move in the game. "Why not stay with me? There's plenty of room at my place."

"And, your wife?"

"My wife? She's in New York most of the time. We don't see much of each other nowadays. "

Ruth did justice to the meal - she'd always had an appetite, and she was enjoying herself. She knew she was selling herself, but for what? for Money? - For the consequences of Money, at any rate: Luxury, Excitement, and Privilege; all those things. You ought to be ashamed of yourself, she thought, but, she smiled, not secretly, but openly - she knew she ought to be ashamed, but she didn't feel like that at all.

"What's amusing you? Tell me" said Arthur; but Ruth didn't answer him directly. It was time for her to take the initiative: that was one thing she'd learnt from Tom, a girl like her should never lose the initiative. She looked at Arthur boldly, and said "You'll have to get me back to camp by Nine tomorrow morning. I've a children's swim to arrange."

She knew she'd surprised him, but he was too cool a businessman to show it. He said "I could arrange for you to move to London right away."

"No" she said "I want to finish the season here. Then I'll join you in London."

Arthur called the waiter and told him to serve coffee in the Suite upstairs. They went up in the lift together, and, if the Hall Porter was surprised he didn't show it - he'll get a good tip, thought Ruth.

It was a proper suite, with twin beds and a bathroom,

and a lobby with chairs.

The waiter came in with the coffee, and, when he went, Arthur locked the outer door of the suite. He said "You must realise how I admire you Ruth. How attractive I find you."

Ruth said "You've got authority, Arthur; and you've got style. And - there's nothing wrong with being rich. Girls find it attractive."

That was it, thought Ruth: Style and Authority; confidence and breeding. She was a sucker for breeding, she knew that: the Officer Class. Definitely. She looked at his hands, the ultimate test: they were well-manicured and smooth. No, she would not mind those hands on her, not at all. More than anything, she hated rough hands, Rankers hands. Even Stan had known that - if a man was ambitious, he had to get his hands right.

"You have nice hands, Arthur" Ruth said.

"And so have you, my dear. The loveliest hands in the world."

He started to make love, in a businesslike way. He said "I expect you'll want to take your frock off. Mustn't get it crushed."

They reclined together, half on and half off the bed, Ruth with her frock off, and Arthur still fully dressed. He kissed her, and she put her hand onto him, not knowing what to expect, she'd had no experience with an older man. But he was erect and ready, and he kissed her hard when he felt her hand on him. His cheek felt quite leathery against hers, so sun-tanned it reminded her of fine leather, and she could smell eau-de-Cologne on his skin.

Ruth started to open his fly-buttons, and he said nothing; he just looked down and watched her fingers and the red fingernails undoing each button. Then, she felt for the opening, and pulled out his cock and held it - it was a bit damp, and its little eye was like a tiny Cyclops, open and unblinking.

She said: "Hadn't we better both undress properly?"

Ruth didn't take long, and then she lay back naked, her legs hanging over the edge of the bed, and spread-out wide, quite brazenly; deliberately brazen and provocative, while she caressed herself between her legs. Arthur looked down at her, and he couldn't disguise his desire, as, for the first time, he lost his sang-froid, and began to fumble, and to snatch at his collar and his shirt-buttons; and the clothes, which he had been carefully folding, were all in a heap on the floor.

He stood naked, and he'd shed some of his air of authority with his clothes; but he was in fair shape for a man of his years - his belly sagged a little, only a little, and he was making a brave effort to hold it in. He was not as rampant as he would have liked: his cock began to droop - he moved towards Ruth, and there was a hint of pleading in his voice. He forced his voice to sound detached. He said "Nowadays, I need more stimulation."

Ruth looked up at him, and knew that she could exert power over him and that it would give her a wicked satisfaction to exert that power. She touched his cock, and it hardened again at her touch. He said "Kiss it!"

"Another time, if you're good," said Ruth. Instead, she pinched the tip between her fingers, and moved them quickly until he was hard, really hard - hard as she wanted him. She said "Aren't you forgetting something?"

He fetched a rubber from his suitcase, and Ruth said "Shall I put it on for you?", and she did it the way she liked, safe and taut, right down to the root. "I'm ready" she said, and he lowered himself into her. She closed her eyes and found herself wishing it was Guy's cock that was inside her, as she rubbed herself sideways, this way and that. Arthur started to move, but Ruth said "Wait!" and she contracted her

129

diaphragm, to make herself tight around him, until he gasped and said "Ruth. You're wonderful. Wonderful and beautiful."

She said "Now, I'm ready Sir. You can move now."

Arthur moved well - he was experienced, of course, she could tell that; not too eager; building up until she was moving with him, and the Jerk, jerk, was giving her that lovely feeling, all tense and jelly-like, all at once. Then, he made his last thrust, and the spasms came, and the lovely twitch, twitch in her as the cock squirted.

Ruth ran a bath, and soaked. Then, they went to bed, separate in the twin beds, and, during the night a moonbeam woke her through a break in the curtains. Ruth lay awake for a time, then she had a mischievous idea to awake Arthur. She found that she felt aroused, and, if he was embarrassed by that, well, serve him right. The thought surprised her, and she almost hoped he'd fail; it would give her a sense of power over him.

At first, she didn't get into bed with Arthur - that would have been too cosy; she just knelt beside the bed. She was naked, but she wasn't cold, the night was so warm: she knelt there and felt for his cock where it lay all floppy, and, as he slept, she tickled the cock so lightly that he didn't wake. He stirred, and turned a little, and she kept on until he began to harden; then, when he was strong and hard, she leant forward and kissed him on the mouth until he half-woke, and tensed-up.

She said "Relax. You're tired."

He said "Aren't you tired?" and she said "No. I'm full of life." Then, she lay on top of him, and gripped his cock tight, between her legs and started nibbling his nipples, and saying the sexiest things she could think of to provoke him, things she could say in the dark.

She turned on the bedside light and fetched a rubber

from where she'd seen him get them from the suitcase; she slipped it over him and tight on him; and then, she straddled him so that her weight was hard down and he was inside, high and handsome.

Arthur was all tense, excited but tense; he had an uncertain, excited, kind of expression. Ruth shouted, not so loud as to wake anybody, a kind of a shout under her breath "Tally ho!" or "Go!" or something; and she started rising in the saddle, up and down and "Yes. Yes!" he cried and then "No. No. I can't. I'm sorry," and he lay back, defeated.

"You asked too much. I'm sorry." He said.

"Never mind" said Ruth; and she found that her feelings were mixed-up - frustration, certainly: that was the obvious feeling; but, in a way, a sort of triumph, an assertion of power.

Ruth said again "Don't worry," and she lay down beside him, and massaged him, squeezing him quite hard to make him rise again.

After a while, he did grow hard, and she straddled him, and rode him. He protested "No. I can't." And "Yes" she said "You will."

So, it was coming up to the Finishing Post, neck and neck and she slapped his flank to bring him in the winner; and "Ah" he said "At last...."

"There you are" said Ruth, "We've won."

Next morning, he took her into Camp in the Rolls." I'll see you in September", Ruth said, and he replied "The house will be ready."

In September, he sent the Rolls to collect her. He'd arranged everything; her transfer to the London office, everything.

The house was in Sloane Square: outside it was just

131

like all the other houses, but luxurious inside; the house of an art-connoisseur. While Tom's house had only escaped vulgarity because it was shockingly opulent, Arthur's treasures emphasised his good-taste.

Arthur said "I expect you would like to have your own room; your own private place" - He was a considerate man and, after all, he'd made his money by giving people what they wanted.

Ruth's room was at the back overlooking the garden. She usually spent the nights in Arthur's room, but, if Arthur was away, visiting one of the Camps, it was nice to have her own room. The Camps always needed attention out of season, and, sometimes, Ruth went along with Arthur. They would stay at some Grand Hotel on some deserted Esplanade, and it should have been fun but it wasn't.

Ruth had an Account at Harrods, or, rather, Arthur had an Account at Harrods in Ruth's name; and she had another Account at Harvey Nicholls. Some of the assistants recognised her from when she used to go with Tom, or from when she did Modelling. Arthur did a lot of business - entertaining. Nobody seemed bothered about her relationship with Arthur; many of the visitors were in a similar position, and, as for Arthur's wife, she might as well not have existed. There were so many business acquaintances, but no real friends; and so much luxury and pleasure.

At Christmas-time, Ruth went home again. She went First Class from Paddington, and, again, there were new faces in the Camp, and herself an outsider, looking in at the officers' Mess. Prunella was home, but, this time, their paths didn't cross; but Ruth did meet her once by accident in London. It was springtime, near Hyde Park corner - Prunella was window-shopping in Knightsbridge, wearing a sort of duffle-jacket, rather under-dressed for London; and Ruth was in fur, the silver-fox jacket, not the Red Fox coat. It was a bright day, but nippy for springtime, definitely Fur weather for Ruth, although, across in Hyde-Park, the buds were beginning to peep.

"Prunella" said Ruth "Do come and have lunch! ", and when Prunella hesitated, Ruth said "I've an Account at Harrods. It's a chance for me to use it."

They walked to Harrods, and Ruth ordered a nice little lunch, Oysters and Chablis; she said "Well. How's Guy?" and Prunella said "Oh. Guy's got a girl." - Ruth had to dig her nails to stop Pru noticing, but Pru did notice her expression. She'd been thoughtless, but, after all, it was all over between Ruth and Guy ages ago, and Ruth was now so obviously in her own glittering world.

Ruth flattened the emotion out of her voice. She said "Good for Guy. What's the girl like?"

"Oh, the usual sort of girl that hangs around Oxford. A society girl. Not an undergraduate."

"Society?"

"Well. Her father would like to think so. He's got an Industrial Knighthood." Ruth's time in London went by, and luxury became a routine, until, one summer day Ruth said "I must have a change Arthur. Why don't we take a holiday?"

"What? Right in the Season? The summer season? We're in the Holiday Camp business, remember?"

But she persuaded him. She said "Your most effective work is in the winter - planning the profits for next Season. Leave High Seasons to the Accountants."

He had to laugh at that; she was right and he had to admire her. So, he booked a Suite at the Carlton Hotel, at Cannes.

4. GUY AGAIN

After Ruth left Oswestry, all the excitement and all the brave glamour of the guns had become for Guy just a dreary posting in peacetime U.K.

He couldn't put Ruth out of his mind, and, of course, he was always meeting the `Q' around Camp.

"Morning Q.! How's Ruth?" he asked. "She's doing well, Sir." Replied the `Q'. "No harm in my writing to her?" asked Guy.

But Ruth didn't reply to his letter.

The other fellows in the Mess teased him a bit "Missing the `Q' 's daughter Guy?" - they couldn't guess how much he did miss her.

Pru came home from Oxford for the Vacation. He could talk to Pru. She said "Look, Guy. I've got a dozen girls lined-up for you at Oxford. You'll forget Ruth."

But, Guy didn't forget her. He thought about her when he went past the Library, and all the memories came back to him: Lady Chatterley; all those memories. He thought of her as he walked around the Regimental Lines, still bouncing his stick as was his habit. He remembered how he used to meet her in unexpected places, and he'd throw up a salute for her, and she'd smile the open smile he loved so much.

But, most of all, he thought about her in bed, in the lonely night when he almost cried for Ruth, and his cock swelled at the thought of her, and he wanted her beside him, pressed against him, and her head against his shoulder.

Often, at weekends, he had an impulse to drive up to Merseyside to find her; to drag her away; a mad impulse. It wasn't a distance; barely fifty miles.

And then, he was demobbed. Just that. Out of the army, two years gone, and hardly anyone to notice it. "Goodbye Guy" said Rufus, and shook his hand "You'll be seeing Pru in Oxford, I expect."

"It was Pru that got Guy into Oxford Society. There were always invitations from Pru "At Home. Bring a Bottle." - and there were usually more girls at the party than men.

I say, Guy" said Pru, on one occasion "Have you seen this month's Vogue?" And, there was Ruth, all glamourised and made-up, full-page, full colour: modelling and posing; not named, of course, but Ruth was unique. The old pulse beat faster, and a girl said "Good Lord. Do you know her? Isn't she glam?"

Another time, Pru opened Tatler and "Look at this" she said. It was a big party, up at Merseyside, some girl's Coming Out Party, and there she was "Miss Ruth Evans and Mr. Tom Vernon" - in that formal phraseology affected by Tatler Magazine.

Guy tried to smile, but he felt cold steel. He said "You'll make me jealous, Pru."

There was a girl at the Party, a sweet girl. Her name was Sarah, and Guy kissed her, and said could he take her home in his M.G. He kissed her goodnight outside her College, but, when he tried to stroke her leg, she slapped his hand, and said "Stop it!"

The car was too cramped for Romance, and the gear-stick got in the way. "I've got to go" Sarah said "They lock the College doors" - Guy remembered that they did the same at his College, and it was murder climbing into College: you went over the wall, and over the roof of the lavatories, trying hard to keep your balls away from the barbed-wire.

He said "I'll see you again" and she said "O.K.", so he took her to the Cinema that week, and at least twice a week for the whole term. Everyone went to the Cinema at Oxford, in the afternoons as well as the evenings. Guy took Sarah to the Cinema, and held hands; and, after a week or two she let him tickle her fanny, and she squeezed his prick; and, if he tried to push his finger into her she went all prim and said "No. Not that, Guy. No." - She wanted to keep her virginity for the "Right Man", and Guy couldn't blame her; her virginity was a valuable commodity.

Guy worked quite hard, studying Law, and it was interesting enough. He had to pass his Exams., Law Moderations, so he worked in the Library, or attended a Lecture. In the afternoons he took some exercise, he always felt better for exercise, and he'd got used to so much exercise in the Army. So, he played Rugger for the College team, and, lots of squash. In the evenings, when he wasn't at the Cinema with a girl; when the mist came up from the Isis and shrouded the Colleges, Guy joined all the other Rugger men deep in the womb of the College, in the Cellar, where there was beer and darts and singing rude choruses. When the Hour came for Formal Dinner he'd pull on a gown, and crowd into Hall, onto an old oak bench for a feast served on an old oak board; with silver sconce and roaring, warm, male company.

Yes; When Guy paused to think - Ruth was right. She had no place here. But she kept her place in his heart.

When they had the College Rugger Dinner half of them were drunk, and Guy was drunk. There were bicycles in the street, and they lifted them over the wall into another College; that was uproarious, and so much fun, all the bicycles jangling and crashing. Then, there wasn't much left to do, and it wasn't that late, so Guy thought of Sarah, why not? He managed to tip himself into the M.G. and find his keys and somehow, to drive to her College before they shut the gates. Sarah let him into her room, and, God, no, he wasn't going to be sick? He managed to avoid that, but he slumped over the bed, and Sarah got angry; and that was the end of that.

136

Another time, Pru was living out of College, in a flat in North Oxford near the Parks, and Guy got a card for Tea. He ought to feel grateful to Pru, and he was grateful; she was like a sister to him, and he needed a sister. She had so much to do, she was in her last weeks, working for Finals, and she still took the time to bother with Guy.

Guy knew most of Pru's friends already, all getting keyed-up for Finals, and toasting muffins at the gas fire and glancing nervously at the clock,as if they felt guilty about a minute snatched from work.

Pru said "Thank God you've come, Guy. These people are getting neurotic about Finals."

There was a different girl, sitting apart, on the window-seat, and Pru said "Lucy- meet Guy. Lucy's Dad is a friend of Rufus."

Guy took a cup, and a muffin on a plate, and parked himself beside Lucy. He said "What College?" and she said "The Crammer, actually." The "actually" was defensive. She added "If I do well at the Crammer, I'll try for Pru's College."

She was a pretty girl, quite petite and healthy-looking. Guy said "So you know Rufus? He was my C.O. during National Service."

Lucy's reply was so predictable; Guy had to laugh, he'd heard it so often. Pru had said it, all the girls said it, or, if they didn't say it they thought it. "Thank God for National Service. Keeps men out of the way when they're at that awful stage, after school."

She was self-assured - she must have been at one of those schools where they picked-up self-assurance - Cheltenham, Roedean, one of those.

Pru came over with some scones. She said "Has Lucy told you? Her Dad's Chairman of Merchant's - the Far East Trading Company."

"Sir Philip Merchant?" said Guy "So, you're Lucy Merchant."

The tea-party was breaking-up, and even Pru was talking about a work-crisis. Guy said "Lucy. I'll drive you home" and she said "My car's outside." He'd noticed the new X.K.120 parked at the kerb, and he said "Not the Jag - I couldn't keep up, in my old M.G."

He waited for her on the doorstep, and he said "How about the Cinema tomorrow?" she said "What's on?" and he said "Does it matter?"

Some of the fellows from College were making up a party for the Eights' Week Ball at Pembroke College, and Guy asked Lucy. It was cosy to have a girl friend you could rely on, and Lucy always looked so good, her Daddy made sure of that.

That afternoon they went down to the river to watch the races from the College Barge: all the Colleges had Barges, top-heavy and decorated, and flying the College flag for the races. They cheered the College crew, which made a Bump, and Lucy met Guy's friends; you could see they all admired her: in her summer frock, she looked lovely.

By the time it was evening, and they were at the Ball, Guy was already half in love with Lucy; what with the marquee, and the music, and everyone happy and joining in the fun. Guy was wearing his new white Dinner Jacket, and Lucy said "Oh, Guy. You remind me of Dad. Dad always wears a White Tuxedo in the East."

After the Ball, in Lucy's Jaguar - Lucy wanted Guy to drive because of her ball frock - after the Ball when they parked up a side-road, Lucy was different, more eager when he kissed her; she'd rather rationed her kisses up to now. Now, when he stroked her leg, she didn't push his hand away, she just said "Oh, Guy," and he could see her expression was tender, in the moonlight.

Guy didn't see Lucy during the Long Vacation. She was always travelling with her parents, they seemed to have an apartment in half the cities around the world; but she sent him cards from Hong Kong, Malaya, and all over.

Lucy was back in the autumn, for the Michaelmas term. She sat the Exams for University Entrance, but even Sir Philip's millions weren't enough to get Lucy into Oxford. But, Lucy stayed: like so many others, she enrolled for Miss Spruce's Secretarial Course.

They did all the Oxford things together. They went to the Varsity Match together, the Rugger Match at Twickenham and, that night, they went to the Varsity Match Ball at the Royal Festival Hall. All the College Rugger men were there, they all knew Lucy. Guy and Lucy danced every dance and afterwards they held hands in the moonlight, under the cold December moon beside the Thames. Lucy said "I love you, Guy."

Guy wondered what to say; so he said "I love you too," rather lamely: he said it because it was expected. That's why he said it, but, anyway, he did love her, he supposed.

He said "I expect we'll marry" and Lucy put her head on Guy's shoulder. She said "You've a long time to go your Finals. We'll wait."

Later, she said "Daddy's giving a Party on Boxing Day. Will you come?"

It was funny. He'd known Lucy for months now, and he'd never met her parents; they always seemed to be abroad. They had a house in London, in a Square off Kensington High Street, not an ostentatious house, but opulent inside. Guy drove up from his parents' place, from Woking, and parked the M.G. like a country cousin amongst the Bentleys and Lagondas. The front door was opened by a butler, and there were some people standing around drinking; fewer than Guy had expected. Lucy came downstairs all excited and sparkling

- she wanted to show him off, but there wasn't anybody their own age: just a group of middle-aged millionaires. Guy noticed the expressions on their faces: this one detached, that one full of bonhomie, but all of them wary, somehow; sizing one another up, like gunslingers.

And the women: all of them so richly dressed, and wearing their jewellery so carelessly; no longer concerned about having the biggest diamonds; far more worried, now, about the imprint of Time.

"Daddy, here's Guy" said Lucy; and Guy faced a man who had been handsome, a lean man with a Tropical suntan that showed up the lines on his face.

The butler announced Dinner, and the dining room didn't seem quite right for England - more like the Officers' Mess of some Regiment of the Raj, full of Indian silver, and jade, and portraits in oils.

It was a banquet, carefully chosen - a banquet for the wealthy; a statement of good taste both literally and metaphorically.

The menu was simple and perfect: perfectly simple: Sole Bonne Femme then Tournedos then Charlotte Russe. The wines were equally simple: Clicquot, then Lafite and then Y-Quem.

Afterwards; after the other guests had left - they didn't stay late - Sir Philip had another whisky. It was the only drink he liked: the wine at dinner was for show, and a whisky and soda, a chota peg, marked him out as an Empire man. Sir Philip invited Guy into his study and he said "What will you do Guy? When you come down from Oxford?"

Guy was expecting the question. He said "Hardly anybody seems to know what he's going to do. I could go into the Law of course."

Sir Philip said "Why not join us?" and Guy said "I

140

know it's a terrific business - but I've only a hazy idea how it works."

Sir Philip said "Monopoly, if we can get it: Monopoly dealership. Export and Import. A particular make of car, for instance: Mercedes say."

Guy said "That's what Jardines' do in Hong Kong don't they?"

"That's the sort of thing" said Sir Philip. "It's not just the Profit - It's the Power. Think about it, Guy" and he added "Lucy is keen on it, you know."

Sometime during the next Term, Guy's relationship with Lucy became a full and sexual one.

It was in the afternoon, one of those gloomy winter afternoons at Oxford with not much to do except work or go to the Cinema. They didn't feel like the Cinema, and Lucy was in Guy's rooms, lying on Guy's bed, and they were wondering whether to make tea. They had been necking as usual, petting and so on, which was becoming rather stale, and Guy's wallet dropped out of his pocket and Lucy began fiddling with it. She was always fiddling with things, she was like that; and a contraceptive packet dropped out of the wallet onto the floor. Lucy picked it up, and read out "Durex! " and Guy didn't know what to say.

Lucy said "Well!" but she didn't sound shocked, she was just pretending to be shocked, and Guy said "I must have had it for ages. Before I met you."

Lucy said "Well. Hadn't we better use it? " just like that.

Guy laughed; and it was simple and deliberate, like a biology lesson. Lucy's matter- of-fact remark had excited Guy; that flat phrase "Hadn't we better use it?" was more of an aphrodisiac than musk.

Guy locked the door: "Sporting his Oak,' was the Oxford expression. "We'd better undress" he said.

Lucy said "I'm nervous, Guy. But I want you." He could see she meant it. She was naked and spread rather untidily across the bed; and looking up at him shyly. He'd often seen her part-naked, and felt parts of her, when they'd been petting - their petting had been prolonged and passionate. But, she'd never been completely naked for him. She was lovely, a lovely girl, small and slender, with trusting eyes.

Guy said "You look lovely, Lucy."

There was no need for foreplay, there had been enough before. Before, when they were petting, she'd been as active as he, squeezing his cock, and opening her mouth to his tongue; but now, she just lay waiting for him; passive and waiting.

He said "Look. The rubber's easy" and he pulled it on. He said "Open wide," and she spread her legs; he felt her with his hand, and she was wet and open, and the hymen relaxed and easy to stretch. He said "I'll not hurt you" and he pushed into her, gentle and slow.

She said "Oh, Darling - It's Heaven!" and he just lay there, for a minute or more, hard and still.

She lay, saying nothing, with her cheek against his cheek and her arms around him. He felt a dampness on his face, and he said "Oh - you're crying" and she said "It's because I'm happy Guy. I love you; and her love was a force to hold him to her, stronger than chains.

It was time to move, to caress her with that part of him that now belonged more to her than to himself. He moved; in and out he moved, to bring her ecstacy. When he felt it, felt the build-up of power at his root, he whispered "Lucy. Lucy now!" and at that whisper, before it happened, ages, seconds, before it happened, she began to tremble and to moan in orgasm; and, when he made his last thrust - hard this time, harsh not gentle, and the spasms jerked inside her, she cried out, and the ecstacy for Lucy was near unbearable.

She said "If you're always like this, Guy, I'm the luckiest girl alive."

Guy said nothing: he was glad he'd made her happy, that he'd aroused her for ever. And it had been wonderful for him too; after all this time, wonderful. But, as he lay beside her, calm and satisfied, he thought of this love that bound him, now, stronger than chains; a memory of Ruth came to him, and he was troubled.

Guy said "We should be married Lucy," but Lucy had an organising mind. She said "We'd decided. After your Finals. Let's not change."

That brought it home to him, how close it was to June, and Final Exams.

Lucy said "First you'll join the Company. Then we'll marry. Later we'll be sent abroad. After a year or two we'll go abroad."

She had it all worked out; she'd arranged it all with her Dad, of course, mapping out their future - Sir Philip mapping out the future of his future son-in-law. It made Guy uneasy, somehow, as though he wasn't master of his own destiny.

They fell into a routine of sex. Lucy was quite passionate, and very trusting, and that's the way it was. Sex didn't interfere with Guy's work; if anything it was helpful- he needed to relax. It was usually in the afternoons and it became a habit - a girl wasn't allowed to stay in College overnight: men had been rusticated, or even sent down for that. Lucy would usually come around for tea, and they'd talk over tea; and, if they felt like it, which was more often than not, they'd undress and get into bed as natural as anything.

There was a Finality about that Final term at Oxford.

Then, before Guy started what Sir Philip called a proper job, they were all to take a family holiday. Sir Philip had arranged it: one of his friends, well, a business associate, all Sir Philip's friends were business associates - one of these friends had a Villa at Cannes, and he'd lent it to Sir Philip for July; and, besides the Villa, Sir Philip rented a boat, a motor-cruiser, in case they got bored with the beach.

So in July, they left London in the Rolls. They left the chauffeur behind, and Guy took his turn at the wheel. They took the car across the channel by plane - Sir Philip couldn't be bothered with ferries - and the Rolls took up half the space on the plane;, and they drove into Cannes late in the evening as the lights went up around the bay.

The Villa was at the far side of Cannes, on La Croisette, the Crescent, just behind the Esplanade. There was a big room with a balcony, and a lot of expensive decor, fin de-siecle, which was the fashionable style amongst Sir Philip's friends - who were really business associates, but you couldn't call them that. Sir Philip called them friends, though you knew it wasn't just for friendship that the friend had lent the Villa.

Guy and Lucy had separate bedrooms at the Villa - you had to keep up appearances; that was important. Sir Philip said "There's a nice little place for Dinner, around the comer - he knew a "nice little place" in most of the Resorts and in most of the Cities around the world. "Freddy's Symphony" was quite a jazzy place, and the food was good, with all the hints of privilege which Sir Philip liked; so that's where they usually dined.

The motor cruiser was a splendid boat, and quite fast, good for showing off around the bay. She didn't compete with the grand yachts, of course, like Onassis' yacht, the Christina which was often at Cannes - Onassis used to move it up and down the Coast, to Monte, or to Portofino; but usually at Cannes.

144

The Cannes Casino was the fashionable Casino that season - not the Municipal Casino, of course, which was a pint-sized imitation of the one at Nice; but the other Casino, at the end of La Croisette, the Palm Beach Casino, out on the rocky tip of the Crescent in the sea.

"Fancy a flutter?" said Sir Philip, in his self-conscious, self-important way. It was after dinner at Freddy's, and, outside the Casino, things were just starting to happen; the Cadillacs and Rollses were jamming-up the roundabout in front of the Casino; chauffeurs were opening doors, and the occupants were taking their time, to make an impression.

Light from the Casino was spilling out, over the lawns and the flowerbeds in front, over the cannas and the bougainvillaeas. Once a car had driven up to the marble entrance and the marble patio, and had established its position there, the chauffeur was out of his seat, in cap and polished leggings, to open the door for whoever it was, for the Shah and Soraya, or for Sir Bernard and Lady Docker, or for Onassis; or a hundred other billionaires, Americans mostly; the women deliberately slow, to show-off their jewels; and some of the women were beautiful, and some were not. There were so many jewels you wondered where they all came from, you wondered if they'd hired the entire collection from Cartier's or Tiffany's, and where they kept all those jewels most of the time.

The man at Reception asked for Passports, and he wouldn't let Lucy go inside because she was under twenty-one; not even when Sir Philip offered a banknote, a big one - it was not worth the risk, the gendarmerie were strict. But Mademoiselle could use the outer Salle where there was Boule; and she was welcome to stay out on the terrace - for a drink and dancing.

Sir Philip and Lady Merchant went into the Main Salle, and Guy went into the outer Salle with Lucy; Lucy was sulky, you couldn't blame her - it was disappointing and

145

unfashionable in the outer Salle. She'd got dressed in her little white frock, the one from Balenciaga, and she'd put on her jewellery, her own jewellery and also a rope of pearls that Mummy had lent her; she looked fashionable and expensive and able to keep her end up with the other women: what an anticlimax to be banished to the outer Salle. Not that Boule was very different - it was just Roulette with a larger Ball for lower stakes. As for Guy, he'd never seen anything in Roulette. It was so mindless: just a ball, and a spinning-wheel, and chance. It was all tricked out with trappings, Croupiers in evening dress and gloves, and a hush everywhere, muted sound; just the click-click of the spinning ball, the whirr of the wheel, and the expensive rattle of perspex chips: all show, and no substance.

If anything, Guy felt relieved that he hadn't to face a series of nights at the Casino. That's what Lucy would have wanted to do, and, if Kings and Captains of Industry were drawn to the tables, why not Lucy?

"I'm bored" said Lucy, and Guy said "It's pretty, out on the terrace. Let's dance."

The terrace was built on rocks, just above the sea; between the Casino behind and the moon which set its beam like a highway across the water. There was a dance-floor, terrazzo, and, on the near side, close to the Casino lights, tables and a bar. On the far side, beyond the terrazzo, a West Indian band was playing Latin rhythms. It was somehow seductive, the inky sea, and the inky faces of the musicians; the musicians with their white, silk shirts, and the white phosphorescence on the water.

"Garcon!" called Guy, and the waiter brought beer and Campari-soda. The band was playing a Samba, and there was nobody dancing; just a few couples drinking at the tables, taking the air before going inside to gamble. Guy sensed the glamour of the scene, and it disturbed him the way it was all being wasted: the style of the musicians, and the music and

146

everything; the moonlight and the shimmering water - it was all being wasted through human perversity: an obsession with money and a little, hopping ball.

"Let's dance" said Guy, and Lucy stood up rather ungraciously: she couldn't hide her resentment at being shut out, like a child shut out of Fairyland. They swayed together to the music, and the man with the maracas put on a tour-de-force, grateful to be appreciated. Lucy's cheek was on Guy's chest, the way it usually was when they danced, but, when he looked down at her, he could see her staring, away from the sea, and into the wide windows of the casino. Her heart was inside with those glamorous people, all crowded around the tables, with their backs to the sea, and oblivious to the beauty outside.

"Here's Mummy" said Lucy. They went back to their table, and Guy said "Can I get you a drink, Lady Merchant?" - as usual, he felt silly at addressing her so formally; but she hadn't suggested an alternative, and Guy wondered if she ever would. The waiter brought a Martini, and Lady Merchant said "You go inside, Guy. I'll keep Lucy company."

Guy said "I prefer it out here. Really." But, she was insistent.

Guy entered the glittering Palace. There were knots of people, close around the tables watching the play, all mesmerised. Guy went to the kiosk and waited while they served someone with chips in exchange for Thousand Dollar bills. He changed his own poor twenty pounds and went over to the table where Sir Philip was seated. He barely acknowledged Guy: jealous even of raising his eyes from the baize. He seemed to be playing a system, Rouge, Impair et Manque, and he'd built-up a respectable pile of chips. He was hoping to win two out of three for even money: it was cautious and rather dull.

Eventually, someone vacated a seat, and Guy took the

place. He, too, played it cautious, Red or Black; Odds or Evens; lose or win. My God, he thought, can this really be me? He became exasperated, put the lot on a single number and lost; relieved to get away, and twenty pounds a small price to pay.

He went over to the bar - there was a long bar, the length of the far wall, marble - topped with a row of swivel stools. Most of the people on the stools were women; and they weren't facing the wall with their drinks on the bar. They were swivelled around with their backs to the bar, and facing into the Salle. The barman was shaking a cocktail - ice-cubes in a cocktail-shaker - and the rattle of the ice-cubes matched the rattle of the balls on the roulette-wheels. There was a background hum of voices, and the rattle of a dozen roulette-wheels, and the flat voices of the croupiers "Faites vos jeux - Rien ne va plus - Rouge, Impair et Manque." And then the soft scrape of the Croupier's rake across the baize.

There were some beautiful women on the Bar-stools; beautiful and rich, to judge by their diamonds: all trying hard to smile, and to hide the tedium of their long vigil, their long wait until their men left the tables.

Guy ordered a beer, and there was a woman, hardly more than a girl, on the stool beside him. He smiled, but she didn't smile back; she just looked vaguely alarmed. Guy thought, many of these women are really frightened women.

Right across, over in the far corner of the Salle, in a bay-window, there were tables for Baccarat and Chemin-de-Fer: a relief from the monotonous wheel. Guy thought he'd finish his beer, then go over and watch. He waited until a spectator moved aside - spectators had been so pressed around that table, you couldn't see the players. As soon as the man moved away, another took his place; but Guy caught a glimpse, and what he thought he saw brought excitement and alarm: wanting it to be a mistake and not a mistake, all at the same time. He turned to the barman - all the barmen spoke

English, or, rather, American - he said "There's a woman at the table in the alcove, with a crowd around her. She has an elegant back. It was her back I noticed."

The barman was polishing glasses, the way barmen do, to look busy. He said "There is only one back like that. Very straight, very proud. She concentrates on her game."

Guy said "She doesn't seem to relax."

The barman fixed his eye on the glass he was polishing. He said "You like a woman's back, Monsieur? You are attracted by a beautiful back?"

"By this back, certainly. Her shoulders are quite perfect."

The barman said "She knows her finest point, Monsieur. For many women the fashion is the low neckline. But - Madame's fashion is the bare back. It is sensational." The barman paused, choosing his words. "A word of warning, Monsieur. You've heard of Monsieur Chandler? Monsieur Arthur Chandler, the Holiday Camp Tycoon?" - He said "Tycoon" with a funny, American, intonation, half-American, half-French as though he was speaking in a gangster-movie.

Guy said "I've heard of him."

"That man is Rich - and Jealous" said the barman. "She belongs to him."

"His wife?" said Guy.

"Wife? - No. But, they have an arrangement. He pays the bills. Such arrangements are common on the Cote d'Azur."

"You mean, she's his Mistress" said Guy "What is her name? Who is she?"

"That even I do not know. They call her La Marina. She plays Chemmy; Baccarat. Never Roulette." He added

"Monsieur Chandler plays Roulette" and pointed to one of the smaller tables with the high minimum stakes. Queen Soraya was sitting at the table with the Shah standing behind her; both were smoking cigarettes, which they did all the time, and both were looking tense and sad. Onassis was standing at one side, watching in his sardonic way, and the Penicillin billionaire was occupying a seat: he was not actually sitting on the seat, but was half-standing at the table, with the seat behind him. He was tilting the seat backwards, and plonking down armloads of large chips like a child with building bricks.

Chandler was seated and impassive; not gambling high, but enough. Whichever way the wheel spun, for him or against him, he showed no emotion - what a waste, Guy thought: such nerves should be tested on a game like Poker. Guy watched for a bit - he could see enough without moving from the bar; and he had to admire Chandler, admire him and hate him too.

The barman said "If the Casino bores you Monsieur, why do you stay?"

Guy replied "I'm bored by the gambling. Not by the gamblers. The Wages of a thousand workers on one turn of the wheel - that makes me think."

"You'd soon get used to that, Monsieur. I'm used to it, and, after all, my own pay is not good."

Guy said "Just to watch is cheap entertainment."

The barman said "It is La Marina who has caught your eye. Leave her alone - I advise you."

Guy finished his beer, and strolled across to the table in the alcove. So, Ruth was La Marina now? - She'd come a long way!

He had to push his way through the people around the table; they were all men, watching: watching the cards; watching Ruth - for, it was Ruth: La Marina. She was

150

absorbed in the game, playing her cards deliberately, and her red nails were like gashes across the cards. She seemed oblivious of everyone, of the men whose eyes bored into her back.

At last one of the men, - perhaps he could bear it no longer, - pressed tight against her chair, and stupidly, perhaps innocently, he touched the bare back. Immediately, she was up, and springing at him like a she-cat, a panther with claws. "Attention!" she hissed, pronouncing the word the French way; and the man backed away mumbling "Pardon!"

Guy said "Hello, Ruth. I'm with some people on the terrace. Would you care to come out for a drink?"

She caught her breath, and put her hand on the table to steady herself. The she recovered, and smiled.

They went outside, and the terrace was deserted - empty but for the musicians who were still playing to the empty sea. Lucy and her mother had gone. Guy called for Champagne, and the waiter brought a bottle in a bucket of ice.

Guy said "La Marina...it's an attractive name."

Ruth laughed "So, you know my incognito?"

Guy said "I saw your picture in Vogue - and the Tatler. Pru told me about you. Who's this fellow Chandler?"

Ruth said "He respects me, Guy. And he's generous. I'm not unhappy."

Guy said "You always had expensive tastes, Ruth. You look expensive now. And beautiful."

Ruth said "Very expensive tastes, Guy. That's my weakness."

Guy said "Those musicians, they're super. Haven't they got style? I feel sorry for them. The way everyone ignores them."

They stood up to dance. The man with the maracas grinned, and led into a Rumba, Cuban Rumba, to cast a spell of the jungle over the couple: Guy and Ruth, Ruth and Guy, who were locked together and moving together, moving to the rhythm, beside the sea, in the night.

They went back to the table, and the Champagne. Ruth said "I'd better go inside, soon. Arthur gets jealous."

Guy said "I can understand that."

Ruth said "I'm staying at the Carlton. We've got a suite there. Come for tea tomorrow. The Carlton Terrace at four o'clock."

Guy said "I'm here with some people - the Merchants. I'm engaged to Lucy Merchant."

Ruth couldn't quite hide the effect of that, and Guy said "I left her here with her mother but they've gone. She can't go into the Salle; she's under twenty-one."

Ruth said "Do you love her, Guy?"

Guy said "In a way. - I don't know. She's suitable."

They went back into the Salle. Ruth went over to Arthur and said "Someone's taking me back to the Hotel. An old friend."

Arthur nodded, and continued with his game, placing his chips in his careful, businesslike way; and the Shah and Soraya, his sad Queen were still there, as though the Casino was a pool of light, secure from the dark seas outside.

Guy went across to Sir Philip who was still absorbed in his game, still under the spell of Big Money.

Guy said "I'm leaving. Lucy and Lady Merchant left early."

As they left the Casino, one of the chauffeurs moved towards a car, but Ruth said "Non - Attendez!"

She had put on a fur wrap to cover her shoulders, a lightweight wrap, a mere token; for the night was as sultry as she. They walked slowly along the empty Esplanade, from one pool of light to the next, between the palms and the flowers on one side and the strip of sand on the other. The bay was inky-black in the moonlight, and they walked past, first, the plage publique, then a strip of sand with furled umbrellas and pedalloes pulled up on the beach, and next a row of volley-ball nets: tomorrow a hundred people, children and adults, would be leaping and laughing around the nets; but now, it was all deserted under the moon.

Guy stopped, and their hands touched. He said "Remember how the Guns looked at night?"

They kissed, quite gently, but Guy felt Ruth was nervous. He said "Are you frightened of Chandler?" and Ruth said "I'm more than a match for Chandler. If it was only Chandler by himself."

Guy said "What do you mean?" and Ruth said "He uses his money. He bribes. The barmen - and the chauffeurs: they're watching me."

They walked on, and the Carlton was still ablaze with light, full of life, and cars with people returning from the Casino. "Tomorrow" Ruth said "At four."

****

The Carlton terrace is the most expensive piece of terrazzo in the world. People were taking tea, but the terrace was not crowded, and there were spare tables and spare sunshades. The sun was hot, and, in front of the terrace, between the terrace and the sea, the world went by: bodies cooked and oiled and nearly naked; excited children; men in dark glasses who looked like gangsters; a few fishermen

153

going down to the port for the evening catch; women past forty who had spent the day at the coiffeuse, and who were now emerging for the promenade; beauties in bikinis; gigolos in Palm Beach suits; ice-cream vendors; show-offs on motor-scooters irritating everyone; whole families from enfant to grandmere.

Ruth was alone at a table under a blue umbrella. She said "Where are the others, your friends?"

Guy shrugged. He hadn't asked them.

Ruth said "Arthur will come later" - but he never came.

The waiter brought tea served à l'Anglais, in a teapot, and eclairs and petits fours. Guy said "How's the `Q'? And your mother?"

"Dad's retiring soon" said Ruth "I don't go home very often."

Guy said "I'm joining Merchant's next month. After this holiday."

Ruth said "The family firm. And when will you marry?"

Guy looked at his plate, as if he couldn't meet her eye. He said, quietly "In the Autumn. It's the best thing."

Ruth spoke slowly, choosing her words. "The best thing Guy - for you, or for Lucy? Will you be happy, Guy?"

He looked out to sea - he was sitting beside her, his arm along the back of the seat behind her. He said "Not happy the way we were, Ruth. The way it might have been."

Ruth had to gulp a little. She said "I don't think it will ever be like that again. For either of us."

A peddlar came close, an Algerian selling carpets, who was making comic faces, to attract their attention. Guy laughed, and a waiter shooed the man away. "Good Lord"

154

said Guy "I didn't mean to be so serious. My tea's going cold." He took a gulp, and a bite of eclair. "They certainly have style in this place" he said.

Ruth said "And I'm living here like Cleopatra. It's funny." Guy said "You'll always be Cleopatra to me, Ruth. You know that."

She had a piece of gateau on her fork, and, on an impulse, she leaned forward and popped it in Guy's mouth. He was reminded of the fun they used to have, and he said "Are you often at the Casino in the evening?"

Ruth said "I go when Arthur goes. He nearly always goes."

Guy beckoned the waiter, to pay, but Ruth put out her hand to stop him. She rested her fingers on his, and for a moment, her hand in his hand was a shared memory. "Everything goes on Arthur's account" she said.

Guy was about to protest, but i wasn't worth the fuss. "Au Revoir" he said, and left.

Next day was a lovely day for a sail - not that it was different from the other days - but Sir Philip announced it was a day for a sail, so it was.

A sail was so easy; just a walk to the harbour, and Monsieur le Capitain and Madame la Capitaine had her ready, they always had her ready - the boat: "la Goulue" was a sexy dancer of a boat, a Parisienne.

They came out of harbour, past the yachts that were moored in a line, as rigid as marines: the "Christina" with her brasses shining, and Onassis and his friends with their morning drinks under the awning; Onassis dapper as ever in navy-blue blazer and co-respondent's shoes, and never removing his sun-glasses even in the shade; and, half a dozen other people, distinguished-looking men; and decorative women to complement the lovely lines of the yacht. And -

155

there was Ruth, in what looked like silk pyjamas and a yachting-cap, in animated conversation. If she was as surprised as Guy, she didn't show it; she just waved and smiled as they went past.

Around the corner, into the bay Monsieur le Capitain boosted the Chrysler engines, and the twin screws thrust la Goulue upwards to breast the waves; as though she was being fucked from behind. She was a brave boat, a dancing boat; and she danced over those waves.

They came into an empty bay, westwards, towards St. Tropez - a sandy bay between red rocks.

It was mid-day and it was hot.

Guy put on fins and goggles, and swam across the bay where the fish darted across the sand below and the surface ripples showed as dappled shadows. Lucy wouldn't come with him, and Guy thought, Ruth would have come.

The sand met the rock, and there were more fish, and crabs, and a squid in a fissure in the rock. Guy looked across to la Goulue which looked like a toy boat in a bathtub, with little figures waving. He swam back, and Lucy said "You're holding up the lunch."

Guy wondered why she was tetchy; it was unlike her.

Madame la Capitaine had made the lunch. Sir Philip called the Captain "Skipper", it was predictable, but Madame was always "Madame". Madame's lunches were very good lunches; right for the Mediterranean in Summer. They were light lunches, so light you could eat too much if you weren't careful; and they were cold lunches, that went with the sea and the sun: a salad; some fish: tuna, anchovy; perhaps a terrine; and, afterwards, a sorbet or a peach; anything you liked to drink: cold beer, or cool wine.

Lucy said "I'm dying to see St. Tropez", but St. Tropez was an anticlimax: the same row of moored yachts as at

Cannes, but the whole place more sandy, less tidy than Cannes: a bit of Tahiti in the Mediterranean and the name of the nudist beach was Tahiti-plage. The fashion seemed to be no-fashion: rope-sandals on the feet, and kerosene-lamps in the bars. They spent the afternoon playing at being Naturists like the other tourists; and Guy was glad when they set out for home.

"We need a good Dinner" said Sir Philip'", and what could be better than the "Little place around the Corner?" - Freddy's Symphony was delightful, of course it was, but Guy found himself resenting the way Sir Philip liked to appropriate the place.

Their table was under a vine. You couldn't tell if it was al fresco, - probably not, in case of rain - but, at night, it looked al fresco with the roof hidden behind vine-leaves; and a gypsy band playing Tarantellas.

The violinist came to their table, and he serenaded Lucy, and he serenaded Lady Merchant, who giggled. Lucy tried hard to be jolly, but Guy saw it was forced. They had Lobster Armoricaine and Champagne, and the Champagne went so fast that Sir Philip ordered another bottle.

Afterwards - it was midnight - Lucy said she was tired and had to go to bed, and Sir Philip said "Lord, yes. We're all dead beat." But Guy didn't feel tired; he felt he'd drunk the elixir of Life - it was the Champagne, he supposed. He said "I feel ready for anything. A swim - anything."

He left them, and walked away at a fast stride, determined to tire himself out. But, it was self-delusion - he knew where he was going. He had his jacket and his tie, and he had his Passport - all that was necessary for entry to the Casino; and he had some money, enough.

She was there - there had always been the chance of disappointment - but, she was there, at the same table playing Chemmy: the same lovely back; a different frock, but the

157

same, plunging back.

He went past her table, into the bay-window where she could see him, and she smiled as though she was expecting him. She finished her hand, collected her winnings, and left the table and the disappointed voyeurs.

"You saw us putting out to sea" Guy said "I feel so fresh. I could dance all night."

Ruth laughed, happy to see him; happy to see him so full of life. And, he was glad to see her, it was so obvious. She said "I'll meet you on the terrace."

He went outside, and it was the same Latin band, the same welcome. Ruth came, and Guy ordered tall drinks, and he said "Did you enjoy the party on the "Christina?"

Ruth said "Isn't she a beautiful boat? - Designed in Heaven! - Arthur knows Onassis." Guy said "And Onassis knows a pretty woman. - Ruth, you look so splendid."

"I want to dance" she said.

He took her in his arms, and the musicians grinned with pleasure; one of them started to sing that haunting Calypso about the heavy night picking bananas "Come Mister Tally-man, Tally me banana" - and, about the relief that came with the Dawn "Day-oh!" Hope and Rest! The hardness of life: the joy of life.

Guy held Ruth to him, lost to everything but Ruth and the Rhythm and the Tropical sound; oblivious to the curious faces at the windows of the Salle Publique, faces no longer turned towards the tables, but staring outwards at the terrace.

But Ruth was not oblivious, and she felt again the protective instinct of a she-wolf for her cub. She said "You must be careful, Guy. Arthur is dangerous, when he's jealous."

Arthur noticed the people at the window, and he

158

noticed that Ruth wasn't at her table. One glance, out of the window, was enough. Somebody, a mischievous nobody said to him "Madame Marina is sensational Monsieur. May I compliment you on her dancing?"

It was spoken with a sardonic twist and it made Arthur angry. He went to the bar. "Paul" he said to the barman.

"Monsieur?" - the barman came quickly: Monsieur Chandler tipped too well to keep him waiting. "Is there anything wrong Monsieur?"

"Wrong? - No. Only mockery."

"Mockery. Monsieur?"

Chandler said "Don't act innocent, Paul. Pour me a Cognac."

Paul reached for the bottle, and a glass, while Arthur stood at the bar, feeling alone and foolish - outwardly as calm as ever, but inwardly seething in the way an unemotional man seethes when the pressure gets too much. He said "The nastiest pleasure, Paul, is to see someone put down. Someone humiliated."

"Pleasure, Monsieur?"

"How they all enjoyed it - seeing her with that - schoolboy! Taking tea at the Carlton at my expense!"

"Mais - non!" - Paul feigned horror.

"Don't pretend you haven't heard" - Arthur could not hide the emotion in his voice

"Everyone has heard. How he wanted to taste her gateau, and took some from her fork." Arthur drank the Brandy, and Paul said "I think you worry about nothing, Monsieur." "Nothing! - The two of them. Together; there, outside. They call it dancing! Look - they have an audience! And everyone's laughing at me!"

159

Paul said "He's obsessed by her! - obsessed by her back. He told me. One should pity him."

"Pity? - Perhaps. But I can only hate him. You must help me, Paul."

"I Monsieur?"

Arthur said "I want to teach him a lesson. I don't want him injured - just punished a little." Arthur took out his wallet and showed some big notes "I'll pay in Dollars - American Dollars. You have friends, I know."

Paul said "The chauffeurs. But, you have your own chauffeur, Monsieur?" "My chauffeur!" Arthur said "I pay him; but he worships her."

Paul said "There are other chauffeurs. Perhaps - when they see the money..." Outside, Ruth said "Guy. Everybody's watching us. Have you noticed?" Guy said "Let's take a walk. Like we did the other night. - I'll wait for you"

When they left the floor the band seemed to wind down like an old gramophone; and the faces moved away from the window.

Ruth went upstairs to the Salle. She said "Arthur. I've been dancing. Such a nice boy - the one who came to tea."

Arthur said "I'm glad you're enjoying yourself." He'd regained control, and was wearing his Poker-face.

Ruth said "He wants to walk me home - you don't mind?"

Outside, Guy was waiting - Ruth must have been delayed, and he wondered if Chandler was being awkward. Then, someone came up to him; it was the barman, Paul, saying "Pardon, Monsieur. Madame Marina waits in the car-park."

"The Car-park. Why?"

Paul shrugged his shoulders, and pointed to the dark park behind the palms.

Guy felt a thump on the back, and a thump in the gut, and a sick pain; but he managed to get one in at something soft, at someone's belly, before he was dragged to the ground and booted; and a hellish pain crashed through his head. He shouted, and got hold of a leather legging and twisted hard. But the man ran off, they all ran off.

Guy lay in the dust, sick and full of pain. Oh God, that Bastard! Chandler had fixed it; and the Barman. The jealous Bastard! Ah, the pain!

He dragged himself, away from the palms and into the light; mumbling "Oh God, I wish Ruth would come."

But, Ruth had already come, and gone. She'd waited for an uncertain minute; only a minute until suspicion became certainty: certainty and anger. Arthur was still at the bar, drinking more brandy. "What have you done with him?" She demanded.

There were people, curious people, and Guy didn't want that; but there was a way around to the back, onto the empty terrace; empty except for the band still shaking their maracas at the sea. Upstairs, Arthur was talking, and what he was saying didn't make sense. Ruth ran across the Salle to the back window, and there was Guy, crouched and stumbling; then he slumped on the ground.

Ruth ran, clack-clack in her high-heels down the stairs, out onto the terrace "Guy. Oh, Guy. The Bastards."

She held him to her and he said "Ruth. I'm all right. No worse than a Rugger match - A few bruises."

Some people had started to come outside, to look; and Arthur came out, too. Guy said "It could have been hospital for me. There were three of them." Ruth said "Would you recognise them?"

161

Guy said "They were chauffeurs. One had leggings. I twisted his leg like Hell." - He laughed at the thought of it, which made him wince.

"Dirty chauffeurs" said Ruth "Paid to do it, of course."

She remembered Arthur at the bar, and how the bar had been unattended. A barman doesn't leave his bar for nothing, and it all fitted.

She said "Why didn't you wait for me in front of the Casino? Like you said?"

"It was the barman. The barman brought a message. To meet you in the car park." Arthur came forward. He said "I hope it's not serious."

Ruth said, in a voice cut with hatred. "Not serious enough for you, Arthur. You paid them to do this."

Arthur said "Nobody mocks Arthur Chandler."

Ruth stood proud. She said "I will never stop mocking", and she ran her red nails down his cheek to draw blood. She laughed "Everyone will mock you now."

Arthur lunged, to hurt her; to maim her: anything to spoil her if he could; smash her nose, anything: like a child trying to smash a toy. But Ruth avoided him, and whipped-out a flick-knife from her bag; she stood, daring him and ready to slash. She said "You touch me, Arthur, and I carve you!"

Guy managed to get to his feet. He said "My God, Ruth. A knife!"

Ruth said "A girl like me doesn't go unarmed. I've learnt to fight."

She put the knife close to Arthur's throat. She said "Arthur will be armed. Frisk him Guy."

Guy started to feel Arthur's pockets, and she said

162

"Take the knife", and ran her hands up the legs and body until she found the pistol. "I'll keep this," she said "It might be useful,"

It all seemed staged: the watching audience, and the band. The musicians sensed that they were playing background music to a Melodrama, and started to play a Bolero; Ravel's Bolero, which follows one crescendo with another.

"And now, Arthur" said Ruth "You are going to do your own fighting. - Guy, can you take him?"

Guy said "You bet. - The cold-blooded bastard. He wouldn't have cared if they'd kicked me to death."

Guy took up an orthodox boxing stance, and Arthur, seeing he was cornered, kicked out at Guy's crotch. Guy punched, and all his fury was unleashed in the punch; and he was punching, punching at that cold, inscrutable face.

Arthur, his little eyes filled with hate looked for an opening; and all the while, the music throbbed, insistent and ever louder; and the black faces grinned in the moonlight.

Guy got in a blow to the stomach, and Arthur fell. Guy was going in to finish him, to boot him; to get his own back for the boots. But Ruth said "Stop, Guy. He's too old for that.'

She said to Arthur "Come with me Arthur. Remember. I've got the pistol; and the knife."

They went up the stairs to the Salle, and they went up to the bar, Ruth said "I want it, Paul. The money. The Blood Money."

The barman was nervous, but he hesitated, and Arthur said "She's dangerous, Paul. You'd better give it."

Ruth said "Four Hundred Dollars - Well! - A hundred each for the three thugs. And a hundred for Paul!" She turned to Arthur "I'll have the rest, Arthur" - the flick-knife was in her hand and she jabbed him with the hilt. He handed over his wallet: another hundred Dollars; and a hundred Pounds; Some Francs.

She said "Give me time. To clear my things at the Carlton - or, I go to the Police. You wouldn't like that, Arthur."

She called the chauffeur, and Guy went with her, to the Carlton, and up in the lift to the Suite. She said "I'll only take the best. I'll leave the rest", and she filled two suitcases with clothes and jewellery. Guy said "Where will you go?"

Ruth said "I'd like to disappear. Who can you trust when money talks? - Arthur always talks with money."

Guy said "I'll help you" and Ruth said "I threatened him with the police. That was a bluff, really. Arthur's vindictive. He'll want his own back on me - on you too."

They left the Hotel together through the foyer. Guy was carrying the cases, and he was amused how the gentleman at the Desk glanced suspiciously in case they were leaving without paying. Then, he pretended not to notice: he knew who was paying that bill!

Ruth told the chauffeur to drive to the railway-station. Then, she sent him away, and there they were, in the dark outside the station waiting for a train to God knows where, at God knows what time.

Ruth said "If I could get to Monte. There's someone there. Somewhere I might hide."

Guy said "Shall we hire a car? A taxi?"

Ruth said "Taxi drivers might talk to Arthur for money. But my friend at Monte. I can trust him."

Guy said, and there was a touch of sadness. "Will he be your next lover, Ruth?" She said "He wants companionship;

164

just friendship."

"Who is he?"

"It was at the Casino. We were at the bar and got talking. He said he was a Rajah - he wasn't boasting, and it's probably true. He's certainly an Indian. Quite dark."

Guy said "He must find you attractive. All men do."

Ruth said "He was considerate, and quite old-fashioned. He wants a companion - a sort of secretary-companion. He's touring Europe."

Guy laughed and said "If I didn't know you Ruth, I'd say you were naive."

Ruth turned, and said "Oh Guy. You're going to get married. I've got to have someone - can't you see?"

Then Guy said "Monte you said? - I have an idea. We'll go by boat."

They humped the cases down to the quay, and la Goulue was there, a shadowy thoroughbred lapping the water. Guy knocked on the cabin; a light went on, and the Skipper came on deck in his pyjamas; and he'd put on his yachting cap to give himself authority.

He looked at Guy, and at the girl with the suitcases; and Guy said "A big favour. Can you sail to Monte tonight?"

The Skipper asked no questions, he just laughed the laugh of a shipmate "O.K." he said, the way the French say O.K., and he beckoned Ruth on board.

"Where's Madame?" asked Guy. "Madame La Capitaine?"

"Ashore" said the Skipper, and left it at that. La Goulue's lights went on, Red and Green; they cast off, and away.

The Skipper didn't bother to change - he was standing at the wheel in his pyjamas and yachting-cap. He's enjoying it, thought Guy - something to break the routine of jaunts for pampered millionaires.

Guy said "I'll crew for you", but when they'd cleared the bay, the Skipper had all the help he needed from the lighthouse and the buoys.

Ruth came forward, and the three of them were in the wheelhouse cabin, with the Skipper standing, and looking ahead, and holding the wheel. He said "Monsieur Guy. I ask no questions - but, you've been in a fight - No? - You want a drink?"

Guy said "Thanks. Will you have one?"

"A large Rum - neat!"

The Rum was symbolic, a touch of the Navy. Guy filled three glasses, and Ruth said "Rum - what fun!" and they all laughed.

The Skipper set the course close to shore, and they were passing Eden Rock, and the Naval School at Antibes. The esplanades were all lit-up, a chain of fairy-lights along the coast; then it became dark and blank, and they were passing rock. The Skipper said "Why don't you two turn in? - Fighting makes you tired!" - he was a humorous man and understanding. He seemed to want to be alone, with his boat and the sea, or, perhaps, he knew what Guy and Ruth wanted, better than they knew themselves.

There were two cabins: the Skipper's cabin, and another cabin where they could relax at last, and Guy allowed himself to feel the pain and weariness. Ruth said "They gave you a dreadful battering" and Guy said "A mad night. An adventure, Ruth."

Ruth smiled "An adventure? - Yes. And I love you."

"I love you. Ruth."

"But" she said "I'm leaving you again, Guy. At Monte. It's best."

They lay together on the lower bunk; and they made love as urgently and naturally as was inevitable.

Guy said "Ruth. We should be together. Always." and she said "You'd lose your chance with Merchant's. You know it wouldn't work."

There was a sealed-glass porthole, just above the sea and level with the bunk, and they could look out at the night and the moonlight sparkling on the foam of la Goulue, where she danced upon the water. They lay, close and happy after sex, and Ruth said "Look, Guy. There's Nice - the Promenade Anglais."

They were close to shore, and they could see the moving headlights of the cars, and all the twinkling lights; and the great Casino where it faced the sea.

They lay together saying nothing. The lights of Nice faded astern, and they were below the cliffs where the Alpes Maritimes plunge sheer into the Med.. Here and there, across that dark blankness, little lights moved like glow-worms, where cars passed along the Corniche roads.

Guy said "Ruth. It's beautiful - like you. The dark beauty of it all!"

She squeezed his hand, and he felt a renewed response in his loins; and, he was grateful to whom he knew not, to Aphrodite, perhaps, Goddess of Love, and Goddess of that ancient Sea.

He said "Ruth. I want to make love again. So that you will always miss me."

He entered her; hard and happy. And he stayed in her, while he kissed her, and nuzzled her, and she touched him

167

with her tongue. She put her hands to his face, and they were gentle. She said "Please, Guy. Please. Now", and he moved, firm and gentle, wanting to give himself, and she, wanting him, wanting to keep him for ever; for ever, ever: until ever was now, and now was Always. Now and Always.

It was done, and Ruth jellied into contentment: him there, soft now and tender; and she: mate and dam - dam and mate, saying "Guy. Oh, Guy. My Love."

They were near Monte now, passing Beaulieu-sur-Mer with its big Palms and its buildings of the Grand Epoque, that were vague shapes in the half-light before dawn. They heard the Skipper's cheerful shout, so they went up. He was brewing coffee, and humming a tune, a tune of the Paris Cabaret, one of La Goulue's tunes. He said "Monte in Teti Minutes. Time for a coffee."

There were some signs of life in Monte-Carlo harbour: early fishermen; a boatman in a dinghy, dipping his oars into the mist which lay on the water. Soon, the morning sun would sear the mist away.

The Skipper cut the engines, and La Goulue changed from Can-Can girl to ballerina. It was like Swan-Lake, gliding over the lake-like harbour, where the yachts and the gulls lay sleeping, side by side on the water. The Dying Swan: it was an image too poignant to express.

Guy went to the bows and waited his moment to jump ashore. The Skipper gave a blip, just a blip to the engine in reverse, and la Goulue made the last shudder of the Swan.

"Merci, Skipper!" called Ruth "Merci - and Au Revoir."

Guy took the suitcases, and they walked together up the quay, past the yachts. Guy looked up, at the steep climb to the town and to the Casino like a Palace of icing-sugar. He said "I'll have to go with you, Ruth. This luggage is heavy."

Ruth said "Put it down, Guy. I'll wait for a Taxi."

Guy started to protest; unwilling to leave her alone and vulnerable. "My God, Ruth. You don't really know this chap. This Indian. You can't even be certain he's here."

Ruth said "You would like him, Guy. I can trust him. I know."

Guy still hesitated and Ruth said "He's like an English gentleman. Only black. Oh - more gentle - and more manly - than most Englishmen."

Guy looked hard at her, and there was a sad dampness in her eyes. He said "You really want me to go?"

She nodded, and he walked quickly back to the boat.

La Goulue seemed to catch Guy's mood, and her homewards dance was a frenzied dance over the sea. The Skipper stood silent at the wheel; he handed Guy the glasses, and Guy focussed on the little group on the quay; the two suitcases and the girl. Then, a car stopped beside the group, and took them away.

It was mid-morning when Guy got back to the Villa; and there was panic. It was only last evening that they had all Dined together at Freddy's - it was scarcely credible, it seemed so long ago.

Lucy was crying "Oh, Mummy. We should never have let him go out alone."

Sir Philip said, testily "Where do you think we are? Shanghai or somewhere?" - the women were trying to make him feel guilty, and he wasn't having any. The boy had no need to go off by himself, and stay out all night. "Dammit" said Sir Philip "I'm damned if I'll do without my breakfast." And he called for croissants and coffee.

They heard Guy as he was coming in. Lucy cried out "Oh, Guy. You've had an accident. You've been in a fight!"

169

They expected him to deny it: people never believe that you've actually been in a fight; they think you've fallen, or something - or been knocked-down by a car. Guy felt so weary. He slumped into a chair, and said "A fight? - Yes - a fight, and other things." There came a confusion of questions "Shut up!" shouted Sir Philip "Let him tell us." Guy didn't want to tell, to go through it all. But, he knew he'd have to say something. He felt so damned tired - but, he'd have to talk - the gossip would be all around Cannes by now: the fight, and the Casino; and Ruth. The whole night, all he'd wanted was to keep going. But now, he had to rest.

"I need some coffee" he said, and Lucy said, hysterically "It was that woman! Daddy saw you with her the other night." So, she knew. It didn't take much guessing.

"She's an old friend" said Guy. "She was in danger - I had to help her."

"You didn't have to get yourself beaten-up" said Lucy "She must be some girl - for you to get beaten-up like that!" There was hurt in her voice, and she didn't bother to hide it.

Guy said "I took a liberty, Sir Philip, I'm sorry. I got the Skipper to ferry us to Monte."

"Good God - Why? - In the middle of the night!",

Guy said "It was the best way. She wants to get lost. And you don't leave footprints on water."

Lucy said "So, that's where you've been - to Monte" she was angry now.

Sir Philip said "If this woman's in danger, it must be from her gentleman-friend; her Sugar-Daddy. He will threaten you too, Guy."

Guy smiled "What - Arthur Chandler? Not when I've got Merchant's behind me, surely? Sir Philip Merchant."

Lucy said "You don't deserve it Guy. That woman!"

There was a silence, then Sir Philip said, deliberately. "I see. Yes. Protection. I wouldn't do it for anyone else, mind. But; for my son-in-law? - Perhaps."

Guy said "It's about time Lucy an d I were married, then." And that was that.

The London flat was Sir Philip's wedding present to Lucy, and Guy moved in right away; even before the wedding. He started-in with Merchant's, to "learn the ropes", in the office, mostly, and with the brokers.

Guy had expected good money, but satisfaction in the job came as a pleasant surprise. There was a little chap in the office, Mr. King, who fussed around Guy and took a lot of trouble - he'd been put up to it by Sir Philip of course. Mr. King took Guy to all the Brokers, the Commodity Brokers in the City, Tea in Mincing Lane and all the others; and they went to the Agencies, the big Advertising agencies with branches around the world; J. Walter Thompson and the rest. Merchant's were starting to market their own Brands in the Far East, so they needed Marketing advice.

The date of the Wedding was fixed: October, an Autumn wedding; "very cosy" said Sir Philip "with the nights closing-in." Guy had to rack his brains about whom he should invite: his people of course, and relations, Aunts and Uncles; and the fellows from School and from Oxford; and the fellows from the Army. He paused at that: those fellows knew too much about himself and Ruth. And Pru? And Rufus? - They'd be coming as the Merchants' guests, in any case.

"It will just be our local Church" said Sir Philip - the Church that was the most fashionable in London. It was one of the weddings of a Season which was getting stale by October, and needed a bit of new life: all the newspapers were there, and the Tatler, and the photographers made a lot of it, a little sensation before the winter.

Outside the Church, there were too many Rollses to

count, and, when Sir Philip brought the bride up the aisle it seemed his Big Day more than hers. They had an organ, and orange-blossom - if Merchant's couldn't get orange-blossom out of season, nobody could. After the service, it was the organ blasting the old tune; the richest show in Town, and everyone with fixed grins and good wishes for the happy pair; and smiles for the cameras; and the confetti; and the crowd outside "Ooh! Look at her dress!", and "Look at those Diamonds! Did you ever!"

Guy smiled and waved like everyone else; he was quite happy, really. After all, it was the best thing, and he was fond of Lucy, very fond. It was Ruth, after all who had said it was the best thing, though Ruth kept intruding in his mind. He tried to blot her out, but she was there, during the Vows and everything, and after that, Guy accepted it was useless: Ruth was always with him; that was that.

More than any other Hotel, the Dorchester looks like a Wedding Cake; and it was the best place for Publicity, which is why Sir Philip chose it. He knew all London would notice the Cavalcade of Rollses up Park Lane.

The Reception was in the big room downstairs, and Lucy played her part perfectly.

She treated everyone to her smile, and to the rustle of her satin - all the Taipans and all the Nabobs were enchanted and readier than ever to trade with Merchant's.

"The Reception was held at the Dorchester" the Papers said "And the Honeymoon will be spent in Rome."

Sir Philip had said "You'll not have much time to spare, now you've started with Merchant's. A week in Rome's enough! "

So, it was Goodbye, Good Luck, and away from the Dorchester with a horseshoe clanking behind - as though the Rolls had a broken exhaust, what an indignity. Lucy was being a good sport, so Guy kissed her, and he asked the chauffeur to stop at the flat so they could tidy-up.

Guy removed the horseshoe and they brushed the confetti out of their hair. Then it was the blur of London traffic in the dusk, and Heathrow, and B.E.A. Viscount, Turbo-prop., to Rome.

Rome at midnight, far warmer than London, and no damp in the air. They were met by a car - Merchant's had arranged it all -, and the Hotel looked splendidly over the Colosseum. Oh, the whole week was splendid, full of things to see, and a car always ready for them. There were nightclubs and the Opera, and the gardens seemed to be having a second Spring after the hot months. The fountains were a honeymooner's cliche; and Ancient Rome with its weight of stone; and Renaissance Rome, so seductive - all marble and gold and Glory to God; and Lucy, in his bed at night. Lucy was happy; and Guy was content.

Then - it was at the Trevi fountain, and they were dropping coins into the fountain like all the honeymooners - Guy turned around, and there was Ruth.

No. Impossible! She'd turned away, and gone. She'd seen him: her gesture showed it, hand to mouth. "Ruth!" he was about to shout; but the sound died before it came. How cruel it would be to Lucy, to spoil it all.

It disturbed and excited Guy, that Ruth was in Rome. Was it chance, or had she come to Rome deliberately? After all, his marriage and the honeymoon had been in the international press. After that meeting at Cannes had co-incidence become something more than chance? Wherever he went in Rome, Ruth's shadow seemed always behind the next column. Even when he was making Love to Lucy, Ruth was there; and afterwards, when Lucy called him her wonderful lover, he knew he'd been a traitor in his heart.

In a way it was a relief for Guy to get back to work,

173

though Sir Philip piled on the pressure as if he was trying to break him; as though father was competing with husband. Perhaps he hoped that Guy would prove inadequate - so often, late in the day, when the lights were on, and the typists leaving; so often there'd be some urgent work, some decision to be made - make or break -; and Guy would work into the night.

Lucy would say "Oh, Guy. You're late again. You work so hard."

Guy laughed it off: he didn't mind, and, that was true: he liked the challenge.

There was a Tanker laden with Palm Oil, Lagos to London, and a chance to buy the cargo on the high seas. Guy took the chance, and, for a fortnight, he felt like Antonio on the Rialto, with Sir Philip waiting like Shylock, and hoping for a loss. But Guy made a profit, and won.

That was the first victory, and there were more: timber and oil and jute - the stuff of Trade. Guy rarely got it wrong: he had the nerve, and he was developing the judgment. Whenever Sir Philip was away, in India or Hong Kong, Guy took his chance to act alone. He had to make himself indispensable.

Guy couldn't sign the big Contracts - he arranged the Contracts, and Sir Philip always signed. After two years of success it was time for Guy to Challenge. He said "If you can't trust me, I'll have to move, Sir. Jardine's would give me a job."

Sir Philip said "My daughter in the enemy camp? - Not Likely!" and he offered Guy a Directorship.

"The old bastard" thought Guy; he said "A Directorship? No empty title, mind. I want control."

Sir Philip said "Directorship before you're thirty! A Directorship of Merchant's! Think of the pay! The power!"

Guy said "I'm glad you mentioned Power, Sir."

Sir Philip said "You can run the show in India, in Bombay."

For Guy it was Triumph, but he'd still not show it. He paused, the way you pause at Poker, when you see the big cards in your hand and you know you must keep Triumph off your face.

He said "India - that's an offer worth considering. Will you have a Contract drawn-up, Sir, and I'll look at it."

Sir Philip looked at Guy with respect. You had to admit it, he thought, the lad's got nerve, the right nerve for the job. He'd never like him; but he'd respect him. He said "Bombay is international. The biggest operation in the East."

Guy said "If Lucy likes it - and the Contract's right. Agreed."

Sir Philip said "You want Authority. I never give anyone full Authority" and Guy said "But I'm not just anyone - you'll see."

5. RUTH ONCE MORE

Sunny was his nickname, and sunny his nature; and in the weeks when she was at Cannes with Arthur, the weeks before Guy came and brought chaos with him; in those dead weeks Ruth's only fun was Sunny.

"My name's Sunil - call me Sunny." He was an Indian, quite dark, quite small, with a schoolboy grin and an Old School Tie - Harrow: he was prouder of that than anything in the world.

It was at the Casino. It was always Roulette for Arthur, but for Ruth it was Chemmy and Baccarat - anything was better than the silly wheel. The cards were sometimes amusing, and all the men, pretending to study her cards, but, really, staring at her back. And "La Marina - Madame Marina" - the pseudonym was amusing. Why not? It was another dull evening, and Ruth didn't know how she'd see it through, a whole four weeks of it - it was even duller than London, and she'd been so excited to come to Cannes. She felt so discontented that nothing amused her, not the luxury at the Carlton, or the shops where Arthur bought her things she didn't really want; a bit of jewellery, a scarf. There'd be the Plage Privee, the Carlton's private beach for an hour or two - Ruth always tanned well, and, it was amusing to cream the skin, and to stretch in the sunshine like a cat, and to pretend she couldn't hear the remarks the young men made deliberately loud. Then, she'd swim in the tame sea, and wish she could join the children and the teenagers playing volley-ball. Once, she hired a pedallo, and pedalled around off-shore, and that would have been fun if she'd had someone with her, to sit in the empty seat and push the other pedals. A young man swam up and rocked the pedallo, but Arthur was up there on the beach, watching her and doing the Crossword; so nothing came of that. She thought, not for the first time, that this was too high a price to pay for luxury; but she'd made her choice. She just wanted to be silly and carefree; to have a holiday. But, Arthur was too old. For Arthur, fun could only be expensive - the more the expense, the more the fun.

It was only for fun, and for friendship that Ruth got talking to Sunny, at the Casino. She could hear the Jamaican band outside - oh, how she wanted to dance; anything, so she could release her energy; be frivolous. Paul was serving at the bar: he was sycophantic, and she didn't trust him; but he could shake cocktails. She said "You must know an exotic cocktail. A barman like you. Mix me a surprise cocktail!"

She heard a cry of delight, and there was this jolly little chap at her elbow. "Good Show!" he said "Give it Hell!"

Then he spoke to Paul "Barman. The same cocktail for me,"

Paul said "Monsieur you don't know what I'm mixing."

"Exactly!" said the little brown man "What fun!"

Paul cracked the ice and put it in a chrome shaker, he wrapped the ice in a napkin and hit it with a hammer -. He had an audience, so he took his time; squeezing the lemon, measuring the sugar; adding the cognac and the curacao. Then, he struck a pose like the man with the maracas, and he began to flourish the cocktail-shaker, holding it wrapped in the napkin against the cold.

The music from the terrace was quite audible, and Paul shook the shaker in time to the rhythm. Then, he set the glasses and poured the liquid so that a cold mist rose from the glasses like steam; and with a final flourish, he rubbed sugar around the rim of each glass.

"Bravo!" Ruth clapped like a child at a party, "What do you call that cocktail, Paul?" "Surprise" said the barman "You asked for a Surprise. Remember? The next cocktail I invent. May I call it La Marina for you?"

Ruth opened her bag to pay, but a brown hand stayed

her. He said "Please!" Ruth smiled with pleasure, and said "A lady allows a gentleman to pay."

He said "La Marina? Romantic! - Will you call me Sunny?"

"Sunny" said Ruth "I like that name."

Sunny said "I'm Sunil really. But always Sunny. They called me Sunny at Harrow, you know," and he touched his tie, a little self-consciously.

Ruth said "Marina's a nickname too. I might tell you my real name sometime,"

Sunny said "I've come over from Monte."

Ruth said "I'm at the Carlton" and he said "How jolly posh!"

The cocktail had a kick and a tang of citrus.

"Gosh. It does taste sunny. - Sunny would be another good name for a cocktail" said Ruth.

He said "La Marina, and Sunny - two jolly good cocktails! Let's drink to that!" and he ordered two more.

Ruth said "I'm keeping you. If you want to Play."

And Sunny said "I only Play if I've nothing better to do. I like talking to you." Ruth asked "Do you go to the Casino at Monte?"

"Monte?" he said "Well, Roulette is the same everywhere. At Monte the clientele seems half-dead. The Casino is like a tomb."

Ruth said "This is the fashionable Casino. The Palm Beach Casino."

Sunny was suddenly serious. He looked down in that Eastern way, as though he was studying his toecaps. He said "You're not happy, Madame Marina."

Ruth said "What you said about a tomb - sometimes I yearn to be silly. To have a friend; an ordinary friend who's fun."

Sunny said "Just pals. Let's be pals, Marina. How about that?"

Ruth smiled "Just pals. Oh, I like that. Sunny."

Then, he did something rather odd; he pulled out a card, a visiting-card, and he said "If you ever need a pal - just in case."

Ruth looked at the card, and at the address in Monte. She said "I'm very touched. But you know what people would say."

He said "I don't care a fig what they say. Just pals - remember?"

He paused for thought "I've got it!" He said "I'm supposed to be learning the business. My dad's business."

"Your father?"

"My father. He was a Rajah, and now he's an industrialist. I need a Secretary. The job's open if you want it."

Ruth kept the visiting-card like a Talisman, and, as she sat on her suitcases on the Quay at Monte, it saved her from Despair. Only when Guy had cast off, and la Goulue was dancing away, over the water, did she allow herself to cry, and to wish that she had taken the cosy way, and gone away with Guy. She wondered at her own obstinacy, and she smiled at herself through her tears.

And, what of Sunny? - Ruth's instincts trusted Sunny, but could she trust her instincts? - Of one thing she was certain, she'd never go back to Arthur, for Arthur had become an ogre.

A taxi came; Ruth showed the visiting card, and the driver took her to one of those streets so typical of Monaco, a prim terrace over the hill. She paid, and waited until the taxi had driven away, then rang the bell.

The door was opened by an Indian servant, and Ruth handed him the Card, uncertain whether to speak to him in French or English. The man left her on the step, and she caught the sound of voices speaking fast - in Hindi, she supposed.

Then Sunny came. He'd pulled a dressing-gown over his pyjamas, and, when he saw her, all he said was "Marina! How kind of you to come" - she had to laugh - it was as though she'd been invited to breakfast, and he'd accepted her troubles, as though she'd handed him her coat.

"Chullo! Chullo!" he said to the man, and pushed him outside to bring the suitcases. "Chota hazri; jeldi!"

"Ek dum. Sahib" the man said, and grinned,

"Come in. Come in, Marina" said Sunny "It's so long since I entertained anyone to breakfast."

He showed her into a back parlour, and, even in her weary state, she noticed the opulence.

Sunny said "I hope you'll excuse a personal remark - but, you look as if you've come out of the jungle!"

Ruth said "I'm in a bit of a fix Sunny. I need a pal. Remember?"

"You need a bath, and some sleep. You're safe here."

The bearer brought the tea and fruit, the "Chota hazri" - early breakfast, and Ruth

noticed that the man had changed into a white uniform, and a turban with a red cockade. Sunny said "Marina. If you can't relax in France - we can leave immediately. I'm on a business tour, remember?"

Ruth sipped her tea, and he saw her drooping in the chair. He said "Come - Gopal is preparing a room for you. You're too tired to talk."

The sun was sinking when there was a knock at her door, and Ruth awoke.

"Master says - Does Memsahib want Dinner?" - so, Gopal did speak English, after all. "Thank you!" she called, and she heard the bathwater running for her. She opened the suitcases to find something fresh to wear, - what she'd brought was valuable but not very useful, and she was reminded of the traveller in the desert with gold but no water. There was a towelling beach-wrap hanging on a hook. Ruth soaked in the bath for a bit, put on some makeup, and went downstairs in the wrap and bare feet.

"I bet you're peckish" said Sunny. "Gopal's made a curry. Gopal's a top-hole cook." Gopal brought the bowl of rice and the bowl of curry, put his hands together in the gesture of namaste, like prayer, bowed, and went out.

Sunny said "Not often can you get a decent Indian curry on the Riviera."

"Prawns" said Ruth "I love prawns" Sunny said "Wine and Curry aren't supposed to

mix. But try this Chablis. I'm afraid I can't mix cocktails like we had at Cannes." Ruth said "Cocktails bring bad memories. That barman, turned out nasty."

"I know" said Sunny.

"Oh! - you know?" - Ruth showed her surprise.

"I've had a day to find out. While you've been asleep. Chandler and the fight, and everything."

Ruth said "You know about Chandler? I don't want

him to know where I am. It's not so much that I'm scared of him. But, he'll never leave me alone. He'll have me followed: I'll never be free."

Sunny said "Stay indoors, Ruth. Tomorrow we'll leave France."

She said "You called me 'Ruth' - you know my name?"

"Ruth Evans" said Sunny "Ruth, why do you run away from Guy?"

Ruth said nothing, and Sunny said "Forgive me. I have no right to pry."

Ruth said "Guy has a big future, He will have no future with me."

Sunny helped Ruth to more curry "I'm glad to see you eating" he said, and added, as though he was still the Harrow schoolboy reciting a poem in class. "Love in a hut, with water and a crust, is Love forgive me, cinders, ashes, dust."

"What's that?"! said Ruth

"Oh, just a poem. We had to learn it at school."

"Say it again" Ruth said.

Sunny repeated the verse, and "It's uncanny" she said "You hardly know me, but you seem to know my secrets."

He said "I want you to feel safe here. I'll never bother you; not like Chandler, I mean."

She said "Oh"...and he noticed the uncertainty in her voice. He said, laughing "Oh

Lord! I know what you're thinking! I'm not a queer. Nothing like that," He paused, to find the right expression "I can have so many girls in that way. You know - our Culture is different in India. We have lots of girls in that way - and our marriages are arranged." He helped her to more curry and

182

more rice, and she said "I'm being greedy." "You'll get fat" he said "And then you can be my nurse - my ayah."

Ruth said she felt bubbly, and it may have been the wine, but it was jolly friendship, too. "You said you needed a Secretary. Not an Ayah." She said.

Sunny refilled the glasses and Ruth said "Will you be Rajah one day?"

"I hope the old man lives for ever!" said Sunny. "Yes. I'll be Rajah of Tarastan one

day."

She said "You're proud of your father, Sunny."

Sunny said "He's a Dad to be proud of, Dammit! He's modernised - gone into Industry. Built up his business. Helped to build India for the future."

"And you?"

"Me?" said Sunny "He thinks I'm like the bloody Prodigal Son - I learnt those Christian stories at Harrow, you know."

"You're not really like that" said Ruth. She said it in a way to show she meant it, and wasn't flattering.

Sunny said "I'm determined, Ruth. To make Dad proud of me. He'll kill the jolly fatted calf for me."

Ruth said "It's exciting, Sunny. I do hope I can help."

He said "We'll go to Rome; and we'll have a holiday on the way. All you need is your Passport."

"It's in my bag" said Ruth "That's one thing I didn't leave behind."

They left Gopal at Monte - there was a Gopal, or someone like him at all the Rajah's places: London, New York, Paris. Places that were plain outside and palaces within.

183

Only in India were there real Palaces to show the world.

They were in the Mercedes coupe, and they took the coast road to Italy; heading East where the cliffs tower like Cathedrals out of the sea; through Menton, and across the frontier towards Genoa.

"We'll stay at Rapallo" said Sunny "It's rather like Cannes, with more adrenalin: la dolce vita;" and they stayed a few days, swimming, seeing the sights; and Portofino down the road.

"Next stop, Pisa" said Sunny. But they got to Viareggio which was like Blackpool in the sun - like Blackpool when Ruth went with the `Q' and her Mum and ate candyfloss. Viareggio was as crowded as Blackpool, and, Mama Mia!, there was a chap at the restaurant with a tub full of Pasta, and that was just the first course. There was the long beach, and the Prom, like Blackpool's Golden Mile, and, all along, sticking out of the sea, a line of swings with "Campari" painted on them, and children swinging.

A swing was vacant, and, before it was bagged, Sunny said "Come on!". Ruth sat on the swing in her bikini, and Sunny stood on the seat, and they swung together, above the little waves.

They went down the road to Pisa to see the Tower, then inland to Florence which was full of heat. But at Sienna it was raining so hard that the gargoyles on the Cathedral were spouting into the square like fireengines.

They could have gone to Rome direct, over the hills, but, when the rain stopped, the heat was so heavy they wanted the sea again; so they took the long road down the coast, to Naples. But Naples, in spite of the sea, was a closed oven. Sunny said "My God, Ruth, It's like Bombay in June. Before the Monsoon." So, they escaped to Sorrento, and to Capri.

There was a breath, just a hint, of cool in the air, if you

wished for it, and believed in it. So, they headed North for Rome, and came to Anzio with its war cemeteries, so brave and sad. Anzio kept them for a day or two, even though the sand on the shore was streaked with black. There was something honest about Anzio that they'd missed in other places.

"At Rome" said Sunny "We start work. But first we see the sights." So, they did the Vatican and the Baths of Caracalla. They shopped on the Via Veneto, and on the Via Condotte. Sunny said Ruth must look fashionable, to impress the customers, and it was an allowable business expense. They stared upwards in the Sistine Chapel, and downwards at the Tiber, and imagined the chariots and the kicking horses in the Circus Maximus. They ate ices at Rosatis and Dinner at Quo Vadis; and drove the Merc. too fast around the Colosseum: like all the Italians, imitating Fangio.

There was one of the Rajah's places in Rome, for them to stay; and Balram to look after them, just like Gopal. There was also one of the Rajah's agencies not a proper office, but an agent who did some work for the Rajah. One day a message came from the agent; a small assignment, nothing much. It was almost apologetic - if Signor Sunil didn't want to be bothered, the agent would understand. But Sunny did want the job; he wanted to make a job of it. And, seeing how much Sunny wanted the job and how he tried to do the job right, Ruth said "You're tired of being a playboy, Sunny."

Sunny said "You're right. But Dad won't give me an important job. Not until I've proved myself."

Ruth said "You can prove yourself in Rome. I'll go and see the agent"

So, Ruth got herself tricked out the way she thought Italian men would like her. She made a hit, and the agent would have propositioned her in a minute, but, she kept it business-like, and she took away a list of business-openings for Sunny.

Sunny was excited "Good Show. Good Show." He kept saying. "What did I tell you? Ruth, you're better than a Secretary. You're a business partner."

It was growing cooler into Autumn, the blessed Italian Autumn. There was a shop selling English papers, and there it was: the wedding photos, the guests, so many famous names; the gushing reports; the wedding-frock. The Reception, at the Dorchester, of course. And the honeymoon...in Rome!

Ruth stopped. I wonder what my true feelings are, she thought; and she even smiled at the futility of introspection. She would have expected, what? - Jealousy? Yes, jealousy she did feel; and sadness too. It was there; it was true, She did feel jealous, and she wanted to cry.

She stared at the paper - it was a Sunday paper. The wedding had been on Saturday, and this was Monday: Guy would be in Rome.

That was how she came to the Trevi fountain. Her mood seemed to give her a thirst for the fountain. Like a diviner, she was drawn to the water; and she knew he would be there. She knew that as certainly as if they'd fixed the rendezvous.

Guy was there, and his wife with their backs to her; and great Neptune in his chariot with spume all around, as though it was the wind-whipped ocean.

Then Guy turned, and they stood for a long second, gazing into each other's soul; then Ruth went away, out of his life.

Sunny had got back before Ruth. "You'll never believe this" he said. He was excited in a way she hadn't seen, and Ruth realised that, before, he'd been excited more like a child - but this was a man's excitement.

"Guess what - Dad's offered me a job." He said it as if he'd been offered a prize.

Ruth tried to hide her depression. "Oh, Sunny, how wonderful!" she said, but he noticed the sad emptiness of her expression. She'd always known, of course, it couldn't go on, this escapade in Wonderland; and now, Sunny was going, and what would she do?

"Oh Gosh!" he said, "You think I'm going to ditch you! - You mustn't think I'm such a rotter!" - His Billy Bunter code of honour was as impossible as Camelot.

Ruth smiled and said "Oh, Sunny. You've done so much for me. You mustn't handicap yourself for me" - and she thought how it could have been herself at the fountain with Guy.

Sunny said "What Rot! You're no handicap, Ruth. You'll be working with me. My new job gives me that authority."

Ruth said "What can I do? - Model clothes - catalogue books. Not much use to you." Sunny said "Ruth. You gave me my start; here in Rome with the Agent."

He added "Dad telephoned. He asked me if I wanted to go on being a Playboy; and I said, "Dad, I'm tired of being a Playboy: it's such hard work." And Dad said "O.K. you can take charge of the Bombay Office" - just like that!"

"So, you're sick of being a Playboy?" said Ruth.

Sunny said "Look at Aly Khan - Rita Hayworth, and all that. I don't want to get like that."

Ruth said, teasing him "In charge of the Bombay Office! You are a Big Shot, Sunny. I'll have to call you "Sir"."

"And you" said Sunny "Will be Departmental Director - of our Fashion House."

He was being serious, she knew; but she pretended it was a leg-pull "Could you see me in a Sari? - What do I know about Indian Fashion?"

Sunny laughed "Saris? - My God! European fashion; American fashion. That's the modern market in India."

So, they caught the 'plane.

"Where shall I stay in Bombay?" said Ruth.

Sunny said "You'll be our guest, of course. Until you find your own flat." Ruth said "What do you mean? - You said 'our' guest. Sunny."

"Why, our guest, of course. Myself and my wife."

"Your wife!" Ruth giggled "Oh, Sunny, you're so funny!"

He said "It rhymes, and he started singing "Oh Sunny. You're so funny!" so the other passengers on the 'plane looked round at them, and Ruth slapped his hand to shut him up.

"Of course I'm married" he said. "I've been married for ages. An arranged marriage, of course."

Ruth said "She may not like me, Sunny."

"Oh, bosh!" he said "Laxmi will like you, Ruth. She's a wizard girl."

Ruth said "Why did you live in Bombay, Sunny? Even before you got this Bombay Directorship?"

He said "My God, Ruth. Bombay is the only place in India I could live. I'd go mad - jungly we call it-: anywhere else is out in the jungle."

She said "The Jungle? - Calcutta and Delhi?"

Sunny said "Even Calcutta and Delhi. Bombay is International. O.K., there's supposed to be Prohibition; but, a fellow can get a drink. And there are decent Clubs - the Willingdon; the Yacht Club."

They landed at Bombay in the evening. The 'plane came low over the sea, and so low over the beach that the palm-trees tossed in the slip-stream as if it was a storm. The sea was blue, the sand was clean, and everywhere else was green, after the monsoon, "The green won't last, I'm afraid" said Sunny.

Ruth said "It looks Technicolor like the films: "Blue Lagoon" or "South Pacific" and Sunny said "They shouldn't give you such a romantic first impression. They should fly over the Bombay slums."

A car was waiting at Santa Cruz, a Chevrolet with a driver who salaamed and drove away like Hell from the airport and into the noise and the crowds, and the lights going on as darkness fell. There were low shacks, and tall new buildings, many in the course of construction, with coolies swarming all over, women as well as men; all balancing on the bamboo scaffolding and balancing bricks on their heads, like a double balancing-act at a Circus; and, all the while the cement-mixers were churning, churning. The construction-sites were lit-up for the night "They never stop" said Sunny. "Day and night. Completed in a fortnight - I've seen it."

They came to a bazaar, and there was a hold-up, a cow blocking the road, and a funeral procession. "They carry the body to the beach" said Sunny "They burn it on the beach."

The driver edged the car past the bier, and the corpse was close to the window, all piled with flowers and just the dead face visible. The procession was surging around the car; the drums and cymbals thumping like a thousand anvils, and boosted by the hooters of a hundred motor-cars, trying to get past.

Ruth felt tense, and vaguely threatened. She looked at Sunny, and he was enjoying it all, glad to be home. He said

189

"We don't have to drive through the City. My house is on Warden Road. This side of Town."

They were driving near to the sea again "The Racecourse" said Sunny "And, down there, the Willingdon Club."

They were passing a Temple, and what looked like an ornamental lake. There was enough reflected light, and Sunny said "Mahalaxmi Temple - most Temples have a water tank for ritual bathing."

The driver pulled the car off the road and up a driveway. He blared the horn and two bearers appeared, wearing the same uniform that Gopal wore at Monte, and Balram wore in Rome: white cotton and a red cockade.

Laxmi was waiting inside, in the big room. She didn't embrace Sunny or anything; she just smiled, and made a salaam. She spoke to Ruth in English, and offered her hand for Ruth to shake, in the English manner. She said "Please treat this as your home. Please call me Laxmi. And I will call you Ruth." Her English was correct, but sing-song to a Western ear: a hint of the Welsh lilt that Ruth had not quite lost.

The bearer announced the meal and Laxmi said "I hope you like curries, Ruth."

They sat together at table, in the European Way, and Sunny said "This makes us modern, Ruth. That's funny isn't it? Men and women at table together - and European cutlery."

Though Laxmi sat silent, she wasn't self-effacing. An aristocrat, thought Ruth, from her pink toenails to the white flower in her hair. Her sari was silk and gold-embroidered. Ruth said "Your sari's beautiful, Laxmi. I must learn to wear a sari."

Laxmi said "We Indian girls are always wanting European dress."

190

Next morning they set out early for the office. Sunny's suit was tropical weight, but, otherwise he might have been dressed for the City of London.

He called the driver, and it was close to the sea most of the way, along Warden Road to Kemp's Corner; Chowpatti beach, and Marine Drive; then away from the sea and into the bazaars and the noise, and the big office blocks. Tarastan House was a solid building, six stories.

"The air conditioning is fairly recent" said Sunny - "It used to be so sticky; the ink used to smudge."

Everyone was waiting for Sunny, the managers, the clerks and the typists, all in a line at the office entrance. The chief clerk made a salaam, a namasti and garlanded the new boss: Sunil Sahib the heir to Tarastan. "Congratulations, Sahib. Congratulations, Director-Sahib" - the man spoke in English: every ambitious Babu spoke English at the office.

"Congratulations Director-Sahib" echoed the chorus-line. They all seemed so happy, Ruth thought - well, sycophantic as well. But that seemed to be the way of India, unashamed of flattery.

Sunny held up his hand. It was a very Indian gesture, not a bit Harrovian: conciliatory and commanding at the same time. It was the first really Indian thing Ruth had seen him do. He said "This lady is Miss Evans. My first new appointment: Management Status."

It took a year for Ruth to prove herself, and, within two years she was indispensable.

Ruth liked to swim; she liked to prove to herself, and to anyone else who might be around, that she was a physical girl, and fit. She was at the Pool, at the Willingdon Club, and there was Roosi, she might have known it - Roosi Modi: looking sweaty and pleased with himself, in white shorts and shirt, squash racket in hand. He said "I've ordered samoosas, and cokes" - He really is a handsome so-and-so, thought Ruth, all aquiline features and a big chap for a Parsee.

The waiter came, and Roosi signed the chit. Ruth said "You look pleased with yourself."

"I beat Sunny at squash. First time I've beaten him."

Ruth said "You know he's got something on his mind."

Roosi said "How about the flicks tonight? There's a good film at the Metro."

Sunny came - he'd changed out of squash kit into bathing trunks. He said "Ruth - that Rotter has knocked spots off me."

Ruth said "How's Laxmi?"

"Fat" said Sunny, and he didn't try to hide the pride in his voice." She may come down later - when it's cool."

Ruth said "It's not fair. You men can play squash, and swim. Pregnant girls have to hang about."

"Not you, Ruth!" said Roosi. He expected a sharp reply, but she said "I sometimes think I'd like a child."

Roosi said "How about me for Dad, Ruth?" - He was only half-joking, Ruth knew. Sunny dived in, and swam a length, in the neat way he did everything. Ruth said "Aren't you going to swim, Roosi?"

The sun was hot; she was nearly dry, so she sat down, under the beach-umbrella, and Roosi offered her a samoosa. He said "I wanted to talk, Ruth. While Sunny's in the pool."

Ruth looked a bit nervous at that, and he said "I'm not going to propose or anything. I'm talking about a different partnership. A business partnership."

Ruth caught her breath - Modi's? - one of the biggest Businesses in the East. "A Partnership?" she said.

He said "Ruth. You're unique you know. A first-class Business woman. You could come into Modi's at the highest level. Director - Partner. Call it what you like."

"And what about Sunny?" asked Ruth "He's your friend."

Roosi said "You don't think I'd go behind his back? - But, he can't stop you taking your chance."

Ruth thought, and the thoughts raced through: all the good times, and all the tough times since she came to India. Two years ago, Good Heavens! The early mistakes, and the worries; the way Sunny had helped her that awful time, when she'd lost the 100,000 Dollars in American Fashion. She'd flown to New York, and she'd made the deal - it was going to make her name. Then, none of the Bombay girls would buy the stuff, and it was a write-off, a loss, with Ruth in a panic not knowing why it was happening, was it an Islamic influence in the styling that Hindu girls wouldn't buy, or was it dirty rivals that started the rumours, oh, cow-fat, and pig-fat in the manufacture: the sort of ridiculous rumours which had started the Mutiny a century before. But, there it was - the whole bloody consignment had to be dumped: the wholesalers wouldn't take it, nor the retailers; not even the stores under European control. The Traders wouldn't even ship it on, to Hong-Kong or anywhere. It was an embargo, and wherever Ruth went, she met a Chinese wall.

She knew who was behind it - that most inscrutable of Trading Houses: Merchant's. Britain's Empire might have gone for ever, but not the Empire of the Trading Houses.

The old Rajah even came to Bombay. He hated Bombay - he'd go anywhere, Hong-Kong, Paris, Bangkok; but he always avoided Bombay. He said Bombay was like a chi-chi tart, ashamed of her Indian blood. The old Rajah came down from his summer palace at Naini-Tal, and said "Sunny. She'll have to go" and Sunny said "If she goes, I go" and he

193

meant it.

The Rajah started to shout "Does she mean so much to you? Is she your Mistress or something?"

And Sunny said "She's not my Mistress, Dad. She's my friend."

So, the old man gave Ruth another chance, because he loved his son, and because 100,000 Dollars wasn't really that much money to him. And, it was a cheap lesson at 100,000 Dollars for Ruth; for, after that, Success was the whole of Ruth's life, and to get the better of Merchant's.

Ruth said "Roosi: I can never repay all that Sunny's done. I would never betray him. Never."

Roosi looked irritated. He said "Anyone would think Sunny was your Lover." Ruth said "You're not the first to say that. He's not my lover. He's my friend."

Roosi said "I'm not fooling. We will make you a Vice-Chairman. That's equal to me!"

- Vice-Chairman of Modi's! - was this how far she'd come; a little Librarian from Shropshire? - Modi's, one of the great Parsee Enterprises, nearly as big as Tata: Tata in Steel and Airlines: Modi in Textiles and Fashion - Modi a la Mode. The offer was immense, and Ruth thought of Satan leading Jesus to the mountain and offering the splendours of the Earth below. If she accepted, she'd never be the old Ruth, envying the wealthy; she'd be the wealthy Ruth, omnipotent.

She said "I'm flattered Roosi. But, no."

He said "I'll talk to Sunny."

Sunny swam to the side of the pool, and came to sit with them. Because he was wet, he sat away from the beach-umbrella, and the droplets on his skin glinted in the sun. He said "Super-doopah Samoosa! If I eat enough, I'll win our next game, Roosi."

194

Ruth said "Roosi's offered me a Partnership in Modi's."

"My God!" - Sunny coughed on his mouthful.

Roosi said "She's the best Fashion Buyer in the East."

"She's not only the best" said Sunny "She's also the most attractive."

Ruth said "Sunny. I'm no turncoat. I owe everything to you. I've told him No." Sunny said "Fashion's only a sideline at Tarastan's. Fashion's Big at Modi's. I'll talk to Dad about it."

"Right!" said Roosi "Then how about the flicks this evening? Bring Laxmi. And, Dinner at the Taj, on me."

That evening, Roosi called for Ruth himself. He could have sent his driver, or she could have come in her own car, but he collected her from her flat in Mafatlal Park. Ruth had chosen the flat because she liked the luxury and the view of the sea.

Roosi came in his Mustang - you might almost have said "on a mustang", the way he drove it, all snorting and bucking. He arrived in the Mustang and drove her through the City to the Gateway of India and the Taj Mahal Hotel. Sunny arrived with Laxmi, and Ruth made a note that, if ever she got pregnant, she'd wear a sari - Laxmi looked so good.

Dinner was never a disappointment at the Taj - Sunny was full of wisecracks, and so proud of Laxmi, and Roosi looked quite dashing; more dashing than the film stars: there were more than a few of those, dining at the Taj. After Dinner they sat upstairs in the circle at the Metro cinema, and Laxmi and Sunny and Roosi knew most of the people there - everyone in Bombay Society knew everyone else. Afterwards, after the show Roosi said "How about dancing?" - Laxmi laughed, and said "I suppose you mean an elephant-dance? - ask me again a month from now." Sunny and Laxmi went home and Ruth said "I'm in the mood for dancing," so they went back to the Taj where it was European-style dancing, of course. They danced close, and it was romantic.

They drove back to Mafatlal Park in the Mustang, and stopped on the oval drive; and Roosi kissed her, which was nice. She said "Won't you come up for a drink?" - It was a clear invitation, and she knew it, and he knew it - he was attractive, and she hadn't been close to a man, for, oh, ages, nearly two years since that time on the boat with Guy. But Guy was married now, and lost forever. Guy had a Merchant's wife now, and he was married to Merchant's with a capital M: Merchant's who were The merchant-traders sans pareil, the Merchants who had nearly ruined her.

Meanwhile, here was Roosi Modi, very handsome and very rich; and, unbelievably, a very nice man, too; a gentleman. What was more, Roosi was in love with her, - as long as she remembered to qualify that: Love never meant quite the same thing in the East.

Ruth's block was one of a crescent of apartment blocks around an oval lawn, and a swimming-pool. They went into Ruth's block, and the chowkidar who was asleep, leapt to his feet, and salaamed.

They went up to Ruth's flat, on the fifth floor, and she said "Drinks in the Cabinet- ice in the fridge. Help yourself." She knew that Parsees would drink anything, and that Prohibition was no problem for them: it was no problem for anyone who had money and influence in Bombay. She said "I'll have a small peg. Plenty of soda and ice." He mixed the drinks, and she came to him; she said "The bedroom's over there. Will you stay?"

After they had made love - he was a good lover: Ruth knew that Indian men thought that was important - after they had made love, and were lying together, Roosi said "Surely, you won't dismiss the idea of marriage now?"

She said "I don't think so, Roosi." He became angry, and said "Do you behave like this with any casual fellow? Any time?"

Ruth was surprised to find his remark had hurt her. She said "So, you think of yourself as any casual fellow? I like you, Roosi."

Roosi was silent for a minute. He said "It makes no difference. The offer - the business offer stands good."

Ruth said "It depends on what the Rajah says."

Roosi said "Come to my place next weekend, and meet the family."

Next Sunday Ruth played golf in the afternoon with an Anglo-Indian girl, a friend of Laxmi's. Then Ruth had a swim, and, afterwards, drove herself to Malabar Hill, to Roosi's place. It didn't take much finding, high up Malabar Hill, overlooking the Bay. The house was a Palace, and not a small Palace either.

Roosi didn't send a servant, but came himself to welcome her. He came down the portico steps, and he was wearing a Palm Beach suit and a rose in his buttonhole. He said "My parents are expecting you."

Sir Cooverji Modi was dressed like a Parsi gentleman of the old school, in a tightfitting black frock coat. He welcomed Ruth with friendly formality "I have heard so much about you Miss Evans. My Fashion advisers think highly of you."

Roosi said "This is my mother; and my sister." The ladies were wearing saris, but, like most Parsi women, they seemed more emancipated than Indian women.

The servant brought tea, which, like everything else at the Modi's, was a happy marriage of East and West: iced cakes that might have come from a French patisserie; and

Indian sweetmeats, jellabi and gulab jaman; everything sprinkled with flower-petals, and almond-flakes. The cups and saucers were English Spode, and the teapot was a silver samovar.

Roosi said "I'll show you around."

He led her out onto the terrace: far below was Chowpatti beach, with all the Sunday crowds, and away to the right, a headland blocked the view along the coast. Roosi said "The hanging gardens are over there. They won't have to take me far when I die." He said it with a grin: Indians are not shy about death.

He said "The Towers of Silence are in the Gardens. They're hidden by trees. We put the bodies there, for the vultures and the kites."

Ruth said "That's cruel."

"Enjoy life" said Roosi "Accept death. We Parsees want to leave the earth clean behind us."

Ruth said "It doesn't seem clean to me: kites and vultures."

Roosi was quite serious, he said "The ancient ideals of Zoroaster: Our ancestors brought them from Persia. That's why we're called Parsees - you know, "Persees" – Persians."

"Why did they leave Persia?" Ruth asked.

"Islam - Mohammet. It was Islam or the sword - or, you got away. The Parsees came to India as refugees."

Ruth found she was interested; so much was interesting in India. She said "The Parsees kept their old religion, then?"

"That's true - a sort of Mithraism and Zoroaster's teaching. We don't contaminate the ancient elements: earth, air, fire, water. The only alternative is scavengers."

They went back, into the house, and up the marble

stairs to the banqueting room, a room as big as a ballroom, with a hundred tinkling chandeliers.

Next day at the office, Sunny said, "I've been on the 'phone to Dad. He wants to see us: There's a plane for Delhi at noon, and Dad will send a car to take us up to Naini-Tal."

By the standards of the Rajah's main Palace in Tarastan which was more like a walled City, the Palace at Naini Tal was a miniature. That's why the Rajah liked it; that, and its setting in the foothills, with the Himalayas blocking-out the sky, and the pretty lake, and the pine-trees - rather like Scotland, except for the monkeys. It had never been an official Royal palace, not even before Indian Independence: it wasn't even in the Rajah's territory, as Naini Tal had been in British India.

But, that was a technicality. It had the air of a Palace, a perfect miniature of a Palace - and, the Rajah still looked like a Maharajah, whatever the government said.

Sunny was impatient to get things settled, but the Rajah insisted that they wait until morning "You're both tired" he said. So, there was another night for Ruth's silly, secret idea to nag at her. It nagged her in the morning while she took her breakfast on the verandah overlooking the lake. There were yachts on the lake and a pine-tree reached up like a mast from the forest-deck, with monkeys on the branches, like sailors on the main- yard.

The bearer came to take away the tray, and Ruth went down to the lake. There was a whiff of wood-smoke in the air like a whiff of England, and, I wonder how Guy is now, thought Ruth.

They sat in the Rajah's study, and he said "I'm sorry you had to come so far to see me."

Ruth said "It's been worth it - just to be in such a lovely place."

He smiled and said "You're always welcome, Ruth, whatever happens."

They are so generous to me, thought Ruth; how can I let them down?

Sunny said "I've explained Roosi's offer. Dad understands."

The Rajah said "We mustn't hold onto you, Ruth. It's not that Modi's Business is better than ours. But we're in the wrong business for you. Fashion is a sideline for us." "Modi's is Big Fashion" said Sunny "You've got to have your chance."

Ruth sat there, and the silly, nagging thought was insistent now: the silly fancy which had begun as a day dream on the 'plane; which nagged her on the drive through the jungle; as they passed the elephants, and she saw them logging, and saw how the elephant beat the challenge of the log; and, in the morning, with the monkeys on the branches as she sipped her tea; and one monkey had done the impossible, had sprung in a great curve and caught a distant branch. She decided then, that all you really had to have was confidence.

Ruth said "Big Businesses can merge, and become bigger Business. Tarastan could merge with Modi - have you thought of that?"

They sat silent: the idea was so disturbing that only silence could hold it.

At last, the Rajah said "Does Sir Cooverji have any idea of this? Does Roosi?"

Sunny laughed "Roosi would jump at it. He'd see it as a way of marrying Ruth. Like a Royal marriage sealing an Alliance."

Ruth said "Marriage is a card I'll never play."

The Rajah said "I'll get the Accountants to work it out.

And, if it fits, I'll come to Bombay."

"Well, I'm damned!" said Sunny. "I can never get you to Bombay. It takes a lady to do that."

The Rajah said "It's taken a lady to see, when we were blind. India needs bigger businesses. To compete with the world."

"To compete with Merchant's" said Ruth quietly.

The Rajah came to Bombay, and they went to see Sir Cooverji in his office on Ballard Estate, the Modi Head Office. Sir Cooverji listened, while Ruth explained.

Roosi said "You want to work for Modi's, but you don't want to leave Tarastan's. Isn't that it?" But his father's thought-process was quicker. You had to admire the funny old boy in the funny frock coat. He said "Can't you see, Roosi? She wants both at once - A takeover or a merger? - Which?"

Roosi said "A Hindu Business and a Parsi Business. It won't work - No!"

Ruth spoke to the man with vision, to Sir Cooverji - "Think of British and American Companies. Indian Companies will have to merge the way they do. To compete."

The Rajah said "She's right. A Merger. Equal Partnerships, of course."

Ruth said "You've only got to look at Merchant's. If we don't do something, they'll strangle Indian Business."

So, it was agreed. They went over the Accounts and they talked to the Bankers. They all visited Modi House and ate Parsi food, and Sir Cooverji made sure there was nothing to offend a Hindu, though he knew well that, in private, neither the Rajah nor Sunny really cared if they ate beef.

The Agreements were signed, and a new business, Modi-Tarastan, was born. Roosi said "It would tie things nicely if we married," and Ruth said "Perhaps - some time, Roosi. Not now."

Ruth kept the Modi name, "a la Mode with Modi," and launched her new Collection with a fashion Show at the Taj Hotel. She even modelled an outfit herself.

More and more girls were buying Modi frocks - wherever she went, Ruth saw The Modi style and that was exciting: at the Dinner-Dances at the Yacht Club, or at Green's Hotel. But, there were still too many girls wearing Merchant's fashions, as distinctive in their way as Modi's, all imported from London, Paris or New York.

The potential Market was immense, the opportunity for Profit limitless: those hundreds of millions of women still in saris, compared with the westernised few.

If anybody was going to win this market, Ruth was determined it would be Modi's and certainly not Merchant's. She saw so many girls in saris, even at posh places- sophisticated girls who refused to be westernised. Nobody, thought Ruth, knew as much about saris as Parsee women like Roosi's sister and mother. So she started the Modi range of saris.

Haute Couture was all very well - brilliant fun and high profit-margins - but millions of girls still made their own frocks, or they went to a durzi, a bazaar tailor, who would make up a frock for next to nothing. Ruth secretly admired those little geniuses with their treadle machines who could copy high fashion to perfection for a few rupees. She knew she could never defeat the durzi - but, she could recruit him!

While, ironically, some society girls were reverting to saris, more and more of the other girls were wearing frocks: perhaps not all the time, but in the evening, at a party or with friends. They'd buy a pattern, Vogue or McCalls, and a durzi made the frock up for them in a day. Nobody could hope to compete - Modi's couldn't compete.

But, why not? It was Intuition and Inspiration again; like when Ruth had the idea that Tarastan and Modi should merge. Of course! The new idea became an obsession, and, for a year, Ruth drove herself to achieve success.

First choose a Model Frock, and buy exclusive rights. Then, get it made up by the durzis at piece-rates. She organised a team of Parsi girls to find the durzis, and the business grew. Modi's Modes became a sensation and a sack of gold for the Business. Fashion for the masses had reached Bombay.

Ruth was wealthy. A profit-share had been written into her Contract, so Ruth was wealthy, no doubt about that. Roosi kept asking her to marry him, but she could afford to turn him down.

As for Merchant's, it wasn't so much that their profits fell; but they lost their market-share. The Fashion market grew so rapidly, and it was Modi's, Modi's all the way.

Merchant's Man in India started to panic, and people started to make those nasty remarks that he was meant to overhear "Poor fellow. Fancy losing out to an Indian Business and to a woman!"

Merchant's man in India overheard, as he was meant to overhear - he heard it at the Gymkhana Club, and at Breach Candy Swimming Club, which was still an all-European anachronism. His wife said "A laughing-stock: ridiculed by Indians!" - She had her image of herself, which she treasured like the Jewel in the Imperial Crown; the image of the Memsahib, one of the old breed.

Merchant's Man was summoned to the U.K., for a word with Sir Philip, the man they called the Burra Sahib, whose word was Law in Merchant's. The Burra Sahib said, coldly "Bill. You've got to stop the rot!"

Bill tried to beat Modi's at their own game. He sent his

men into the bazaars, recruited durzis, offered better rates of pay. The durzis took Merchant's money, but they didn't give up their work for Modi's. They worked for Bill by night and Ruth by day.

The Merchant frocks were made and merchandised - but the frocks didn't sell. For some unexplained reason, they didn't sell: perhaps they were too sophisticated, not quite innocent; or, perhaps the colour was wrong against a brown skin. The girls tried them on "Oh, my! Mummy - what a pretty frock!" but Mummy said it didn't suit, and they bought the Modi frock instead.

The strain was too great for Bill's heart, and his Memsahib had to arrange the funeral in a hurry, the way you have to in the heat. "Won't I be glad to get out of this bloody country!" she said.

That was how Sir Philip Merchant came to offer his son-in-law the top job in the East : Head of Bombay Office. Oh, he had offered it before, to tantalize Guy, and then he'd contrive some reason, some plausible reason, for delay.

6. RUTH AND GUY

Ruth knew. As soon as Guy arrived in Bombay, Ruth knew. Really, she'd known long before - known, without knowing. She'd known it would be Guy.

As soon as the other man had died; as soon as he'd died and his obnoxious wife had gone - no, "obnoxious" wasn't fair: "sad" was fairer, sad like a pachyderm doomed to extinction; even then, Ruth had known it would be Guy. Sir Philip Merchant, the Burra Sahib, would send Guy.

Guy didn't even know that Ruth was in India, but Ruth knew exactly where Guy was staying: at the Merchant Company flat; and she knew where he worked, his Offices, and the Director's private office.

Merchant's was too big to fall just because of the Indian Fashion trade, but Guy might fall. Ruth thought, it's not beyond Philip Merchant to have planned it all.

It was a Sunday afternoon when Ruth saw Guy. It was after her usual round of golf at the Willingdon - she'd taken to golf the way she'd taken to skiing - and she was waiting to meet Roosi, who usually played tennis or squash to work up a sweat. She wasn't really surprised to see Guy - he'd been in Bombay for a month, and the boss of Merchant's could jump the waiting-list of any Club.

He was by himself, sitting near the pool in his bathing-costume and a towel round his shoulders; and just to see him again was exciting.

He saw her, and he can't have known anything about her - his face showed such incredulity, and joy, and hesitation, all at once.

He just said "You?"

She smiled, trying to be casual; after all, she had the advantage of surprise. She said "Hello, Guy. I bet you didn't expect to see me in Bombay."

Then Roosi came. He was ready for a swim, and already wet from his shower. He looked fine, Ruth thought, dark and fine, with his wet hair shining in the sun. She kissed Roosi on the cheek, as a sort of tactical statement, and she said "Guy. This is Roosi Modi; my boyfriend."

"Modi did you say?" exclaimed Guy "My God - Modi. And I work for Merchant's!" He held out his hand for Roosi to shake, Roosi shook his hand and said "Your last man- the last Merchant's boss. He'd have died before he'd shake hands with a Modi. He's dead in any case, poor fellow."

Guy said "Roosi. When I saw Ruth, I couldn't believe it. I last saw Ruth at Monte- Carlo;" he paused, and added in a puzzled tone "No - Rome. It was you, Ruth, in Rome; at the Trevi Fountain."

Ruth said frivolously "I'm like a conjuror - popping up at you when you least expect it."

Roosi was trying hard to smile - even Roosi can't help feeling jealous, thought Ruth. So she said "Guy - how is your wife? I hear she's with you in Bombay."

Guy said "You haven't told me, Ruth. What are you doing in Bombay?"

Roosi said "She works for Modi's Modes. We're proud of her."

"Good God!" said Guy "Modi's Modes, So you're the girl."

Guy knew he'd have to tell Lucy, and, that night, he told her.

Lucy said "I thought we had got away from that woman for ever."

Guy said "There's another chap in Ruth's life. Rich and

handsome: Young Modi no less."

Lucy said "I don't trust her, Guy. Perhaps Dad would agree to move us. To Hong Kong or somewhere."

Guy said "I've come out to do a job - for Merchant's."

Lucy said "If we stay - Dad will expect Victory. Victory over Modi's."

A week later, the Invitation came through the Post. The card was vulgar by European standards, all gold-embossed and illuminated:

"Sir Cooverji and Lady Modi request the pleasure of your company at a Ball and Supper at Modi House....."

Lucy said "How dare they" and Guy said "We can't refuse. It would look like surrender. " The Party was the sort of Party only Parsis can give - unashamedly ostentatious, a Party to impress. The Modi millions were on display, and it was an extravaganza.

There were marquees in the garden, and bands playing Rock-n-Roll. Inside the house, the tables were heavy with meats and sweetmeats, and anything you wanted to drink - this was a private party, and Roosi wasn't going to let Prohibition or Religion spoil the fun. Half the guests were Hindus, and some were Moslems, and nobody seemed to be on orange juice, not even the girls. All the younger men wore Dinner Jackets -white ones, mostly, Tuxedos, American-style; while the older noblemen, all bejewelled and turbanned, were trying to outdo one another by the splendour of their plumage. As for the girls, many wore evening frocks, unmistakenly Modi; but it was the evening saris that took the eye, all nine-carat embroidery and colour.

Guy had ordered the Company Cadillac - you had to show the flag, quite literally: all the cars had fluttering pennants, those emblems of Rajahs and Big Business. At Modi House, they had to wait in a queue of Cadillacs and

Rollses before the Head Bearer announced "Mr Guy Baker and Madame Baker."

Sir Cooverji said "Welcome," and Roosi was there saying "Guy - meet Sunny, my greatest friend."

Ruth said "Guy knows how much I owe to Sunny."

There were Bearers everywhere, and Champagne and Whisky-pegs, like in the great days; the Bearers in white with sash and buckle - red sash, brass buckle - and starched white turban and cockade.

"You haven't met Laxmi" said Ruth, and Laxmi said "Hindus don't have God-parents, but Ruth is like a God-mother to our baby."

Then, Roosi was asking Laxmi to dance, and Sunny was asking Lucy, and there they were, Guy and Ruth. He said "Remember the first time we danced? At the Garrison Hop?" Ruth said "The Garrison Hop! It was so funny!"

They were dancing now, in a formal sort of way, despite the crazy music, the latest thing from America, Rock 'n' Roll. Guy said "It's like a duty dance, isn't it? We can say anything and nobody would hear in all this blaring sound. But, we can't hold close."

There was a sit-down banquet for the older people, a chance to show-off the Modi gold plate "But the young people like a Buffet" Lady Cooverji said. And there it was, the Buffet, ready and exotic: curried this and curried that; pilau; prawn, guinea-fowl, pheasant, duck; and anything you wanted to wash it down. And the sweetmeats: a castle of cakes; jellabies, ludhu, gulab-jaman; all covered with rose-petals and silver flakes.

Ruth found herself next to Sunny. He said, quietly "You still love Guy" and Ruth said "Is it that obvious?"

Sunny said ""Thank God for an arranged marriage. It's

much less complicated."

Guy danced with Lucy, and he tried, he really tried with her. She's a lovely girl, he thought: the wrong, lovely girl. He took Lucy outside, onto the lawn, out of the music and into the moonlight. He held her hand, but all he felt was emptiness; and Lucy said "You'll go back to her, Guy. I know."

Guy began to deny it, and he thought of Peter denying Jesus. Lucy stopped him, and said "I know you can't help it, Guy."

Guy said "What do you think of Ruth, Lucy?" and she said "I hate her - because you love her, Guy."

Guy said "I've no illusions about Ruth. She's betrayed other men. She might betray me."

Lucy said, sadly "I hate her - but, I know that's not true. She'd never let go of you, Guy."

They went over to where the lawn overlooked the sea, and Lucy said "You seem to be drawn together like magnets - Cannes, and now, Bombay. And, there was Rome."

"You know about Rome?" that shocked Guy.

"I saw her; and I saw how it disturbed you."

Guy didn't answer. He looked out to sea, then he said "I'm sorry, Lucy."

She said "Nowadays, when you make love to me, you're like a 'plane on automatic pilot. Did you realise that?"

He said "I'm sorry, Lucy."

She said "I'm going home, Guy."

At first he thought she only meant that she was leaving the party, but she said "I mean home, Guy. Back to England."

Guy said "We can both leave India."

Lucy said "I don't think Dad would agree to your leaving. Dad will never surrender." So, Lucy left India and Sir Philip Merchant was in Bombay within a fortnight.

He said "Lucy's my girl, Guy, and you've let her down. You're letting down my daughter and my Company."

Guy said "I've failed with Lucy. But I've not let Merchant's down."

Sir Philip said "The godowns are full of Merchant's Fashions, and no Sales. And you say you're not letting us down."

"That was Bill's legacy" Guy said "But I've learnt we can't compete with Modi's." "Fuck Modi's!" said Sir Philip, "Oh yes - that's a bit too literal, isn't it Guy."

Guy said "You're offensive, Sir."

"It's you who should be offensive" said Sir Philip "Take the offensive. Get on the attack. Spend what you like - but beat Modi's."

He's obsessed, thought Guy, and said "I can boost our Profits on everything else - all Merchant's business: cars, electrical goods. But Fashion is a loser. We've got to cut the loss."

"So; you want to surrender?" Sir Philip's voice was scornful.

Guy said "If you insist on Fashion - I'm not your Man for Bombay."

Sir Philip said "Your job is to beat Modi's - and that woman!"

Guy said "If I leave Bombay, there is still a chance for Lucy and me together."

Sir Philip said "First, prove your loyalty to Merchant's - Merchant's or Modi's; which is it to be?"

Guy said "You're asking the impossible - to beat Modi's at fashion. You know that." Sir Philip said "Do you think the big Trading-Houses, Jardines, Matheson's Merchant's, got where we are by the Rules?

"Surely you wouldn't use force?" Guy said, and Sir Philip answered "Threats should be enough."

Guy said, sadly "If you really mean, that, Sir, you'll force me to leave the Company" and he added "Perhaps that's what you really want."

Guy left Sir Philip, and went back to the flat. Sir Philip was staying at the Taj Hotel - he always stayed at the Old Hotels, Raffles and Shepheards and the Taj; those Hotels.

At the flat, the bearer served Guy's dinner, but it was bloody lonely; he found he was missing Lucy's company, and, in a way, he was almost glad that he felt miserable: it was a paradox, but it made him feel less guilty.

The 'phone was there, and he could have lifted it so easily and talked to Ruth; but he hesitated out of pride, or guilt - or fear, perhaps, that she'd not respond to him: better to keep Ruth like the last appeal of the condemned man; the appeal for Mercy.

But Ruth was not put lightly from his mind - out of Melancholy came irrational Panic; and, out of Panic, Action. He remembered Sir Philip's talk of Threats, and he sensed a signal coming through the night. He wanted reassurance - what harm, just to go and watch? Ruth need never know.

He looked for a weapon - he wished he had a pistol, or a good knife, and he thought he'd ask the Bearer or the Cook. Even a Cook's knife would be better than nothing. But, the Servants were all Merchant's men, and he couldn't trust them.

He went into the kitchen like an intruder, and he took a kitchen knife and a rolling- pin, and he chuckled at the rolling-pin - how droll!

211

He put the knife and the rolling-pin in his briefcase, and told the Bearer he was going out and might be late. The Driver had gone off duty, which was just as well and Guy drove himself to Mafatlal Park. He knew it was Mafatlal Park, and he knew the number of Ruth's flat - he knew her 'phone number, come to that: he'd looked her up so often in the Book,

Mafatlal Park at night was a place of contrasts, dark and light, a dark centre and a periphery of light.

Guy stopped in a patch of shadow, and kept watch, waiting for he knew not what; for nothing at all, or what? for a car-load of Gangsters like Chicago?

There was nothing at all, of course, and was he such a fool as to wait all night? Then, no, it was imagination; yes, a movement on the wall of the apartment block, between the lighted windows.

Guy moved quickly, expecting to alert a chowkidar, but the entrance was deserted. A vague fear of being trapped made him avoid the lift and he ran up the staircase two at a time to the Fifth Floor. Should he rap or ring? Either might alert the human snake, who was slithering up the wall. So he knelt and called softly through the letter-box "Ruth. It's Guy."

She came to the door full of welcome, but she caught his urgency. He whispered "Someone's trying to break in through a window."

She said "Wait here until I call" and she left him in the lobby. The door was ajar, and from where he was hidden in the dark lobby Guy could see the brightly-lit room, and Ruth on the settee with her handbag beside her. There was no noise, no noise at all, but just a movement where the curtain parted, and a glint of light on steel. Ruth casually opened her handbag, as if to take out a handkerchief, and she pulled out the little pistol they had got from Chandler. Quick as a mongoose, she aimed at where the human snake was ready to strike. That was speed - Ruth's speed. Then stillness. The stillness of confrontation. Then speed again - the man-snake's speed. To slither away like a snake under a stone. The snake slithered, faster than sight, and the pistol popped into the void; while the snake-man held death in his fangs like a cobra - the deadly sharp blade of the knife. He slithered into the dark lobby, and Guy bludgeoned him down with the rolling- pin.

Ruth was shaking with shock, and Guy said "There may be others."

"I'll 'phone for Sunny" said Ruth. "He'll come."

The snake-man lay uncoiled, but oiled. Guy said "We'll have to tie him up. Look at the grease."

Ruth brought rope, and pointed the pistol while Guy tied the man. She said "Chandler's pistol - Remember?"

Guy said "I think I know where this snake came from. Philip Merchant as good as warned me."

Sunny came, and two of his servants. He said "The Bombay Police. Hand him over to the Police."

Guy said "My father-in-law is responsible, and I've hurt my wife enough. I'd rather keep the Police out of it."

Sunny said "Tarastan – the raj of Tarastan - was feared before the first Merchant Adventurers came to India. I'll make this snake so frightened that he'll talk."

Then Sunny began to speak in Hindi, and the snake began to show his fear.

Sunny said "He'll do anything I tell him. The Thugs, you know, the jolly fellows who made human sacrifice to Kali. You British never quite managed to suppress them in Tarastan."

Guy said "Philip Merchant's staying at the Taj."

"Good show!" said Sunny "I know the Manager. He'll be expecting us" - and he picked up the 'phone.

The two servants held the man-snake prisoner in Sunny's car, and Ruth went with Guy. They drove through the midnight City, past Chowpatti beach and round the moonlit crescent of Marine Drive; across to the harbour and the dark slab that was the Gateway of India, and Green's Hotel still lively. The cars stopped outside the Taj, and Sunny had arranged it all: unchallenged entry for the strange group - a Rajah's son, two Europeans, two servants, and a dangerous near-naked man.

Guy knocked and said "It's Guy, Sir." The door opened, and Guy jammed it open with his foot. Merchant saw the danger, and moved fast, but no faster than Guy, who got between Merchant and the coat; it was hanging over a chair and Guy guessed there would be a gun in the pocket.

Guy said "I think you know Miss Evans. And you know the naked gentleman, as well."

Sunny said, "Sir Philip - we should hand this fellow to the Police - you as well." Merchant said "I've never seen that man before."

"You're wasting your time," said Sunny "Tarastan has more power than Merchant's.

This fellow has talked already."

Ruth said "None of us are safe while you are in India. We want a signed confession." Sir Philip said "What if I refuse?"

Guy said impatiently "We're giving you a chance. For Lucy's sake."

Sir Philip said "Lucy? - You only care about this tart here."

Ruth lashed out in anger across his face. She said "A slap's a small revenge for attempted murder."

Sunny said "Tarastan can be as cruel as Merchant's -

but India is not Hong Kong. This snake here is terrified of the Thugs."

Sir Philip stood uneasy, glancing here and there, assessing his chances - the 'phone? the bell? At last, he said "All right, a signed confession; and a promise to stay out of India."

Sunny said "If there's any threat, to any of us - Ruth here; Guy; myself - we will find you. Anywhere."

There was a desk in the room, and notepaper headed "Taj Mahal Hotel." Guy sat and wrote, and, as he wrote, Sir Philip watched, and the others watched Sir Philip.

Sir Philip signed, and said "You no longer work for Merchant's, Guy" and Sunny said "Guy is working for Modi's - from tomorrow."

Guy looked surprised, but said nothing. He felt the coat, and sure enough, there was a pistol in the pocket. He took it and said "Ruth. Add this to your arsenal."

They left the Hotel, and Sunny spoke in Hindi to his servants "Take this budmarsh to the office. Get the Chowkidar to help you. Take his thumb-print and a photograph. Then let him go." The servants went off in Sunny's car, one driving and one in the back with the prisoner, and with the man's own knife pressed to his ribs.

Guy said "Sunny; I'll drive you home," and, on the way Sunny said "Be careful. Merchant may still try something."

Ruth said "We've got two pistols now."

Sunny said "Look. Why not go out to my shack? The shack at Mallard, for a day or two. At least until that bastard's out of India."

He took a key out of his pocket, and gave it to Ruth, "You know how to find the shack. Why don't you take a week's leave? - You've earned it."

Ruth said "Sunny - didn't you think about Roosi? - When you said Guy could work for Modi's?"

Sunny laughed, and said "This is the best way to bring Roosi to his senses about you. He's got to learn, Ruth."

Guy pulled into Sunny's drive, and the chowkidar came out to meet them. Guy said "We had better go home first. To collect some things."

Sunny said "You'll find everything you want - food, a razor. It's all there." Ruth said "He's right, Guy. Better for both of us to disappear for a few days."

Sunny got out, and Ruth said "Thanks - oh, thanks, Sunny - my love to L.axmi and the baby."

They drove away, and Ruth said 'Oh God. I've got the shakes - reaction I suppose." Guy said "Relax. Just direct me."

They headed out of the City past Mahalaxmi Temple, and past the Willingdon Club where the road was always restless, even at night; past the shanties and prone figures everywhere, rolled up in rags, or just lying in the dust. Past the racecourse and the cavalry-stables, the smell and snort of horses; and through the bazaars, still lit by kerosene and people already stirring before dawn.

A. cow moved out of shadow, and Guy had to blast the horn. Ruth jumped and said "Oh God. I'm nervous."

Now, the road was clear and there were buffaloes in byres, dark statues in the night; and mosquito-fires blowing acrid smoke across the road.

They drove through a village with a mosque, and vultures asleep on the minarets, and Guy thought "All this death - how unimportant we are, really; and the things that have happened tonight."

They were on the embankment now, above the salt

pans. They could smell the salt tang, and, ahead was the line of palm-trees that marked the sea.

Guy said "Which way?" - Ruth sat up, and pointed down a track. She said "A servant is coming from the fishermen's huts." The man had heard the car.

Ruth spoke slowly - her Hindi was not yet fluent - and she showed the key. She said "Sunil Sahib." The man salaamed and helped them to open-up the shack, taking the slats from the windows and lighting the lamps.

He went away, and returned carrying water - he had a bamboo, with a kerosene drum of water at each end. Guy thanked him and gave him a coin, and he left them.

Guy said "Sunny said there's everything here - but, with no electricity?"

Ruth said "There's food in the fridge. It works on bottled gas - it's no longer primitive out here. Soon there will be electricity and running water. It will be a shame."

There was a break of light in the sky, and the dawn came furious with the sun. Guy said "Do you feel safe now, Ruth?"

She nodded, and said "I'm all tensed up. I must sleep."

The beds were ready, made-up under mosquito-nets. Ruth said "You need a net out here."

They undressed, just dropping their clothes anywhere, and went together, under the same net like a Bedouin couple in a tent. Ruth put the two pistols under the pillow "Better be sure" she said; and they lay together, naked, on the bed.

It was getting quite bright now, even under the net, and Ruth was already half- asleep, already less tense. She turned her lips to be kissed, and moved her hand to where his manhood stood, honest, and hard for her; and soon, they fell asleep.

They awoke in the blistering afternoon, and Guy rolled out, from under the net. He saw the sand as white as metal in a furnace, and he said "Shall we swim before we eat?"

The beach was quite deserted, so they ran, naked, onto the sand; and it was like fire- walking. Then, straight into the sea, a warm sea but fresh; and splash, and dive into the waves. They swam quite far, trying to drive away the tension with their efforts; and they dived into the waves and splashed like children.

Then, they lay in the shallows to get their breath; there, in the shallows with the ripples lapping their navels, and Ruth's hair wet and shiny-black. She cupped her hand to splash him playfully, and she saw, there beside her, that he was hard and manly for her; there, below the surface, and breaking the surface like a periscope.

Guy laughed and said "I can't hide my feelings" and Ruth said "Oh, Guy" and she bent forward and kissed him there, and pressed him to her lips. He pulled her to him, and the wet sand shaped itself to their shape. He said "Oh, Ruth. It's been so long."

She whispered "Oh, Guy. I'll get pregnant,"

He answered only "Well?" - and it might have been a question, or a challenge.

He said, again "Well?" and she said "Yes. Oh, yes, Guy. It's been too long."

He rolled over, to shade her from the sun, and she was under him: the lovely part of her like an anemone in the sea, with ripples around it. Guy reached down, and waggled himself like a fish-tail, to wash away the sand; and he went like some marine tentacle, like some denizen of the reefs, slippery and eel-like into the anemone. The anemone opened for him, to hold him, and contract around him; and Ruth's fulfilment was like the shriek of a seabird over the waves.

218

They ran back over the sand, and the fisherman had set-up the shower for them: it was just a kerosene drum full of water, which tilted when you pulled the rope, and that was fun: everything was fun.

There was food in the fridge, and a cooker that worked from bottled gas - it wasn't really primitive at all: it was only playing at Robinson Crusoe; but it was fun. There were some chuppatties that were not too stale and some tins of curry; and beer and coke in the fridge.

"I'll probably get pregnant" said Ruth.

"Yes" said Guy - there was no use pretending. "Yes" he said. Then "Good." "Oh!" said Ruth. Then she smiled "Oh, yes" she said "Good."

Guy said "You'll have to marry me, after all."

Ruth said "You're married already. Or am I wrong?"

Guy said "Lucy's not vindictive. Not like her father."

Ruth said "I wonder what job Sunny had in mind? For you at Modi's?"

Guy said "Why not Fashion? - number two in Fashion. You'll be my boss! You'll need someone to stand-in for you - if you're pregnant."

Ruth said "It's funny. Just the one time without a contraceptive and we assume I'm pregnant."

Guy said "Somehow. I'm sure" and Ruth said "So am I."

Guy wiped the last of the curry from his plate, and chewed his last bit of chuppatti. He said "Ruth - what about Roosi?"

Ruth said "I know. I feel rotten about Roosi. He's such a good hearted fellow." "And handsome too," said Guy.

Ruth laughed and said "He's so generous - he'll be glad for us - in time."

"Well, that's settled," said Guy. "I'll stay with you in your flat - if I'm invited. And, as soon as things are settled, we'll marry."

Ruth said "You must be quite sure Guy. Remember who you will be marrying - La Marina: a woman of a certain reputation."

"If you promise me you'll be true - you will be true, for sure."

"Yes" she said "You can be sure of that."

About the author : -

John Rigby

The son of an expat, industrialist, John spent his early years, including the war years, in India. He returned to a catholic public-school in England. Two years national service followed, as a subaltern in the Royal Artillery, then Oxford University where he won a rugger Blue. He followed his father into industrial management for 10 years before a more congenial period as a public-school master. He has always enjoyed sport: he was an England reserve at rugby and a competitive swimmer. He enjoys music, particularly opera, and good theatre. He is married and has two daughters and three grandchildren.

Lightning Source UK Ltd.
Milton Keynes UK
20 December 2009

147787UK00001B/6/P